MAR 1985

ELK GROVE VILLAGE PUBLIC LIBRARY

3 1250 00162

P9-CBE-301

ARY

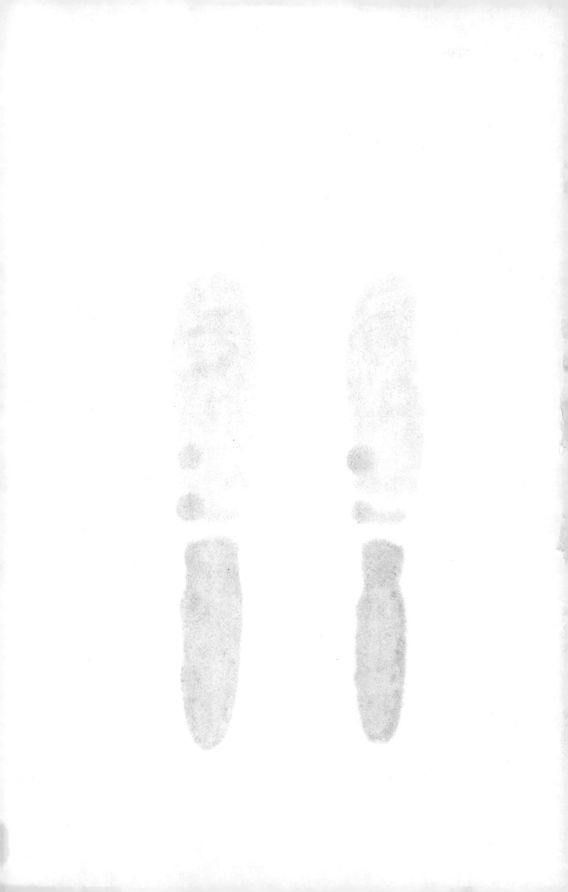

OTTO'S BOY

BY THE SAME AUTHOR:

Telefon

Sledgehammer

Viper Three

Swap

The Playwrights Speak

City Under the Ice—Camp Century

The Girl Who Split

Time of Reckoning

My Side

Blue Leader

Blue Moon

Blue Murder

Designated Hitter

Walter Wager
OTTO'S BOY

MACMILLAN PUBLISHING COMPANY   New York

ELK GROVE VILLAGE PUBLIC LIBRARY

All of the names, characters and events in this book are entirely fictitious. Any resemblance to or connection with real people or incidents is both coincidental and unintended.

The U. S. Army's Office of Public Affairs in New York City and the Pentagon, Dr. Herbert Peyser and chess savant Fairfield Hoban are among those who provided valuable counsel and information. If any of the facts on chemical warfare, psychiatry or chess are incorrect, the fault lies solely with the author.

Copyright © 1985 by Walter Wager

All rights reserved. No part of this book may be reproduced or transmitted in any form or by any means, electronic or mechanical, including photocopying, recording or by any information storage and retrieval system, without permission in writing from the Publisher.

Macmillan Publishing Company
866 Third Avenue, New York, N.Y. 10022
Collier Macmillan Canada, Inc.

Library of Congress Cataloging in Publication Data

Wager, Walter H.
  Otto's boy.

  I. Title.
PS3573.A35O88 1985   813'.54   84-21870
ISBN 0-02-622510-7

10 9 8 7 6 5 4 3 2 1

Designed by Jack Meserole

Printed in the United States of America

To CYNTHIA AND LEE ALDERDICE,
good friends and two of the noblest Texans
of them all

W. W.

OTTO'S BOY

CHAPTER 1

HE COUNTED EACH STEP.

Thirty-six . . . thirty-seven . . . thirty-eight . . . thirty-nine.

He knew exactly how many paces it was across this main concourse of Pennsylvania Station. He had walked to the stairway on the other side of the large chamber many times, but he still liked to count the steps. Measuring things in numbers made him feel good. It gave him a sense of control. That was important.

Forty-two . . . forty-three . . . forty-four . . . forty-five.

He counted silently. Only he heard the reassuring numbers echoing inside his head. His lips did not move and his eyes showed nothing as he circled the travelers lined up to buy train tickets. Pausing to avoid colliding with a portly priest, he glanced up at the big clock.

5:01.

He was right on schedule.

He had planned it all meticulously, and he had timed each stage of the operation over and over. As a disciplined soldier should, he had rehearsed every detail a dozen times. No, twenty. He had counted that too.

Now the staircase was directly ahead. It was eighteen steps down, he recalled automatically. Holding the package firmly in his right hand, he descended at an even, careful pace. He could not afford to stumble here. He wouldn't, of course. He didn't make mistakes.

At the foot of the stairs, he turned left into a stream of people hurrying down a wide passage. It was the start of the evening rush hour, and they were on their way home. Just sixty-two paces away was the entrance to the subway branch that New York City officials called the Independent division. The patient passengers who regularly rode its clattering, graffiti-splattered trains through the bowels of the metropolis spoke of these services as the Sixth or Eighth Avenue lines.

A lot of people would be talking about the Eighth Avenue line tomorrow. *Millions*—and not just in the United States. Suddenly he realized that he was smiling in proud anticipation. He changed his expression at once, replacing it with the blank look that was on so many of the faces around him.

He must not be noticed or remembered.

Either could be extremely dangerous.

There were the turnstiles—a dozen yards away. As he approached them he saw the large "I Love New York" poster on the wall, and he barely managed to suppress a grimace. He hated this city and he despised its people. This polyglot mass of blacks and Hispanics, Jews and Orientals filled him with loathing. It was this turbulent tide of racial garbage that made the city one great sewer, he thought as he took the subway token from his pocket.

5:04.

An "A" express train heading uptown had left this station thirty seconds earlier. The next "A" going north would depart at 5:08 and a half, stop at 42nd Street, and reach Columbus Circle at 5:15. From there the express would rattle and roar nonstop to 125th Street in Harlem, traveling the sixty-six blocks in eight minutes.

That was the evening rush hour schedule for weekdays. He had tested it again and again. He had meticulously written the times in his notebook. After he had memorized the numbers, he had torn out the pages and burned them. Then he had pulverized the ashes before flushing them down the toilet.

There must be no clue, no link that might betray him to his many enemies. He must maintain maximum security precautions at all times. His mother had raised him that way. He must keep the family secret, fulfill the great dream.

5:05.

The density of the crowd swirling around him was building, and the blank-faced people were moving more urgently, impatient to get home. As soon as he dropped the yellow metal token into the turnstile, he moved to hold and protect the package with both hands. He cradled it as if it were a baby while he warily made his way to the uptown platform.

5:06 and a half.

Two minutes.

He had chosen both the place of attack and the time of the train quite deliberately. The plan required an express to a major center of "racially inferior" population. One Hundred and Twenty-fifth Street—heart of black Harlem—was right. So was an uptown train that left this 34th Street–Pennsylvania Station stop just after 5:08 P.M.—early in the rush hour. The cars would be fairly crowded but not so jammed that other passengers would press too closely against the package or impede his exit.

His eyes blinked as he remembered.

He swallowed hard twice.

During one of last month's test runs, he had ridden a later train packed so tight that he couldn't wriggle or push his way out at Columbus Circle. Trapped in the tangle of arms and torsos, he had been forced to go all the way to 125th Street before he

3

could break free. Even now his heart pounded as he recalled all those dark faces.

He had been angry and afraid.

Not of *them*, he told himself. No, it was the package. There was nothing unmanly about that. Anyone would be afraid of it. In a few hours, tens of millions of people would be terrified. The incident that took him to 125th Street meant nothing now. It had happened on April 23. Today was May 1, and he wasn't the least bit afraid as he walked to the middle of the platform. If his pulses were beating faster than usual, it was exhilaration. After all the planning and preparation, he was about to do it. Mama would be so pleased.

An uptown local came and went.

Then a downtown express arrived.

As it left, he heard the growing roar of another train approaching from the south. He turned to look. The metallic thunder grew into a tidal wave of sound that drowned the entire station.

There it was—the uptown "A" train.

Now he counted to himself again as it slowed to a stop. Nine . . . no, ten cars; a score or more people standing in each. Then he wondered whether the train was on time. It was annoying that he couldn't glance at his wristwatch, but he had to protect the package with both hands.

The exteriors of two cars were defaced by the garish fantasies of spray-paint savages. Only a city as utterly undisciplined and degenerate as this would permit such barbarism, he thought bitterly as the doors opened. These animals *deserved* the package.

Passengers were still getting out as others began boarding. Some bumped or brushed against those rushing the other way, but not a word was exchanged. It was as if they didn't even see each other. The man who counted was among the last to get on, and he took a place in the middle of the car.

This was a delicate moment. He had to find the right metal

4

column or handle to hold. In a few seconds the doors would close, and the train would start with a lurch. That could send someone reeling into him—and the package. So could an abrupt stop or start at 42nd Street, the station where the "A" halted before clattering on to Columbus Circle. A sudden stop might even send him stumbling into someone. When that had happened nine days ago, he had dropped the dummy parcel. He could not risk that again.

Now he found an overhead handle to grasp and encompassed the package protectively with his other arm. The doors closed with a thud. As the train charged from the 34th Street station into the dark tunnel, he tried to ignore the noise and the vibrations beneath his feet and the yellow lights rushing by outside. He had to go over his mental checklist again.

No eye contact with anyone.

No behavior of any kind that might make other riders remember him.

Look bored and work weary as they did, but inside stay totally alert. Don't relax for an instant.

And watch the time very carefully. He had practiced doing that by counting his own heartbeats. He was accurate to within five seconds per minute. He was proud of that.

Forty-second Street.

Seven passengers got out, but a mass of others crowded in immediately. Seeing them, he strained to keep a glow of pleasure from his eyes. Two of the arrivals wore dark suits, large black hats, and long sideburns that identified them as Jews of a Hasidic sect—one of the most Orthodox groups. He hated Jews even more than he despised blacks. These two were like a gift, he thought.

The train was rattling north once more. He resumed counting off the seconds in his head. He could hear the moments ticking by. He could not deny himself the luxury of another furtive glance at the Hasidim. Pretending to scan the advertising cards promoting Eastern Airlines, Miller beer, Carlton low-tar cigarettes, he savored one appraising look at the two men before his eyes moved on to a route map half-obliterated by spray paint graffiti.

Two and a half minutes.

In one hundred fifty seconds he would walk out of the car at the Columbus Circle Station, stride briskly through the connecting tunnel to the IRT line, and take a Broadway–Seventh Avenue local south. He would be four miles away when it happened. He would be out of the state eighteen minutes later.

One minute—and counting. It was like those space-shot launchings he had watched on television. No, he was much more clever than those highly publicized astronaut crews. He was doing it all by himself—something no man or group had ever dared before. He was greater than any of them.

Just half a minute; it was time. He sighed as if he were tired, glanced around to see if anyone was watching, and nodded. No one was paying any attention to him. Each passenger was in a private world of thought or half sleep, ignoring others only inches away. The man who counted put the package down on the floor between his feet. The seconds ticked away steadily.

Suddenly the train slowed, and the "A" slid out of the tunnel into the 59th Street–Columbus Circle station. He started for the door at once, pushing purposefully but trying to avoid any confrontation. Controlling his anger, he managed to circle a trio of chattering young Puerto Rican women and squeeze out onto the platform—just seconds before the door closed.

He took a deep breath. Then he turned to look into the car that he had left. The two Hasidim were still aboard. Pleased, he nodded happily and glanced at his wristwatch. The "A" train clattering north was forty-five seconds behind schedule.

At 5:24 P.M. it reached the 125th Street station. The doors opened, and passengers poured from nine of the ten cars. Nobody emerged from the fourth car of the train. The only thing that came from the open doors was a terrible stench, a sickening smell as if fifty people had vomited and defecated.

Appalled by this nauseating odor, several of those hurrying

to board the fourth car froze in their tracks. Clarice and Aretha Jackson didn't. Afflicted with bad colds, neither of the middle-aged sisters could smell anything. They were speaking to each other earnestly as they stepped into the car. Then they stopped talking and began to scream. Ten seconds later they collapsed. Three minutes after that they were dead.

CHAPTER 2

6:19 P.M.

Seven miles south of 125th Street.

Three important men sat in a high-ceilinged office on the first floor of an historic building. This was the "new" City Hall erected in 1812 to replace an earlier one gutted by fire. Only two minutes ago they had been discussing how to present the Police Department budget at tomorrow's press conference. Now they were staring grimly at a television set that looked incongruous amid the fine nineteenth-century furniture and paintings.

The screen was filled with nine or ten blue-and-white police cars, at least as many ambulances, and dozens of uniformed patrolmen. Most of them were spread in a wide arc, holding back some three or four hundred black civilians. Women were screaming. Children were crying. Men were shouting and pointing at white-garbed medical teams carrying stretchers into the subway entrance.

". . . may be among the worst disasters in the city's recent history," the off-camera television reporter continued. "The police aren't letting us down into the station, so we don't have exact casualty figures yet. There are all kinds of rumors. One—unconfirmed—is that there may be as many as fifty dead and even more injured."

Leaning forward in the leather swivel chair, Mayor Thomas Astor Warner winced as if he had been hit. There wasn't a trace of that famous campaign smile on the tall politician's handsome face as he shook his head in concern.

"There's still no word on just what happened. There's no smoke, and fire fighting equipment has not been summoned," the invisible journalist reported. Now two men emerged from the subway entrance. One was a young black intern; the other was a powerfully built police commander whom the reporter recognized.

"Captain! Captain Maccarelli!" she called out loudly over the uproar.

He sighed and walked toward her slowly. In seconds other TV newspeople and a score of newspaper reporters and photographers crowded around him.

"This is Captain James Maccarelli, who commands the Twenty-sixth Precinct," she identified briskly. "Captain, was it a collision?"

The tight-lipped policeman shook his head.

"Explosion?" demanded a *Daily News* reporter.

Maccarelli shook his head again.

"Then what was it?"

"Something I've never seen before. I've seen a lot of rough things up here in the Two-Six. And I saw worse when I was in the infantry in Korea, more than a year of combat. But nothing like *this.*"

"Like *what?*" a TV newsman asked.

"It's unbelievable," Maccarelli said in a harsh, choked voice. He seemed dazed and distant, as if he wasn't speaking to this surging media mob at all.

"Captain," a *Times* reporter in Ivy League clothes appealed, "could you please—"

9

Maccarelli didn't seem to hear him.

"They're all covered with vomit . . . and urine . . . and . . . and excrement. The smell is sickening. Bodies all tangled up—it's *awful!*"

Several journalists began shouting questions:

"What bodies?"

"How many dead, Captain?"

"Survivors?"

The veteran policeman glared at them angrily. He had dealt with the press in crises before, but this time he had difficulty controlling his temper. He threw up his hands in signal. The barrage of questions stopped.

"No survivors," he said. "They're all dead. Every man, woman and child in the car is dead. Eighty or ninety people—all dead!"

For a moment the reporters were stunned into silence. Ten yards away the black intern who had come up from the subway with Maccarelli was leaning against an ambulance, unable to stop crying.

"Oh, my God!" the watching mayor whispered.

Then he turned from the television set to the other two men in his office. One was Charles Rosenthal, a chubby and balding Associated Press alumnus whose political savvy and wry wit helped make him an effective press secretary. The other was thirty-eight pounds lighter, a decade younger, and a lot more nattily dressed. Police Commissioner Vincent Xavier Grady was dark-haired, bright-eyed, and charismatic in the classic "black Irish" way. Able and ambitious, forty-four-year-old Grady was as hard as the boulders that drove his farmer ancestors to leave the rocky fields of Connemara for opportunity in golden America.

"He did it, Vince," Warner said bitterly.

"Did *what?* We don't really know much yet," the cautious police commissioner replied.

"Between four and six P.M. on May first—just as he promised. Have you forgotten?"

It wasn't easy dealing with these emotional liberals, Grady

thought. They were so quick to panic, so eager to welcome guilt.

"We'll have lab teams and our best detectives up there in half an hour," Grady assured. "The medical examiner is already on his way. They'll find out *scientifically* what killed those people."

The troubled mayor looked back at the screen, saw it was now filled with firemen battling a three-alarm blaze in Brooklyn, and tapped the remote-control unit on his desk to lower the sound.

"We should have done something, Vince," he insisted.

"I'm sure we did."

"Eighty or ninety dead," Warner mourned.

"You're not blaming my people, are you?" Grady challenged.

Warner did not answer.

"Tom," the exasperated police commissioner reminded defensively, "you get nut notes every week."

It was at this point that Rosenthal got a chance to ask his question.

"Is this something that I should know about?"

Warner hesitated. Grady didn't. He picked up one of the desk telephones and dialed the direct line of his top aide. In seconds, he was issuing orders. The mayor of the City of New York listened, nodded, and took a deep breath.

"Well, Charlie," he began, "about four or five days ago I got a letter."

"And one more thing," Grady continued. "Get that son of a bitch Bloom—*now*."

CHAPTER 3

ASIDE FROM its green door, there was nothing unusual about the appearance of the four-storey brownstone building at 23 West 10th Street. It resembled many others in this pleasant residential neighborhood on the northern border of Manhattan's celebrated Greenwich Village. The exterior gave no clue to the fact that some of the most cunning and ruthless men in America regularly assembled inside to wage a special kind of war.

In the small room on the second floor overlooking the back garden, two combatants were locked in no-holds-barred battle. One of them—square-faced and frowning behind bifocals—was an ex-frogman and underwater demolitions expert who had become an outstanding brain surgeon. His adversary was a quarter of a century younger, an earnest and good-looking thirty-five-year-old with a .38-caliber pistol in his shoulder holster. He had curly hair, brown eyes, and a compulsion to tell the truth that had won him many enemies. Less than a year ago one of them had tried to kill him as he left this building.

The two warriors faced each other across an ornate and famous table. This was their battlefield. It had originally belonged to the late Frank Marshall, the great U. S. champion for whom this prestigious chess club was named. Since these players were two of the huge city's best, a dozen other members ringed the confrontation in silent study. They waited, almost breathless with concentration, to see whether Dr. R. Edward Hackett could escape Bloom's trap.

Lips pursed, the surgeon stared at the pieces intently. A minute ticked away before he made his choice. He moved the white knight. Bloom looked at the historic table on which so many champions had played, but he was thinking, not seeing. Considering the various alternatives, Bloom computed and recomputed before he advanced the black king. Delighted that his foe had taken the bait, Hackett pulled the white queen back with a dramatic flourish.

The watchers nodded in admiration. He had broken the vise, and ingeniously. Suddenly the match was a battle again. Aglow with pride and fresh confidence, Hackett might finally prevail if he continued so creatively.

Now something began to flutter inside David Bloom's jacket. It was a radio beeper, the kind that vibrate in silent signal instead of sounding noisily. Focused on the battle, Bloom ignored it for several seconds. Then he reached inside the jacket, one finger brushing the holster under his left arm as he turned off the electronic device. Having done that, he advanced the black queen.

The surgeon flinched.

He wasn't smiling anymore.

He understood, and so did the spectators. In three more moves Hackett was finished. He had no chance. As a gentleman and a well-bred chess player, he knew what he should do. The surgeon knocked over his king in concession, rose stiffly, and forced himself to thrust out his hand. Bloom shook it and turned.

"It really isn't proper," Hackett grumbled. "Beepers should be barred from the club."

The fact that Bloom's device made no noise and had vibrated

after the surgeon's fatal move meant nothing to Hackett. Bloom elected to avoid the senseless confrontation.

"You're right," he agreed. "Tell the club president."

"But you're the president, David!"

Bloom walked quickly to the phone and called his office. He identified himself. Then he listened for twenty seconds.

"I'll be waiting outside," he said.

As he left the building he automatically glanced left and right. It was more than ten months since he had exposed a ring of corrupt narcotics cops. He didn't expect any more attempts on his life tonight, but such caution was a habit now. Besides, his reassignment to antiterrorist duties had brought Lieutenant David Bloom a whole new set of violent enemies.

6:37.

The unmarked police car pulled to a halt in front of 23 West 10th Street, and Bloom recognized the mustachioed driver. Sgt. Gabriel Velez, who had a degree from John Jay College of Criminal Justice and a useful knowledge of Caribbean and Latin American revolutionary groups, was Bloom's streetwise assistant.

"How bad is it?" Bloom asked as he entered the car.

"It's heavy. Eighty or ninety stiffs, and nobody knows what the hell happened. Siren?"

"The works."

Velez put the flashing light atop the sedan, turned on the siren and pressed down the gas pedal. Born in the Bronx of a Colombian father and Puerto Rican mother, he was a "New Yorican" with a passion for fast driving. Bloom had told him that this was a macho thing, but Velez didn't care. Speed made his adrenaline flow. Besides, he was one of the best drivers on the whole police force.

The sedan accelerated swiftly. Velez had an encyclopedic knowledge of the city, its streets and traffic lights and shortcuts. He had planned his route on the way to the chess club. One Hundred and Twenty-fifth Street in nine minutes. No sweat.

The screaming siren helped. The intimidating sounds parted traffic like a cleaver as the unmarked car raced north. As usual, a few drivers were slow to yield the right-of-way. He knifed between their vehicles expertly, enjoying his own skill as he slid through with five or six inches to spare. A blonde woman behind the wheel of a white Cadillac cursed, and the driver of a green station wagon gestured obscenely. Velez ignored them.

Traffic began to thin out above 79th Street, and the staggered lights on Amsterdam Avenue helped him maintain speed. He didn't slow down until the unmarked car crossed 110th Street. Velez didn't want to risk hitting anyone in front of either St. John the Divine cathedral at 112th or Columbia University two blocks north.

As they rolled past the old brick dormitories that housed Columbia's male undergraduates, Bloom thought about his college years here—for about ten seconds. Then his mind automatically refocused on the question that had been bothering him since they had left the Marshall Club. Why should a detective lieutenant on antiterrorist duty be rushed to a subway disaster? He was still considering that when Velez slowed the sedan to a halt on 125th Street at the edge of the crowd.

In the subway station below, some twenty-six policemen did their jobs. A dozen were spread along the platforms used by passengers heading downtown, to make certain these passengers left the station by exits furthest from the death train. It was still there, blocking the uptown express tracks like a metal tombstone.

The others were on the uptown platform. Their job was to keep everyone away from the car filled with corpses. They had been here for nearly an hour. Some were uneasy, others bored, and several were curious. What had happened here? Why were all those passengers dead?

Among those most tantalized by the mystery was Officer Lester Wellesley. He was a twenty-three-year-old rookie who had joined the force only seven months earlier. He didn't have the stolid patience of the veterans yet. This certainly wasn't a routine case. This was fantastic. Nothing like it had ever happened in the little town upstate where Wellesley had been born. Hell, the whole population of that mountain hamlet was barely six hundred. Could there really be eighty or ninety dead in that one subway car?

They had probably been electrocuted. Sure, some freak accident with the third rail. Everybody said that the city's subways were a mess—short of money and way behind on all kinds of maintenance. Yeah, the electrical thing would explain why the stiffs were covered with their own filth. Wasn't that what happened to murderers who took the big jolt in the electric chair? Wellesley had heard such a story, but he had never quite believed it—until now.

He certainly didn't believe that garbage about germs Sergeant Costello had been saying. That was just science-fiction crap. No way any virus could wipe out everybody in nine or ten minutes between 59th and 125th, Wellesley told himself. Even the Russians didn't have that kind of bug. If they or anyone else did, why the hell use it on a New York City subway?

Now he recalled an old gangster film he had seen on television. "You're gonna fry in the hot seat, Tony," a cop had threatened some 1920s hit man. They had called the high-voltage electric chair the hot seat back then. That was another reason for the awful smell. These people had literally fried.

That was a scary idea. Wellesley had to see for himself. Some four-eyed doctor with glasses as thick as windowpanes had taken one long look, panicked, and yelled to the ambulance crews not to come near. Another M.D., a black fellow, had shouted the same order seconds later. Neither doctor had gone into the car to examine the bodies. Their explanation was that it was up to the medical examiner's team to do that, but they were probably just chicken.

Somebody could still be alive in there.

It simply couldn't be that dangerous, Lester Wellesley thought. He and thirteen other cops had been standing here— no more than fifteen yards from the car—for at least forty-five minutes. Nothing had happened to any of them.

Damn it, what if some man or woman in the car could be

saved? There might be several survivors—unconscious or too weak to appeal for help. Wellesley looked at the car again, but from this distance he couldn't see anything definite through the dirty windows.

He had to get closer. The rookie glanced left and right, saw that no one was watching, and decided to take the chance. If the sergeant got sore, Wellesley would have to endure his tongue-lashing. It would be a small price for saving a human life. There might even be a commendation for it.

Wellesley hurried to the open door. He would be careful. He wouldn't actually enter. As he neared the entrance, he sucked in air and held his breath. That would spare him from the worst of the horrible odor inside. It was bad enough fifteen or twenty yards away, and it had to be worse at the door itself.

"Hey, Les!" someone shouted.

"Stay away from there!" another patrolman called out loudly.

Wellesley was at the open door. He was shocked by the sight of the incredible tangle of bodies, but he forced himself closer. He had to know. Holding onto the door frame so he wouldn't fall or slip into the car, he leaned in and tried to concentrate on searching for any sign of life. His eyes swept left and then right. Hoping against hope, he listened.

Nothing.

Not the smallest movement.

Not a single sound.

He pushed himself back and walked quickly toward his post.

"What the hell were you doing, Les?"

"I thought someone might be— Well, they all look dead," he replied.

"The sarge'll rip your ass, Wellesley," an older patrolman warned.

Lester Wellesley shrugged and sniffled. He reached for a handkerchief. Better take a load of vitamin C, he thought as he blew his nose. This could be the start of another lousy cold.

Barely fifteen seconds later he had to use the handkerchief again. His nose was running. Tonight he would try to get ten hours' sleep. That always worked for colds. He paced back and forth. Damn it, his nose was still running, and his chest felt tight. It might be the flu.

Or some sort of allergy. There were so many kinds. He tried to recall what he had last eaten.

Suddenly his vision blurred. His stomach knotted in terrible cramps, and he staggered in pain. He heard someone calling his name but he couldn't see anything. His whole body was burning with agony.

It was all happening so fast. He opened his mouth to call for help, but no words came from his lips. He moaned. Then he began to retch.

CHAPTER 4

"NINE MINUTES from Tenth Street. Not bad, huh?" Velez said as they left the car.

"Fine," Bloom answered mechanically and started through the crowd toward the police perimeter. Velez hurried to keep pace. Soon they were close enough to see a fleet of blue-and-white police cars, several Emergency Service trucks, and a dozen ambulances.

"Smile," Velez advised.

He nodded toward a small army of newspaper, wire service, and broadcast journalists. There were nine or ten radio reporters with tape recorders and minitransmitters. Every television station in the city and all three networks had news teams here, with cameras, sound gear and lights at the ready.

David Bloom turned sharply left to avoid them all. For two months last year the press had given him much more attention than he had wanted. They had made him a media hero. It was easy for them to zero in on him. Good looking, a Phi Beta Kappa and ex-Ivy League fencing champion, Bloom had played the major role in exposing an entire ring of crooked cops. He had disliked the publicity as much as many officers scorned him for getting it. He still shuddered when he recalled the *New York Post* photo caption labelling him Super Cop.

Determined to dodge the cameras, Bloom circled away from the bustling media mob. But there was another problem straight ahead. Four of the dishonest cops whom he'd helped send to prison had been attached to this precinct. It was almost certain that they had friends still working here—some of them probably within yards of Bloom at this moment. Even though the great majority of New York City police despised the "bad apples," Lieutenant David Bloom could not count on a warm welcome here in the Two-Six.

The flaxen-haired patrolman guarding the way in recognized Bloom at once, but he pretended that he didn't. He'd teach this righteous creep a lesson.

"You'll have to stay back with the other reporters, buddy," he said.

It was pure provocation, but Bloom coped coolly. Swiftly raising one hand in signal to stifle any outburst from his loyal aide, Bloom took out his blue-and-gold lieutenant's badge with the other.

"Sorry," the malicious patrolman lied and stepped aside. As Bloom walked on, Velez paused to study the spiteful cop's nameplate.

"*Stennis,* huh? My name is Gabriel Velez. Remember that, *buddy.* I'm gonna remember you, Stennis. I *never* forget wise guys—or sloppy ones."

Before the patrolman could say a word, Velez angrily thrust his golden sergeant's badge to within three inches of Stennis's startled eyes.

"Aren't you going to check *my* ID?" Velez demanded.

"Sarge, I was only—"

Velez brushed past him to look for Bloom. There he was—approaching a visibly worn Captain James Maccarelli. The precinct commander was arguing with a potbellied assistant medical examiner.

"Those people out there will go crazy if the ambulances leave," Maccarelli predicted. "They've got to stay until the trucks arrive."

"But other emergency calls are coming in to hospitals every minute, Captain."

"I can't risk a riot here, damn it," Maccarelli answered and looked at his watch.

"Trucks'll be here any time," the physician assured.

"Then we'll wait. This is all weird, Doc. You won't let us count the bodies or move them or even come near them. You sure you know what you're doing?"

"If I did, I'd be practicing dermatology in Beverly Hills," the assistant medical examiner answered. "Listen, Captain, I'm just following the standard procedures set down for disasters of this kind."

"What kind?"

"I'll tell you after the autopsies. I'll be right back."

The doctor walked away toward the ambulances. Maccarelli shook his head in frustration a moment before he saw Bloom.

"He's scared, Dave," Maccarelli said, "and so am I."

Then he asked the question that Bloom had been expecting.

"What are you doing here?"

"Obeying orders from the PC's office."

"Does the commissioner think this is a terrorist thing?"

"All I was told," Bloom answered carefully, "was to get up here—*fast*, look around, and report to the PC's office at eight o'clock."

Maccarelli might not have accepted this account from several other lieutenants, but he believed David Bloom. Even those who envied or hated Bloom realized that he didn't lie.

"How much have you heard?" Maccarelli asked.

"Something happened in the subway, and you've got a car with eighty or ninety corpses."

At that moment a uniformed sergeant emerged from the subway entrance and hurried toward them.

"That's about all there is, Dave," Maccarelli said. "Everybody in one car is stiff, and not a goddamn scratch on anyone else. What is it, Sergeant?"

"I had no idea he'd do it, Captain," Costello swore. "He was a new guy, but he'd never broken orders before."

"What happened?"

"This Wellesley got the idea there might still be someone alive. Before anybody could stop him, he got to an open door and stuck his head—just his head—in the car to check. Only fifteen or twenty seconds, Captain."

"Is he okay?"

Costello shook his head.

"I think he's dead."

Bloom could not hold back the question.

"Think?"

"After they saw him throwing up . . . and then the convulsions, nobody had the nerve to go near him. He's stretched out on the platform, all covered with vomit and crap like the ones in the car."

"Pull your men further back," the precinct commander ordered.

"Only fifteen or twenty seconds," Costello said angrily. "What the *fuck's* in that car?"

"Keep everyone at least a hundred feet from the car," Maccarelli told him. "I don't want to lose anyone else. That includes lieutenants."

"You don't want me to go down there?" Bloom tested.

"You couldn't see anything from a hundred feet, Dave, and there's no way I'll let anybody closer."

The commissioner wasn't going to like this. Punctilious and demanding, he would expect a full report.

"Would you mind if I asked the sergeant a couple of questions?" Bloom said.

"Not at all."

"This rookie—did he do anything else? Did he touch any-thing?"

"You mean the stiffs? I don't think so," Costello answered.

"I mean *anything.*"

Costello rubbed his chin as he tried to recall.

"I don't— Wait a second. They said he hung onto the door frame."

"Thank you, Sergeant."

Now Costello turned to his precinct commander.

"Captain, what do we do about Wellesley?"

"*We* don't. *They'll* take care of his body and the others."

Maccarelli was pointing at three big trucks coming through the police lines. As Costello walked toward the subway entrance, the vehicles stopped and young men in coveralls emerged from each. They immediately began to unload a variety of metal boxes and plastic bags. There were no markings on the olive green trucks, but Bloom knew.

"Army decontamination teams," he identified.

"With Geiger counters, germ and gasproof suits, and a lot of other Buck Rogers stuff," Maccarelli confirmed.

There would be an explosion of media activity once the mili-tary unit took out their exotic equipment and put on the strange-looking protective gear, Bloom thought. The effect on all the neighborhood people waiting tensely for relatives who hadn't come home on time might be even more extreme.

"I think we'll head downtown," Bloom said. "By the way, Captain, this is Sergeant Velez. He works with me."

Maccarelli nodded in acknowledgment and wondered what Bloom might tell the commissioner.

"Keep in touch, Dave," Maccarelli said.

The message was clear: This case belongs to the Two-Six. If Bloom should learn anything, he was to share it promptly.

"You can count on that," Bloom told the precinct com-mander.

The decontamination teams were opening their boxes as Bloom and Velez approached the police perimeter. All the journalists would be focused on the men in coveralls, Bloom told himself. With a little luck he would be in the unmarked car and on his way without being spotted.

"Lieutenant Bloom! Hey, Lieutenant Bloom!"

One sharp-eyed TV correspondent, an attractive woman with shoulder-length brown hair and enough energy to run a locomotive, had seen him. With her camera crew in swift pursuit, she was running toward him.

"Liz Trotta—CBS," she announced as she swung her microphone in his direction.

"I know," he replied without breaking stride.

"Is this a terrorist—Lieutenant? Lieutenant?"

Bloom kept walking. Within seconds he and Velez were hidden in the crowd, out of sight of the indignant journalist. Annoyed but realistic, she turned her attention back to the men in coveralls. The ambulance crews were beginning to climb into their vehicles. Surprised and curious, the reporters pressed forward to find out what was going on. It didn't make sense for the ambulances to leave now—empty.

Then Bloom and his assistant heard the sound.

It was a great scream and a roar—a terrible noise.

"They're putting on the sealed suits," Bloom said.

He was right. The sight of the decontamination specialists donning what looked like space suits stunned the press and terrified the already frightened civilians. Startled by the uproar, Velez unlocked the sedan quickly, and both men got in. Velez relocked the doors immediately.

"Holy shit!" he said.

Then he started the engine. When they were three blocks away, Velez noticed how warm it was in the car and rolled down a window. They could still hear the screaming.

24

CHAPTER 5

7:43 P.M.

Two blocks north of City Hall and fourteen floors above the Manhattan streets.

The first thing Bloom noticed as he entered the big office was the windows. The panoramic view of the East River and Brooklyn beyond must be splendid from up here, he thought. Then he remembered that the man who faced him across the desk was an ambitious workaholic. Ruling this entire building and some twenty-seven thousand police and civilian employees, Vincent X. Grady was much too busy—and driven—to "waste time" looking out windows.

"You're seventeen minutes early," Grady said as he nodded toward a chair.

"I thought this was urgent," Bloom replied and sat down.

"I like people who are early," the commissioner assured. "And as for this being urgent, it's the highest priority case we have."

"Case? Is this police business?"

Grady ignored the question.

"Just tell me what you saw at One Hundred and Twenty-fifth Street, Lieutenant."

"I saw three or four hundred scared civilians on the verge of a riot and Captain Maccarelli trying hard to control the situation. It was getting pretty rough as we left."

"It got worse," Grady announced. "We moved in more men ten minutes ago. But that's not what I want to talk about. What did you see in the subway? In the car?"

"I never got down there. Captain Maccarelli said I couldn't. You see—"

"What the hell's the matter with Maccarelli?" Grady demanded.

"It's not Maccarelli. It's a cop named Wellesley. He—"

"Who's Wellesley?" Grady interrupted irately.

"He isn't—not anymore. He's dead."

Then Bloom told a startled police commissioner what Sergeant Costello had reported, and explained Maccarelli's decision.

"It was probably prudent," Grady conceded stiffly. "You say Wellesley did this on his own initiative?"

"Yes, Commissioner."

"In violation of orders?"

Bloom nodded, and Vincent X. Grady sighed in relief.

"Then the city certainly can't be held *responsible* for his . . . ah . . . demise, Lieutenant."

"I'm not a lawyer," Bloom answered.

Grady, who had been an assistant dean at Fordham Law School for six years, blinked in discomfort—for just a moment. Then he looked righteous again.

"It's a terrible thing," he said piously. "A cop tries to do something humanitarian and gives his very life for it."

He'd use those same words at the press conference, Bloom thought, and maybe at the funeral too. Vincent X. Grady was good at funerals.

"Going back to the dead civilians," Grady resumed smoothly, "has the cause of death been determined?"

26

His voice was too silky.

His glance was too cool.

He knew something.

"We should have that by morning," Bloom said. "The army doctors should have finished some autopsies by then. You heard about the army teams, didn't you?"

"I was informed of the medical examiner's decision to, ah, implement disaster procedures. That's a Department of Health matter, you know. I never meddle in other agencies' business."

Why was he being so careful?

Why was he separating himself from the question of a disaster?

"The military decontamination units ought to be moving out the body bags now," Bloom estimated. "The whole thing should be on the late TV news on every channel. There were network crews too—cameras and reporters all over the place. I barely managed to stay off CBS myself."

Something unpleasant gleamed in Grady's eyes.

"I hope there wasn't any trouble, Lieutenant. We've tried to maintain good relations with the media, you know. Full cooperation—that's my official policy."

Suddenly it made sense. Grady had sent Bloom rushing up there to be seen. He was *supposed* to be on camera. The cunning commissioner wanted the public to know that Vincent X. Grady cared enough to send his glamorous "Super Cop." Bloom had simply been *used*. The whole deal was a calculated media event. David Bloom found himself thinking of Wellesley and the others who died in the subway, and he wanted to hit Grady. It took several seconds to control that impulse.

"There was no trouble, Commissioner."

"Glad to hear that. I'm sure that you, as an educated man, appreciate our duty to keep the community informed," Grady pontificated effortlessly. "In a free society, people have a right to know."

As he finished this quote from his recent speech to the B'nai B'rith, Grady's eyes flicked to the locked desk drawer that held

27

ELK GROVE VILLAGE PUBLIC LIBRARY

the file. Was this the right time to tell Bloom? Why tell anyone else until the autopsy results were complete? After all, it was possible that the person who had signed the letter "O. B." had nothing to do with the subway incident.

"Is there anything else, sir?" Bloom asked hopefully.

"Not right now. Remember what I said about the media."

"Yes, sir," Bloom answered as he rose to his feet. "There's one more thing I'd like to discuss—if you have a minute."

The commissioner looked at him warily.

"Have there been any phone calls claiming responsibility for what happened in the subway, sir? Is this a terrorist case?"

"No phone calls," Grady snapped. "Good night, Lieutenant."

Bloom said nothing of what had happened in the commissioner's office until he and Velez were outside the building. It was one of David Bloom's routine precautions, part of the personal security system he had adopted even before being assigned to antiterrorist duty.

"That prick is lying, or at least not telling something, Gabe," Bloom concluded.

"Those are two popular sports, Lieutenant. Fact is, you're the only saint I know who isn't on a church wall."

"What's he hiding? Why is he playing games?"

Instead of answering, Velez pointed a finger toward Chinatown, and Bloom nodded in assent. They ate an excellent dinner of dim sum—assorted dumplings and other hors d'oeuvres—at a large restaurant on the Bowery. They left the Silver Palace at 9:35, and Bloom entered his one-bedroom apartment on West 79th Street just in time to turn on the radio for the ten o'clock news.

It's going to be awful, he thought.

It was worse than he expected.

Maccarelli had been wrong.

There were not eighty or ninety corpses.

When the army men in "space suits" had untangled and bagged all the bodies, a major had counted the dead—twice.

The final tally was 117.

ELK GROVE VILLAGE PUBLIC LIBRARY

CHAPTER 6

AT 4:53 A.M. the autopsy results were definite.

At 5:01 a telephone rang in an office in the "D" ring of the second floor of a huge building across the Potomac River from Washington. There were a score of other offices here in the Pentagon that also operated around the clock, but the men and women who worked in those suites knew exactly what they were doing. This office had been in operation twenty-four hours a day for almost twenty months. Not a single one of the military personnel who served here knew the unit's mission.

It was a small office with little furniture. There was a coatrack, a chair, and a desk. There were two telephones on the desk; one of them was regulation black, and the other a bright blue. It was the blue one that was only for incoming calls. Violation of that order would bring immediate court-martial, and everyone obeyed the directive. But there never were any incoming phone calls.

There was another order. Nobody who worked here could say so—not even to another officer who might have the highest security clearance. When First Lieutenant Simon Bagley had joined this unit eleven months ago, he had wondered about that. After so many boring hours here—more than one thousand nine hundred, he had lost interest. The phone would never ring, so it didn't matter.

He was astonished when the bell sounded. 5:01 A.M. on the morning of May 2. Maybe it was a wrong number. There was a procedure for determining whether the call was an error. Bagley knew exactly what to say and do. They had rehearsed it many times. He put down the computer textbook he had been reading to advance his career and picked up the phone.

"Interstate," he said.

"I'd like to leave a message for Mr. Northshield."

It wasn't a wrong number.

"Northshield?" the young officer tested.

"Robert Z. Northshield in Purchasing."

The countersign was correct.

It was *the* call.

"What's the message?" Bagley asked tensely as he reached for the pad and pencil.

"Please tell him Mr. Woodlawn called. W-o-o-d-l-a-w-n. Have you got that?"

"Yes. And the message?"

"It's just one word. Avalanche. A-v-a-l-a-n-c-h-e."

Bagley printed the word carefully and then spelled it back aloud as he had been trained.

"I'll tell him," he said.

"Thank you."

Then Bagley heard a click and a dial tone. The man had hung up. Bagley did the same and reached for the pouch. It held a key. This bag and an automatic pistol were passed to each officer who took over the shift. Bagley extracted the key, unlocked the safe built into the desk and took out a small plastic-covered notebook.

There were numbers and addresses written on the first three pages, but he ignored them. He had been told to do that. He didn't know that they were fakes or why the next four pages were blank. All he knew was that he must dial the telephone numbers on page eight—at once.

It was 5:03 in the morning. Somebody might not like being called at this hour, but orders were orders. Bagley dialed, heard several rings, and then a male voice.

"Yes?"

"This is Interstate," Bagley recited, "and I've had a call for Mr. Robert Z. Northshield."

"What is it?"

There was a tone of authority in that question. After three years in the U. S. Army, Bagley recognized the sound of command.

"Well, sir, it was only a single word. The word is Avalanche."

He heard a sharp intake of breath.

"Shall I spell it, sir?"

"That won't be necessary. Who left the message?"

"A Mr. Woodlawn. W-o-o-d-l-a-w-n."

Now there was a sigh.

"When you telephone the others, I want you to add something. Tell them that there's a meeting in my office at oh-seven hundred."

"How shall I identify you, sir?"

"Just say I'm the man you called first."

In accord with his instructions, Bagley then dialed the other numbers. In each case he found himself speaking to an adult male. That quality of power was in their voices too, and none of them sought any identification beyond "the man I called first."

Bagley was finished with the list by 5:10, and he felt a little uneasy. Was it all over? Would there be more calls for Robert Z. Northshield in Purchasing? If it was all over, what would happen to Bagley and the other Chemical Corps officers who manned this phone? He still didn't understand why this unit was staffed solely with Chemical Corps personnel.

They would probably never tell him that or what the message meant. They were like that. Bagley shrugged and picked up the computer book again. As he opened it, his mind turned to the man who had telephoned. Woodlawn? That was the name of a cemetery up in New York, wasn't it? Imagine going through life carrying the name of an old cemetery, Bagley thought.

Then he found his place in the book and resumed reading. He continued until his shift ended nearly three hours later. The blue telephone did not ring again.

CHAPTER 7

THE MURDERER awoke at half-past six. It was a habit left over from his twenty years in the army. The thirty minutes of vigorous calisthenics he immediately began were also part of his daily routine. Mama had always emphasized that he must be fit and strong. It was the powerful who would prevail over the others—the lesser ones.

"Seventy-two . . . seventy-three . . . seventy-four," he chanted.

He enjoyed the pushups. This morning he might do an extra hundred. He felt wonderful today, exceptionally alive both mentally and physically. It was the exhilaration of success and conquest, the thrill of smashing the enemy totally.

"There is nothing like it, Ernst," she had said so many times. "Your papa told me—over and over when he came back with his medals from the Russian front. He looked so fine with his medals. It is a marvelous feeling to crush the enemy, and it is our duty to civilization too. Those were his very words."

Remembering that made him exercise even more fiercely.

He had worked up quite a sweat by the time he reached for the television set at seven o'clock. Flicking the remote control, he went back and forth at twenty-second intervals from CBS to NBC to ABC. It was on every network—the lead story.

"Worst subway disaster in decades . . . one hundred and seventeen dead . . . shocking slaughter . . . the mayor said . . . one hundred and seventeen casualties . . . mystery still puzzling the authorities . . . military units called in to assist . . . according to the head of the Transit Authority . . . hysterical relatives and friends . . . chaos in the subway system . . . decontamination teams from nearby bases . . . extra police units . . . full investigation . . . not a single survivor. . . ."

He stared in total fascination. Mouth open and eyes wide, he watched the decontamination units emerge from the subway entrance and carry the bags to the green trucks. There were so many sacks. It was fantastic. The colors were so bright in the glare of the lights. More body bags . . . still more. The crowd of blacks—faces like African masks twisted in anguish—was screaming. The sound was excellent too, he thought.

It was so exciting. The pleasure was almost sexual. He felt the thrill coursing through his body. Now he sensed the swelling in his loins. No, that was bad. Mama had told him that again and again. It was *dirty*. He must not permit it. Until he had avenged his father, all such things were to be shunned. Blood and honor came first.

But the desire would not go away. Click, click, click, he changed stations swiftly to drive the bad from within him. He tried to blot it out with the images on the screen, but his body would not yield. Ashamed and angry at his weakness, he turned off the set and hurried to the shower.

He must not touch himself *there*. It was forbidden. It was weak and filthy and disloyal. It was a betrayal of Otto Henke, who had chosen death over dishonor. Struggling against the hunger, the murderer twisted on the cold water—full blast. It was his only hope. The shock of the icy torrent was acute and painful.

The blow to his nervous system obliterated everything else. It hurt. That was good.

Yes, Mama. Yes.

Now he adjusted the shower so the water gushed down in stinging needles. He raised his face up to welcome the full impact. It was good to lose himself in the cold needles. Quite deliberately he defied the frigid assault upon his senses for two minutes more. Other soldiers had joked about his ability to "take" icy water. They had said that no one else could remain in a cold shower as long, and they had boasted that their sergeant was "a tough ole bird."

He wasn't *that* old, he thought as he turned off the water. He certainly didn't look old. Though born in 1943, he was trim and devoid of flab. "Lean and mean" was still his motto though he had left the U. S. Army twenty months ago. He was still on active duty—in the Henke Army.

Only he and Mama knew that it existed or that he existed. The U. S. Army and the Social Security idiots all thought that he had died in Utah. He had fooled them so completely that Mama had collected his GI insurance and was receiving a monthly pension check as well. And she was still getting the other army money every thirty days as the widow of Warrant Officer Jerry Bob Letherby.

The man who counted stepped from the shower and used the thick towel vigorously. Then he dressed for the bus ride to New York. It would be so thrilling to see in every newspaper what he had done, to hear all those people talking of it in awe. He would secretly savor the dread and uncertainty in their puzzled eyes. That look would change very soon. The mayor must tell them of the letter. Then the whole city would be afraid.

Their bellies would be knotted in terror. Their throats would be dry with dread. Each would study the others uneasily, wondering whether he or she could be the unknown destroyer. There might even be panic, he thought as he combed his thinning hair over the bald spot.

35

After he finished brushing his teeth with the fluoridated mint-flavored paste, he carefully applied an extra-strong antiperspirant beneath his arms. As an additional precaution, he squirted a scented breath spray into his mouth. All these acts were as much a part of his ritual as the enemas he took each night before going to bed. He was not ashamed that he still lived by Mama's slogan—"Clean inside and out."

At 7:55, he boarded the bus that would carry him from green and quiet Montville down to the Lincoln Tunnel and under the Hudson River to the Port Authority terminal. He glanced at the other commuters—some dozing, others gazing vaguely out the windows, and many immersed in newspapers. He swallowed in pride when he saw the four-column headlines about his first attack.

He would let them sweat for a day. Tomorrow he would mail the next letter with his orders. He would tolerate no delays or infantile efforts at negotiation. His terms were fixed: unconditional surrender. They would be searching for him, of course, but it was hopeless. He was much too clever and powerful for their police. He was a superior being, the son of an SS hero. As Mama had whispered so many times, he was Otto's Boy.

CHAPTER 8

9:25 A.M.

Grady looked as if he had been up most of the night. He had, and fresh clothes and a perfect shave couldn't hide it. There was a saw-toothed urgency in his voice that flatly contradicted his businesslike manner.

"In one hour and five minutes, the mayor will hold a press conference," he told Bloom. "I wanted you to know what he'll say first—because this is *your* case."

"The subway thing?"

"Yes. I now have enough information to answer the question you asked last night. What happened in the subway was the work of one or more terrorists. All those one hundred and seventeen people were murdered."

"Gas?"

The police commissioner nodded.

"How did you know?" he asked.

"I didn't know, but I thought about it a lot last night and nothing else made sense."

37

Grady nodded again. Bloom was an independent and intellectually arrogant son of a bitch—and a very smart detective. Right now, a very smart detective was what Vincent Grady needed more than anything else in the world.

"Other than the autopsy reports, Lieutenant, we don't have a lot to go on yet. There was a letter to the mayor six days ago, no proper signature or name, just the letters O. B. at the bottom."

"Doesn't ring a bell," Bloom replied, "but I'll talk to my people, and we'll run it through the computer. I'll check with the FBI and CIA too."

"As soon as possible," Grady snapped.

His fear was almost tangible. David Bloom had never seen him this troubled before.

"Right away. Now getting back to the letter—"

"It received the full treatment. I can assure you that our lab people went over it very carefully," Grady said defensively. "Not a print, not a clue of any kind. Paper and envelope sold at every Woolworth store in the country."

"Typed, written, or printed?"

"Printed—in the *New York Post*. Words and letters cut from the paper and pasted onto the cheap stationery. The postmark was Brooklyn. That's a large borough, Lieutenant. More than two million people."

It was as if he was rehearsing what he would tell the press.

"This is a great city, Lieutenant, with a huge population. The mayor gets all sorts of crank letters and threats almost every week."

"What was the threat in this one?"

Grady shook his head and smoothed his foulard tie.

"It was more than a threat," he answered. "It was a promise to do something terrible between four and six p.m. on May first. Those were the exact words."

"Did the letter say why?"

"To prove that O. B. has the power to do such things. That's another quote. And if we don't want another attack, we'll have to pay five million dollars."

"*Attack?*" Bloom tested.

"That was the word used. The last sentence said they'll send instructions on payment soon. These men are mad dogs, Lieutenant. One hundred and seventeen corpses to show us their power? That's insane!"

"Yes, but it worked. They wanted to shock and frighten the whole city, and they did."

The commissioner sat up stiffly in his big swivel chair.

"They haven't intimidated *me,*" he announced. "I can assure you that we'll do whatever is necessary to protect our citizens."

"So the city won't pay the five million?"

"Various solutions are under consideration," Grady said evasively and fingered his expensive tie again. "We can't go into details yet—for obvious security reasons."

"What will the public be told?"

"Well . . . we certainly don't want to cause any panic, Lieutenant. I believe that the mayor will cover the basics at his press conference. He won't touch on things that might compromise your investigation."

The words were artfully chosen, but the message beneath the politician's jargon was clear: They would hold back as much as possible, using the standard pieties as their excuse.

"And in accord with the department's usual procedures," Grady continued briskly, "we're also setting up a Homicide Task Force in the Two-Six to work on this. That's the site of the crime. I'm not really counting on them. Off the record, you and your unit are the point men in my book."

"I won't tell that to the FBI," Bloom said.

"Of course not. The Bureau has good personnel and a great deal of it. Fine technicians and equipment too. Their resources and cooperation may be very useful, but I'm hoping we can crack this big one ourselves. It would be fine for the city's morale."

And the career of Vincent X. Grady.

"Here's the file, including photocopies of the letter and the autopsy report. Good hunting, Lieutenant."

He handed Bloom a sealed manila envelope a moment before the phone rang. Grady picked it up immediately.

"It's the mayor," he announced. "Keep me fully informed, Lieutenant. . . . Hello. . . . Yes, Tom. . . . Whatever you say. . . . If you feel my presence at the press conference would help, sure."

Then he pointed to the door, and Bloom left with the eight-by-ten-inch envelope. When he returned to the antiterrorist unit's office on the fourth floor, he found Velez and a black detective named Gillespie waiting.

"It's our deal," Bloom said and began to open the envelope.

"Do they know what killed those people?" Velez asked.

"Poison gas."

"I don't like poison gas," Gillespie said slowly.

"Nobody in his right mind does," Bloom said as he sat down to study the contents of the file.

"Do we know whom we're looking for?" Gillespie questioned.

"Somebody in his *wrong* mind," Velez answered.

"Maybe a gang of somebodies," Bloom said. "All we've got to go on is a nasty letter signed O. B.—and that's not much."

"O. B.? Never heard of it. Want me to kick it through the computer?" Velez offered.

"Fast."

"You got it. Oh—Len Fredericks called."

Leonard Fredericks was the competent supervisor of the terrorism squad of the local branch of the Federal Bureau of Investigation. He was the senior FBI representative on the Joint City–Federal Task Force on Terrorism on which David Bloom also served.

As the door closed behind Velez, Bloom dialed the FBI office three blocks away. It took less than a minute to arrange for a meeting of the joint group. Bloom wondered why it couldn't be before 10:45, but he knew better than to ask. The FBI had its own rules and reasons, procedures and priorities. It rarely discussed them with other agencies.

"Okay, 10:45," Bloom agreed. "In the meanwhile, would you check on any outfits or individual terrorists known as O. B.? That's O for orange and B for baker. You might try the Spooks on this too. Thanks."

Bloom went back to reading the documents in the thin file. He went over the letter again and again, searching for something—anything he hadn't noticed during the first five readings. He could see nothing unusual in the spelling, phrasing, or use of language. Still he wasn't satisfied. He handed the letter to Gillespie. Only twenty-eight, the young detective with the neatly cropped Afro haircut had a practical mind that Bloom respected.

"What do you think, Johnny?" Bloom asked.

John Gillespie read the page twice before he shook his head.

"Five million? These mothers are greedy," he judged.

"I mean the text. Anything odd?"

Gillespie looked at the letter again.

"Attack?" Bloom tested.

"That's a military term, Lieutenant."

"Exactly what I was thinking."

At that moment, Velez returned.

"Zip . . . zero . . . *gurnicht* . . . *nada*," he reported.

The computer scan had failed.

CHAPTER 9

IT WASN'T normal. There were three things you could count on when dealing with the FBI, Bloom thought. They were neat and conservative dressers, worked in fairly large teams and were always on time. Being late was as unthinkable as not wearing a white shirt and tie.

The supervisor of the FBI's local terrorism squad was a twenty-two-year veteran of the Bureau. Leonard Fredericks had always done everything by the book during the nine months that Bloom had known him. It was 10:58—thirteen minutes after the time set for the meeting. He had never kept Bloom waiting before. Why today? Was something wrong?

Bloom looked around the "reception area" on the twenty-sixth floor of the Federal Building, exchanged glances with Velez, and checked his stainless-steel Omega again. First the mayor had pushed back his press conference to eleven o'clock and now this. Perhaps it was childish or maybe Bloom was getting paranoid, but he didn't like either development.

"Mr. Fredericks will see you now," a trimly barbered young agent announced. It was Collery, Fredericks' assistant. He was wearing a gray suit. FBI agents did not come in shirt sleeves to escort visitors, and no outsider walked these corridors without escort. This was a maximum-security floor. Bloom suspected that it also housed counterespionage operations, but that was another subject one didn't discuss. Without a word, the two New York policemen followed Collery to a door marked Conference B.

Fredericks, long-jawed and solemn behind metal-rimmed glasses, was seated at the far end of the twenty-foot table. Three other men filled adjacent chairs. Bloom recognized the sandy-haired one as an FBI agent named Gunderson. Facing him was a pair of wary-eyed men in their thirties. David Bloom had never seen either of them before.

"Lieutenant Bloom and Sergeant Velez of the NYPD," Fredericks announced. "I don't think you know Arthur White and Martin Smith."

"Part of your squad?" Bloom asked as he sat down.

"Weapons specialists," the FBI supervisor replied.

"So you've heard about the autopsy results?"

Fredericks shifted in his chair and nodded.

"Here's a copy of the report—and something else," Bloom said. Then he handed Fredericks an envelope containing duplicates of the material Grady had given him.

"It's a letter," Bloom explained. "I think it's from the people who put the gas in the subway car."

None of the FBI agents even blinked at the word gas. It was clear that they already knew. Not one of them said a word as Fredericks opened the envelope and began to scan the contents. While he read, Bloom turned to the weapons experts.

"You fellows familiar with gas?"

Their heads bobbed in assent.

"Good. All I know is what I got from an encyclopedia article I read this morning. As I see it, the way those one hundred and seventeen people died suggests *nerve gas.*"

"Holy shit!" Velez erupted in astonishment.

"Is that possible?" Bloom tested.

The weapons specialists hesitated and exchanged glances. Several seconds passed before the taller one cleared his throat and spoke.

"The information we have seems to point to some type of nerve agent," he agreed cautiously.

"Are you Smith or White?"

"White."

"Which type of nerve agent, Mr. White?" Bloom asked.

"It's difficult to be certain, Lieutenant. There are various kinds."

"The Germans invented the basic product in the thirties, during the Hitler era," Smith volunteered in a strong New England accent. "They called it Tabun. Later they came up with an improved version they named Sarin, and then they went on to Soman. A thickened form of Soman is what the Soviets have been stockpiling in huge quantities. The Red Army is believed to have more than five hundred thousand tons of various nerve agents. They claim that's to deter anyone else from using such weapons against them."

"What about U. S. nerve gas?" Bloom probed.

White cleared his throat again.

"I understand we haven't made any for more than fifteen years," he replied.

"*Atropine,*" Velez said abruptly. "When I was in the army, they told us that the only antidote was an injection of atropine—*fast.*"

"How fast?" Bloom asked.

"Sixty to eighty seconds," Smith told him. "I believe that's why, in combat situations where an enemy nerve agent attack seems possible, each U. S. soldier carries his own gas mask and a hypo filled with atropine."

Velez winced as he remembered.

"You were supposed to inject yourself in the leg. They showed us how."

"How quickly does this stuff kill?" David Bloom asked.

"That might depend on the person," Smith said.

"Or atmospheric conditions," White added conscientiously.

"Roughly?"

"It could be two and a half to three and a half minutes," White estimated. "I've heard that it's fifty times more powerful than hydrogen cyanide. Even a very tiny dosage would be fatal."

Bloom tried to recall the details of what he had read.

"Odorless?"

"Both odorless and colorless, Lieutenant."

Bloom found himself thinking of the men, women, and children who had died in the subway.

"Those people had no warning?"

"None."

"So they never had a chance," Bloom said grimly as he reached inside his jacket and took out a cigar.

"Not really," White confirmed. "Would you mind not lighting that? I'm allergic to tobacco smoke."

Bloom put the corona back into his pocket.

"Thank you, Lieutenant. If you're interested in how the gas works, it neutralizes the enzyme in our bodies that regulates the flow of nerve impulses. They control physical activity. With the transmitting system wrecked, we have unregulated physical activity."

It was all impersonal—as if he were reading from a textbook.

"What does that do?"

"It causes—very quickly—intense sweating, dimming of vision, and the filling of the bronchial passages with mucus. Next comes uncontrollable vomiting and defecation, followed by convulsions. The final stages are paralysis and respiratory failure. That's terminal, of course," the weapons specialist concluded in the matter-of-fact voice of a classroom lecturer.

"You're saying the victim literally stops breathing and dies," Bloom summarized.

"One might put it that way," Smith answered. "Military manuals generally use the word target rather than victim, but in this case either would do."

Bloom took a deep breath before he spoke again.

"How many countries have made this stuff, Mr. Smith?"

"At least four or five. And it's entirely possible that other governments have managed to secure quantities from them in one way or another. The transaction would be secret, as just about everything concerning chemical weapons is."

"Could this be gas from some old German dump?"

"No way," White assured. He explained that the safe shelf life of nerve agents was no more than eighteen or twenty years. Keeping it longer was extremely dangerous, for the powerful gas would corrode its container and begin to leak.

"That happened at the Rocky Mountain Arsenal near Denver five or six years ago," Bloom recalled. "I saw it in the *Times*. They burned some of it and moved the rest to another base away from any city."

The phone rang, and Fredericks lifted the instrument immediately.

"Yes. . . . Yes. . . . It's Captain Maccarelli for you," the FBI supervisor announced as he handed the telephone to Bloom.

"Hello, Captain. . . . Yes, that's what the PC ordered. . . . Absolutely—a joint effort. . . . You know it. . . . What? . . . That's terrific."

Bloom put one hand over the mouthpiece.

"Good news. They may have found the weapon," he exulted.

"If we can help in any way—" White offered.

The FBI's technical expertise could be invaluable. Bloom did not hesitate.

"Captain, what do you think about asking our federal friends to check this cylinder out? As I see it, they have the best labs and technicians in the business. . . . Fine. Please send it down to Leonard Fredericks at the FBI office here right away. . . . Yes, it may be very important—and still dangerous. . . . Because

it might have contained nerve gas. . . . That's still confidential.
. . . Thanks, I'll get back to you."

Bloom hung up the phone and turned to share the news:

"They were finishing the decontamination this morning.
Then they cleaned up the car. In the process, they went through
a lot of mess, including shopping bags, purses, and bundles scat-
tered around the floor. One of the last things they opened was
a package about the size of a shoe box. Inside was a metal cylinder
with a timing device."

The federal agents all leaned forward.

"Three inches in diameter and seven inches long—a cylinder
of bright blue metal."

Both weapons experts blinked rapidly several times. White
coughed. Like Smith, he was avoiding eye contact with David
Bloom.

"Maccarelli's sending it right down by police car," he told
them. "I hope you don't mind examining it."

"We're always glad to cooperate," Fredericks replied briskly.
"And on that O. B. identification, there should be word from
Washington this afternoon. Will you be in your office?"

"Probably. Nice to meet you, gentlemen," Bloom said as he
rose. Then he extended his right hand to Smith. The weapons
expert stood up and held out his own right hand as protocol
required. Bloom noticed that it was damp with sweat. White's
was dry but rigid when Bloom shook it moments later.

"You fellows got a minute for one more question?" Velez
asked as he got up from the table. "The stuff in the gas—would
it be tough for somebody to get?"

"The ingredients are not exotic," White answered.

"Exotic?"

"They can be bought without any great difficulty," Smith
translated.

"And once you've got them, is the gas hard to make?"

"Very. The manufacturing process is both highly complex
and extremely dangerous. Sophisticated equipment is required."

"So a crazy college professor couldn't cook up a batch in his lab?"

"I think that would be just about impossible, Sergeant," White said in a voice that a patient teacher might use to a child.

It was 11:25 when Bloom and Velez got back to their office.

"You were right," Gillespie announced as they entered.

"The mayor didn't mention the five million?"

"Not a word, Lieutenant. He was outraged and he was concerned—the usual jive. The PC was with him. He was sincere but confident."

"About what?" Bloom asked irritably as he took off his jacket.

"About the ability of our hardworking police force and its capable antiterrorist unit led by Lieutenant David Bloom to deal with these savage criminals."

Bloom shook his head in disgust.

"We've already had eight calls from newspaper and TV people," the black detective continued. "Three camera crews, an ABC radio guy, and a photographer from some West German magazine are on their way. And a lady psychic from New Jersey phoned to offer her assistance."

"No astrologers?"

"Not yet, Lieutenant."

Bloom took off his jacket and hung it up.

"This is a real crazy case," Velez said. "The Feds said those people died of nerve gas."

"Jesus!" Gillespie gasped.

"The only folks who can make it are four or five governments, and they're sure to have heavy-duty stuff like this in max security holes one hundred feet underground," Velez said, "so how the hell did these loonies get their hands on it?"

Bloom took out a cigar, lit it, and puffed.

"What kind of people would do this?" Gillespie wondered.

"Very sick ones," Bloom said. "That's it. Thank you, gentlemen."

"For what?" Velez asked.

"Come on, Gabe, there's just one thing to do when someone's

really sick," Bloom chided as he reached for the Manhattan telephone directory on a nearby shelf.

"What's that?"

"You call a doctor."

Phone book in hand, Bloom walked back to his private office.
There were pages and pages of Cohens. It was twenty-five seconds before he found the one he wanted and began to dial.

CHAPTER 10

THE PENTAGON.

Suite 3E-880.

"Are you absolutely sure?" the man in the blue pinstriped suit demanded.

Clark Millard had been president of General Motors before accepting his second invitation to become Secretary of Defense. Dedicated to numbers and the "bottom line," he always wanted everything to be absolutely sure.

"Our people in New York have examined the cylinder carefully," General Younts replied. "It's definite."

Millard's eyes clouded as he heard the bad news.

"And just how long have your people known about this development in New York?"

"First word came in 'bout oh-five-hundred this morning," the army chief of staff reported. "That was the flash call from Woodlawn."

"Who?"

"It's a code name, Mr. Secretary. There was a big list of them, each one a cemetery near some large city," Younts explained in his soft Tennessee drawl. "Woodlawn meant that nerve gas had been used or found in the New York City area."

"Was this list some idiot's idea of *cute?*" Millard bristled.

He was probably working up to blaming the army, Younts thought. Politicians and the media usually did.

"I wouldn't know, suh," the four-star general answered evenly. "I can assure you the army has moved expeditiously. Within minutes after the Woodlawn signal, General Stark called a meeting of—"

"When did *you* hear about it?" Millard interrupted.

"I was briefed at oh-nine-thirty."

Millard studied the thin gold Rolex on his left wrist.

"It's two twenty-five in the afternoon, General. That's almost a five-hour delay. Why wasn't I informed before this?"

This was no time for a petty argument, the veteran soldier decided. He paused for several seconds to slow the tempo before he answered.

"We were waiting on final confirmation 'bout the blue cylinder, suh," Younts told him. "That came in only an hour ago. I tried to reach you directly. I was told you were out to lunch."

Thwarted and tense, the Secretary of Defense pointed at his leather-bound desk calendar. *"Five days,* General," he announced. "In five days I'm going up on the Hill to request approval for us to resume production of nerve gas—the new binary agent. They'll never buy it now."

"But binary is much safer to store," Younts said. "It doesn't become dangerous till the two components are united. That happens only when the shell or bomb is in flight."

"I believe you, and I believe the reports that our stocks of nerve gas are deteriorating and dwindling. I also believe that the Soviets have great quantities of fresh nerve gas. But after yesterday's massacre, our whole civilian population has to be in a state of shock. Shock and reflex revulsion."

"Do you think—"

"I *know,* General. With one hundred and seventeen corpses

up there in the morgue, there's not a member of Congress—not even the half senile ones—who'd come near approving more nerve gas. It would be political suicide."

"But, Mr. Secretary—"

Millard broke in again.

"They may be mediocre, but they're not stupid—not about their jobs. And nobody has a real lead on who killed all those people. What a mess!"

"Yes, suh."

"And it's going to get worse," Millard predicted fiercely. "It's going to be another media circus. They'll be out for blood. Anybody's. Everybody's. The foreign press will have a great time cutting us to pieces. Those sanctimonious snots love to rip the United States any chance they get."

Then he paused to catch his breath.

"Maybe the situation can be contained," the army chief of staff said in an oddly confidential tone.

"How?"

"The cylinder is in our hands—on the way to Washington by special courier. No reason to add fuel to the fire by giving pictures of it to the press. Let the media concentrate on the manhunt. Let them focus on the FBI and the New York police. Hell, Mr. Secretary, they're much more glamorous than we are."

Millard shook his head.

"I appreciate your lack of confidence in the maturity and wisdom of most journalists, Younts. Off the record, I share it. However, there are some who think and work and do more than attend press conferences or rewrite mimeographed hand-outs."

"Only a few," the Tennessean argued. "The odds are with us. For the vast majority, terrorists are better copy and better pictures than chemists anytime. Look, only six people even know we've got men in New York. They won't talk to the press, and there's always the chance that the FBI or local cops will catch the terrorists before the five days. Then we're okay."

"No, we're not. I can't risk it, General. I don't think you can either."

"I'd like to try unless I get a direct order not to," the chief of staff said earnestly. "We need the binary."

Millard evaded the unspoken question and the risky responsibility.

"Thanks for the briefing, General. I'm sure that you'll do what you think is best from a professional military point of view," he announced noncommittally, "and I'll do what I have to do as a member of the cabinet and National Security Council."

"Might I ask what that will be, suh?"

"Well . . . I'll have to discuss the entire situation with the President."

Less than a minute after the general left, Millard was speaking with the White House appointments secretary. When Millard explained that his business was urgent, they agreed that the Secretary of Defense would see the President at nine the next morning.

CHAPTER 11

OTTO'S BOY left work at five o'clock. There was no subway ride in his plan for tonight. Instead, he followed his usual routine. He made his way through the bustle of crowded Pennsylvania Station and walked over to Eighth Avenue. Then he started north in the late afternoon warmth.

The spring sun was shining brightly, and the temperature was a pleasant 74 degrees. He hardly noticed either as he trudged up the street. He hated Eighth Avenue. It was noisy and grubby, lined with cheap shops selling fast food, discount luggage, bolts of cloth, cut-rate liquor, sandals and other low-priced goods from India, Korea and Taiwan.

He thought of those products as rubbish. He felt the same way about the humans on this street. It wasn't only the winos, the hookers and the shabby loiterers. The majority of those he hurried past were black and Hispanic working people, and he despised them just as much. Everything about them—even the way they spoke and laughed—filled him with loathing.

He walked among them carefully. He didn't want any of

54

them to brush up against him. He didn't really like anyone to touch him. Even as a child he never had. Part of it was because Mama had warned him about dirt and disease, but that wasn't all. Physical contact frightened him.

When he reached 40th Street, he stopped and turned left to cross Eighth Avenue. He always did that at this corner. He had to wait for the light to change. As he paused, a leggy prostitute in a leather miniskirt and tight purple blouse smiled her offer from a nearby doorway. He choked for a moment in fear and something else—something twisted and shameful. Then he found the hatred, and he was safe. He could breathe easily again.

It's all right, Mama.

This slut was no threat to his mission. He had killed one even younger and shapelier only last year. That had been a necessary step in his operation—an impersonal execution. Yes, that was probably the simplest way to rid the cities of these disgusting and disease-ridden whores. Exterminate them.

Now the light was green. He walked to the west side of Eighth Avenue and turned right to proceed to the vast bus station. Hundreds of other people were streaming to the same building to board the commuter vehicles that would take them out of the metropolis. It was at a newsstand in the huge terminal that he bought a copy of the FINAL edition of the *New York Post* and slipped it into the nine-by-twelve-inch manila envelope acquired a month earlier.

At another newsstand at the far end of the concourse he purchased a second copy. This one was for reading. He made his way to the bus he always took, managed to get a seat and settled down for a journey of pure pleasure. This late edition would have lots of pictures of his triumph. The big letters of the shock headline that filled the front page promised what he could barely wait to enjoy: an account of the mayor's press conference.

This was something to savor, and he always saved the best for last. It was one of the childhood habits he hung on to blindly. So he began reading the back page even though he had no interest in sports. He paid no attention to the main story about the ninth consecutive victory of "the amazin' Knicks," the local pro basketball team. He was equally indifferent to an account of the latest dispute between the owner and the manager of the baseball Yankees.

The murderer forced himself to scan the rest of the sports pages, the section devoted to various sorts of entertainment and the business reports. The bus emerged from the Lincoln Tunnel into the New Jersey dusk as he glanced at the two pages of comics. He stared at the cartoons for several minutes, seeing nothing.

Then he turned to the front section of the tabloid. The story—*his* story—completely filled pages two and three. The headline that sprawled across both pages was two inches high. That was good. But the quality of the photo reproduction was mediocre, and the black-and-white pictures did not compare with the color of the images on the TV news broadcasts.

Now he read the text. The account of the press conference was disappointing. There was no mention of his letter. Why hadn't the mayor told the whole story? Why was he keeping the power of O. B. from the city? . . . from the world? Was it some cheap politician's trick or the stupid spite of a devious demagogue?

This was disgusting. They must *all* know about him—even if his name remained a secret. They had to fear him. That was part of his plan. Four decades earlier, other inferior and racially impure beings had been numb with terror at the thought and sight of Otto Henke. Now they must dread his son.

He turned the page and saw a photo of a U. S. Marine just back from the tense Middle East. Suddenly the picture changed. Before his eyes it became his father in a very different attire. As in those faded snapshots Mama kept hidden, Papa wore the proud uniform of the First SS Panzer Division, the famed *Leibstandarte* SS Adolf Hitler. It was the toughest of all the *Waffen* SS battle units, which was why it was designated the Führer's "own."

And the point of the cutting edge had been the crack First SS Panzer Regiment, an invincible and fast-moving armored unit of tanks and half tracks. Corporal Henke had been part of the regiment's *Kampfgruppe* Peiper, the battle group commanded by Lieutenant Colonel Joachim Peiper. Mama had told him how brilliantly this combat team had fought in the invasion of Russia in 1941 and 1942, and how ruthlessly it had stamped out enemy guerrillas in 1943.

It was triumph after triumph until mid-1944. Then the Americans, British and Canadians had put masses of troops ashore in Normandy under cover of giant aerial armadas. By November all of France and much of Belgium was in the invaders' hands. But the Führer had a great plan for a gigantic counterattack, one that the glorious First SS Panzer Division would lead.

And *Kampfgruppe* Peiper was to be the spearhead. The strategy was to launch a huge surprise attack through the wooded Ardennes in foggy mid-December. Swift armored columns would slash to the port of Antwerp, trapping four entire Allied armies to the north. They'd be crushed, buying time for the Reich's V-2 missiles and other new "wonder weapons" to turn the tide of the war. It was in all the history books on World War II that Otto Henke's son had read so intently.

In the predawn hours of December 16, twenty-five German divisions struck less than a third as many American troops spread thin across seventy miles of the snow-covered Ardennes. The surprise was complete. Aided by English-speaking saboteurs wearing U. S. uniforms, the Germans crashed forward on the southern and central sectors. But the stubborn Americans somehow rallied to contain most of the attack in the crucial north.

Only one German unit broke through in the north: the *kampfgruppe* in which Otto Henke served. *Obersturmbannführer* Peiper's tanks—twenty-six-ton Mark IVs, fifty-ton Panthers and seventy-two-ton Tigers—ripped through the GIs quickly at first. "We sliced them open like a bayonet through lard," Corporal Henke had written home two weeks later. Mama kept that letter and secretly read it to their son many times. She loved secrets.

Peiper's tanks were rolling ahead on the seventeenth when it happened. The American account was a complete lie, of course. Mama had explained that. The Americans even had the name of the place wrong. They had called the incident the Malmedy Massacre, but it actually took place at a crossroads near a smaller hamlet. The word "massacre" was equally false. It was probably the idea of devious Jews in U. S. military intelligence, as Mama believed. The only solid fact was that the corpses of seventy-two American GIs who had been captured by the Germans were later found in the snow. Peiper's unit was the only German force in that immediate area, but what did that prove?

Without warning, the picture blurred. The man who counted found himself looking at the photo of a U. S. Marine again. Where had Papa gone? It wasn't important. He could always be found in the metal box hidden in the little house in Montville. Otto Henke's only son looked at his watch. The bus would be in Montville in forty-eight minutes.

It was on time. Four people got off—as usual.

" 'Night, Tony," a salesman named Edward Archibald called out casually.

"Good night, Ed," the murderer replied. He was known in this small community as Anthony Sommers. He had no interest in the salesman or anyone else in Montville, but it could be dangerous to be openly aloof or guarded. That might attract attention, so he went along with these superficial amenities.

When he got home, he double-locked the door and adjusted the blinds so no one could see inside any of the four rooms. Then he stripped to the skin, hung up his clothes, and dressed in the coveralls that were his battle uniform. He washed his hands and face with soap, dried them, and studied his face for any pimples or blackheads. His skin, like every other part of his body, must be clean.

After drinking a glass of cold water, he entered the large

bedroom closet and opened the hidden panel he had built into its back wall. He took out the metal box, carried it to the kitchen, and put the heavy container on the table. This box contained his most precious possessions. He was careful as he rotated the dial of the lock set flush in the steel top. This was the security transport cell he had stolen from the Chemical Corps. It contained a detonator and incendiary charge that would destroy the contents if the combination was not dialed correctly.

He opened the box and took out the scrapbook. Mama had collected all the clippings from American and German papers and magazines, but it was her devoted son who had mounted them on the pages. The whole story was here. There was the picture of one group of the SS men on trial for allegedly murdering unarmed prisoners at Malmedy. Otto Henke was in the back row.

Lieutenant Colonel Joachim Peiper and seventy-one of his men had been charged as war criminals. Instead of fighting the Russian barbarians who meant to poison the whole world with filthy Communism, the stupid Americans had persecuted courageous *Waffen* SS troopers. Of the twenty officers and fifty-one lower ranks, forty-three were sentenced to death, twenty-two got life imprisonment and the rest received terms of ten, fifteen, or twenty years.

A decade later, all but one of the seventy-one so shamefully convicted were free. The Americans claimed that he had killed himself in prison after a mental breakdown, but it was a lie. They had murdered him when he refused to testify falsely against his comrades in arms. The psychiatric records were all forgeries, of course. Papa would never commit suicide; only a coward would take his own life. Otto Henke had died bravely, a loyal warrior of the *Waffen* SS and the great Third Reich.

Otto's Boy fought back the tears—as he always did when he read that clipping. There was one more, dated 1976, twenty years after the last of the others had been released. Lieutenant Colonel Peiper had been living in retirement in a rural cottage in France. When the local people discovered his identity, some of them—Reds, no doubt—had butchered him and burned his home to cinders.

Both Otto Henke and Joachim Peiper must be avenged, the sincere psychopath thought as he closed the scrapbook. It had to be done. No sacrifice would be too great. That was why Mama had married the American soldier in the Army of Occupation in 1950—to get them a new name. If Ernst Henke was to avenge the SS martyrs, he had a much better chance of success as Ernest Letherby, "son" of a gullible GI from Meridian, Mississippi. Ernie Letherby had even learned to speak in the soft southern way of his stepfather. Mama had insisted on that. There wasn't a trace of a German accent left in his speech.

Mama had made him the total American boy, the perfect one. She had forced him to read the U. S. history books about the wars and the generals, and also to learn about the baseball teams and their players. Ernie Letherby knew about all of them. Other GIs' sons asked him questions, unaware that he had spent hundreds of hours secretly memorizing facts as if they were multiplication tables. He did the same for football. Though he detested both games, he forced himself to play them, pretending enthusiasm. He rooted for the St. Louis Cardinals in baseball, spinning tales of Dizzy Dean and Joe Medwick and Stan Musial. In football he focused on Ol' Miss—the glorious University of Mississippi.

And it hadn't stopped there. There was so much more to learn: movie stars, candy bars, comic strips, presidents, soft drinks, and racial jokes. He had to memorize all the right attitudes and taunts about blacks and yids and wops. It took a lot of time. Many afternoons when the other kids were playing, he was working on his role with Mama and books she got from the U. S. library. She brought records too so he would be familiar with Bing Crosby and Frank Sinatra and a dozen others. She asked questions to make sure he had it right. He had to have it exactly right—all of it: chili dogs, grits, corn flakes, John Wayne, Gary Cooper, Ava Gardner—everything.

So the man who now called himself Anthony Sommers had

become the purest of American stereotypes—externally. No one suspected that this was a homicidal Huck Finn. When the Letherbys moved from base to base as army families do at three-year intervals, none of the children or adults they met thought that there was anything unusual about young Ernie. He was just another good-natured boy, smarter than most and a friendly lad who never got into trouble. Even his teachers liked him, and other mothers wished that their sons were as nice. He was so well behaved, a sensible kid who was always helpful, neat and very clean.

He was still neat and clean. After he relocked the security cell and hid it in the closet, he washed his hands before he went to work. First he placed the glue and the scissors on the kitchen table, and then he put on the thin gloves of white cotton. He covered the part of the table he would be using with a large sheet of the red-and-green wrapping paper he had bought at half price after Christmas. After he had taped it in place so it couldn't slide, he took the second copy of tonight's *Post* from the envelope.

This was the safe one, the one he hadn't read. His fingers had touched only the first and last pages. He threw that sheet of paper aside. Then he began to read. It took eighteen minutes of careful scrutiny before he found most of the words he needed. The others he would have to make by assembling individual letters cut from other headlines.

He worked patiently. When the words and letters had been pasted in place on the Woolworth stationery, he paused to let the glue dry. While he waited, his eyes roved over the ruins of the paper. There was a photograph on page four that he hadn't noticed before. It was a picture of a skilled detective who the police commissioner had announced was heading the investigation:

Lieutenant David Bloom.

The name was obviously Jewish.

The mass murderer, who had had so many names himself, studied Bloom's face for almost half a minute. It might be useful to learn more about this man. It was basic military tactics to know your enemy. He would begin by finding out where Lieutenant David Bloom worked and lived. Such intelligence could be very useful if Ernst Henke had to kill him.

CHAPTER 12

NINE MINUTES later, Bloom entered an apartment house on East 87th Street in Manhattan. It was a solid old building of gray stone a dozen yards west of Madison Avenue, ten storeys high and equipped with a green canopy and a tan-uniformed doorman. He had a ruddy face and a polite smile.

"Dr. O'Donnell," Bloom said crisply.

"Five-B, sir. The elevator's on the right."

The large lobby and its Victorian furniture were well kept, the detective noticed as he walked across the gleaming marble floor. He looked at his wristwatch a moment after he entered the elevator. It was three minutes before seven—*good*. Being late would be rude. Born into a family that included several physicians, he had been raised to respect doctors and older people. As an authority on the terrorist mind, M. C. O'Donnell had to qualify in both categories.

Maybe O'Donnell wouldn't help at all, Bloom thought. Perhaps O. B. wasn't actually a terrorist group but something else. It could be a gang of professional criminals, but how would they get the damn nerve gas? That was probably much more important than the abstract speculations of some well meaning psychiatrist. Well, it was worth risking fifteen or twenty minutes with O'Donnell on the chance. The worst that he could be was a jargon-spouting bore, like the pompous father of a Barnard senior whom Bloom had dated years ago. He had been awful.

When Bloom got out on the fifth floor, he found himself in a small foyer with doors marked A and B. Between them on the wall hung an oval mirror. The detective paused before it, nodded when he saw that his tie was straight, and pressed the bell of apartment B. Then he entered a waiting room that held a small couch, a leather armchair, a very good print of a John Marin seascape, and a desk. Leaning over some papers on its surface was a woman perhaps thirty or thirty-two years old. She had a sleek full figure, rich chestnut hair in a bun, and an expression of concentration.

"Excuse me," Bloom said to get her attention.

She looked up, and he saw that she had large blue eyes.

"One moment, please," she told him.

Then she glanced down at the desk calendar and turned a page.

"My name is Bloom," he announced impatiently. "I have an appointment with Dr. O'Donnell."

"Uh huh."

"Lieutenant David Bloom," he pressed. "This is Police Department business, miss."

Now she looked up again. She was quite pretty, but Bloom was too annoyed to care.

"I know," she said.

"Well, may I see the doctor *now?*" he demanded.

She turned, walked to a door eight feet away and opened it.

"The doctor will see you," she said coolly.

Controlling his irritation, Bloom strode past her into the office. It was adorned with madras drapes of a cheerful Indian design, fresh flowers in a blue glass vase on an end table, a pair of Italian brass floor lamps and a large bookcase. Near a double window were three chairs and a simple desk of light wood. The psychiatrist was nowhere in sight.

"Where's the doctor?" Bloom asked testily.

He heard the door close behind him and saw the young woman with the large blue eyes walk past him. She said nothing until she was seated in a chair behind the desk.

"Yes, Lieutenant?"

"*You're* Dr. O'Donnell?"

"I have been for eight years," she replied in a voice that was almost glacial. He heard a trace of an Irish accent that he hadn't noticed before.

"I'm sorry, Doctor," Bloom apologized. He eyed her red-brown hair and shook his head. "My uncle told me to see Dr. M. C. O'Donnell. He said that nobody knew more about the pathology of the terrorist mind than Red O'Donnell. He didn't mention that Red O'Donnell was—"

"Female," she supplied. "Am I to gather Dr. Sidney Cohen is your uncle?"

"For a lot more than eight years. He's my mother's brother."

"And chief of psychiatry at P. and S. where I trained. My professional respect for him is the reason I made this appointment on such short notice. What can I do for you?"

The words came from her lips like missiles. There wasn't a trace of warmth in those large blue eyes.

"You can understand my mistake, Doctor. I certainly didn't mean—"

"Would you please get to the point of your visit," she challenged bluntly.

"Sure. I need your help, Doctor. I'm in charge of the Police Department's antiterrorist unit."

"I've read about you in the newspapers. Can we move on to the problem?"

Mine or yours? Bloom wanted to ask her, but he couldn't afford the luxury.

"I'm one of the people working on the murder of those one hundred seventeen men, women, and children in the subway. It was nerve gas."

"Children?"

"Five of them."

"Why don't you sit down, Lieutenant?"

Her voice had changed—just a bit.

Bloom handed her a photocopy of the O. B. note and lowered himself onto an armchair.

"We believe that the individuals who sent that may be responsible, Doctor. We don't have much else, so I'm hoping that you might tell me something—anything—about what kind of person or group would do this."

"Would be *capable* of doing this," she corrected.

"I'll settle for that. I'll take any ideas or comments you've got."

She read the note, sighed and read it again.

"Don't expect any miracles," she warned as she put the note down on the desk. "I'll tell you what I can, but I don't have a crystal ball. I'm a doctor, not a psychic. My specialty is certain types of violent people—individuals who commit terrorist acts. I'm no authority on radical politics."

"There isn't any in the note."

"Not a single slogan or ideological demand," she agreed.

"What do you think that means, Doctor?"

"It could mean that the writer is nonpolitical or simply shrewd. Wiping out so many working-class people isn't likely to win popular support for any cause."

"Like the bombing in the Italian railroad station that killed forty or fifty a few years ago," Bloom thought aloud. "Right-wing terrorists were suspected, but nobody ever claimed responsibility."

"Or demanded money," she reminded.

"Could this be simple extortion?"

She shook her head.

"If it is extortion, it isn't simple. The unusual way it's being done and the weapon used prove it's complex. That suggests that the people who did it are too."

"What can you say about them, Doctor?"

She tapped the note before she answered.

"We have three sources of information: what they wrote, what they did, and what we know about others who've committed generally similar mass murders in recent years."

"Murders for money?"

She nodded. "Now let's consider the note, Lieutenant. In terrorist operations they have found such messages are usually written by one person, even though others in the group may have some input. That person is generally the leader or among the leaders."

"Male," Bloom said.

"You've done your homework. Yes, almost all terrorist or revolutionary groups are just as sexist and macho as the society they seek to destroy."

"So this note was probably written by a man?"

"A man on what you might call a power trip," she told him. "It could be a man who hasn't had much power and has built up a lot of anger about his past impotence."

"Do you mean that literally?"

"I didn't, Lieutenant, but it's entirely possible that this man has major sexual problems. There's practically no chance that he's a happily married man with a wife and two children in a middle-class suburb. This man doesn't live that kind of life."

"Because he's angry?" Bloom tested.

"Furious—even if he manages to conceal it from others. He may seem like a quiet and orderly person outside, but inside he's burning to show the world how powerful and important he really is."

"So he might not act visibly strange or be noticed?"

"Absolutely. He could be good at hiding his rage and other feelings. A lot of people are."

"Is he likely to have a psychiatric record?" Bloom tested hopefully.

"Not necessarily."

Bloom shook his head.

"Going back to the note, Lieutenant, this writer wants to be feared. I don't know why, but he wants to frighten everybody. It's submission, not approval, he's after."

"Like a military dictator?"

She studied the detective for a few seconds.

"Why do you ask that, Lieutenant?"

"The choice of weapon and the use of the word attack in the note suggested a possible military connection."

"Of course," she replied. "Burglars and bank robbers don't use nerve gas. . . . It was very perceptive of you to pick up the military term. I didn't."

"You would have if you'd read the note ten times the way I did."

"No, you read it with a detective's eye," she corrected coolly. "Now let's take a look at what they did. They sent a warning *before* they attacked. That takes a lot of confidence. Actually, it's *arrogance*. They wanted to worry and then humiliate the mayor and the police."

"And they wanted to kill black people," Bloom added. "They had to know that half or more of those who'd be in that car on that line would be black or Hispanic."

She considered his statement, and then her wide blue eyes gleamed in agreement.

"I think you're right, Lieutenant. They're probably racists—bitter ones. People clever enough to acquire and use such a weapon would pick their targets quite deliberately. Looking at what O. B. did, this had to be a very carefully planned attack."

"So there could be a political ingredient even if it wasn't spelled out in the note?"

"On the basis of what they did, yes. Very few terrorist groups massacre women and children, as you know."

"Only the crazies," Bloom said bitterly.

"That's not a word doctors use very often, but I won't argue with you. Killing one hundred seventeen civilians, including women and children, certainly indicates some acute mental disturbance."

"What kind?"

"That takes us to the third point—what we know about the kind of people who do these things," she answered. "I can't be sure, but the pathology here could be paranoid schizophrenia. Paranoid schizophrenics live in their own worlds with their own reality. They believe very deeply that *they're* the victims."

"Of what?"

"Of persecution, hostile conspiracies or terrible injustice. They justify their own behavior and deeds on the basis of getting even for what they think has been done to them."

She leaned forward as she spoke, and the vibrant red highlights in her hair caught Bloom's eye. He wondered why he hadn't noticed them sooner.

"So these people have no compunctions about mass murder?" he asked.

"No compunctions before and no guilt after. They're often rather righteous about what they consider *virtuous violence.*"

"That's quite a phrase, Doctor."

For a few seconds she looked at him warily, uncertain as to whether he was being complimentary or critical. Then she decided that what this good looking detective thought about her didn't matter. The opinions of young police lieutenants, even those as earnest and publicized at this one, were of no consequence.

"Do you have any other questions?" she asked.

"Is there anything more I should know about paranoid schizophrenics?"

She decided not to mention her recent article. He would probably see it as an effort to impress him, and he wouldn't understand it anyway.

"I can think of two things," she answered as she glanced at the battery-powered digital clock on her desk. "First, there are many more of these cases walking around the city than most people recognize. Second, the great majority are not likely to hurt anyone. Only a small segment are violent. If the people you're after haven't committed any violent acts before or haven't been caught at it, it may be difficult to find them."

She realized that he was looking directly into her eyes. It was hard to know whether that was concentration on psychoses or on herself. Could it be a signal that he wanted more than to talk about terrorists?

"I hope that I've been of some help," she said abruptly as she rose to her feet.

"You have. Thank you. If you should think of anything else, Doctor, I'd be very grateful."

Feeling just a trace of guilt at ejecting him this way, she paused for a moment.

"Well, there's the age question. On the basis of past experiences, the odds are that these murderers are between twenty-five and forty, give or take a few years," she told him. "And most have at least a high school education."

Bloom got up and nodded. He was still looking directly into her eyes.

"I'm sorry to rush you, Lieutenant, but I have an appointment."

"May I give you a lift?" he offered.

He could see her stiffen.

"No, thank you. Good-bye, Lieutenant."

As he reached the street a minute later, David Bloom found himself wondering what she would look like with that mass of extraordinary hair hanging down and free. And what names did the initials M. C. represent? She could hardly be a Mary. She seemed too complex and sophisticated for that.

Then his mind turned to another pair of letters:

O. B. They had to mean something too.

Thinking about that as he walked toward Madison Avenue, he did not notice that he was being followed.

CHAPTER 13

NINE A.M. on May 3.

The West Wing of 1600 Pennsylvania Avenue, N.W., in the District of Columbia. The Oval Office.

"I hope your urgent problem isn't too bad," the husky man behind the historic desk said as the Secretary of Defense entered. "Every damn thing I just heard at this morning's CIA briefing was trouble."

"I'm afraid I've got more of the same for you, Mr. President," Millard replied stiffly.

So it's going to be another one of those days, Kimball thought. He had faced so many in his sixteen months as president. His eighteen years in the Senate and two terms as governor hadn't really prepared him for this endless pressure. Still, Robert B. Kimball was coping. He had to.

Millard sat down and swallowed twice.

It had to be serious.

"You'd better tell me what's wrong," Kimball said.

"This wasn't our fault, Mr. President. We weren't even in office when it happened . . . well, when it began."

The President tensed. The situation had to be really bad for Millard to make such a vehement disclaimer.

"I assure you that I knew nothing about it until yesterday afternoon," Millard continued. "The army was, with the best of intentions, keeping it a secret. That was improper, and I've made that clear to General Younts. Even though he wasn't chief of staff when it happened—"

"When what happened?" Kimball demanded.

The Secretary of Defense swallowed hard again.

"I assume you've heard about the one hundred seventeen people killed in the New York subway two days ago," he said cautiously.

Kimball nodded.

"It was our nerve gas, Mr. President."

"What?"

"U. S. Army nerve gas stolen twenty months ago in Utah."

The President's mouth opened in shock.

"Jesus H. Christ!" he exploded. "How the hell could it happen?"

"It was very cleverly done by professional criminals. A whole team of them—at least six."

Kimball shook his head angrily.

"Weren't there guards, damn it?"

"There were eleven armed military police escorting the shipment when the convoy was ambushed," Millard reported.

"And what the hell did they do?"

"Ten of them died, Mr. President."

"Oh, my God!"

Kimball shook his head again.

"They were cut to pieces with automatic weapons, I'm told. Younts says it was in a tunnel running through a big mountain."

Kimball stood up and began to pace the famous room.

"Every standard precaution was taken, Mr. President. The normal complement of guards and usual security procedures were used. The time and route of the convoy from Tooele were Top Secret."

"Tooele?"

"It's a chemical munitions depot in Utah. Most of the army's remaining nerve gas is stored there. It's a well protected base in a somewhat remote area. The convoy was moving an assortment of gas cylinders, including two big ones, to the Dugway Proving Grounds less than fifty miles away."

The President of the United States stared out the French windows at the rose garden for several seconds, still stunned.

"There had to be an informer at Tooele," he reasoned.

"The army thinks it was an MP named Arthur Addams. He was riding shotgun beside the driver of the truck carrying the gas."

"And Addams was the one MP who survived?"

"That's the belief. His body was never found."

Kimball paced silently for another fifteen seconds.

"Then how do you know about the six criminals?" he asked.

"Their bodies were found about twenty miles away. They were machine-gunned, just like the MPs in the tunnel. They were all carrying forged driver's licenses and false ID, but they had criminal records. Their real names were provided by checking their fingerprints."

The President returned to his desk chair.

"Let me get this straight," he said with sudden hostility. "You're telling me that sixteen men, ten of them army, were shot to death on public roads and nobody ever heard a word?"

"People heard that they had died. The army had to notify the MPs' families," Millard explained. "But no one was told that any of the sixteen were killed by gunfire."

"Then what the hell did the army say?"

The Secretary of Defense crossed his legs and swallowed again.

"That's a mountain area, Mr. President. The official story was that they all died in an avalanche. There actually was one on that road the same day."

73

Kimball tried to make sense of what he had just heard. He couldn't.

"I don't understand, Clark. Why this bizarre cover-up?"

"According to Younts, it was to avoid panicking the public. General Joel was chief of staff then. He believed that the impact of this news could be extremely disturbing."

"To the public or the army's next budget?" Kimball challenged.

Millard flinched.

"Maintaining confidence in the armed forces may have been a consideration," he admitted, "but I don't know. I wasn't in the government then, so I can't say."

"And General Joel can't say either."

"He died eleven months ago—a heart attack."

"Leaving us his mess. God Almighty, he must have been out of his mind!"

Then he saw the guarded look in Millard's gray eyes.

"If there's more, Clark, you'd better tell me now."

This was going to be the tricky part, but the Secretary of Defense was ready. He had rehearsed exactly what he would say.

"You should know that the army has mounted a major effort to find Addams and the gas, Mr. President. Dozens of CID investigators gave it thousands of hours. The FBI was alerted to watch for any news or hint of nerve gas, and a special unit was set up to handle Avalanche reports."

"Avalanche?"

"That was the code name," Millard explained. "It was a maximum security operation. Even those hunting for Addams weren't told about the theft. That was part of the attempt to keep the hijacking of the gas secret."

Kimball shrugged.

"That massacre in the subway took care of your secret, didn't it?"

"General Younts doesn't think so," Millard answered evenly.

"He believes that the situation can be contained, at least for a while."

"What the hell are you talking about?"

"There's no reason yet for people to think that it was *our* nerve gas, Mr. President. Other countries make it. They might have sold their nerve gas to third countries, or their gas might have been stolen by some extremist group. With the New York canister now in army hands, Younts believes we shouldn't let anyone, especially the media, see it."

The President frowned.

"I hope you're not saying what I think you're saying," he warned.

"I'm not. I'm reporting what Younts said. He thinks that there can't be any positive identification of whose gas it is so long as nobody else gets a look at the canister."

"It wouldn't work, damn it. And even if it did for a while, there's no goddamn way you could hold the lid on this one for long."

"A while might be long enough, Mr. President."

"For what?" Kimball tested cautiously.

"For Congress to okay production of the new binary agent that the army needs—needs badly. That's what General Younts believes."

"Younts is as crazy as Joel was. Two insane army chiefs of staff back to back. That's terrific," Kimball grumbled.

Then he looked at Millard.

"What do you believe, Clark?"

"I believe that we need the binary as a deterrent, and as soon as possible."

Kimball thought and shook his head emphatically.

"No way. I'll say it again. *No way.* You may be a top corporate executive, Clark, but you've still got a lot to learn about how government works. I'll give you a fast lesson. One word. Okay?"

Millard nodded.

"Watergate! I'll spell it out in case the message isn't absolutely clear. The American people have had it *up to here* with cover-ups. They're ready to step on any politician who fools them by hiding any serious misdeed, and I don't blame them."

Millard hadn't counted on this.

"I realize that you're a man of high principle, Mr. President."

"Don't humor me," Kimball erupted. "I'm no angel, and I don't claim to be. I've cut a few corners on the way here, but now I'm here and it isn't quite the same. Years ago, when another president betrayed the trust of the whole nation, I made myself a promise. If I ever got here, I'd never sweep scandals under the rug or try to fool the country—not on anything important. No, we're not going to bury this one!"

"But I'm not suggesting that we do. I'm thinking in terms of a brief delay—maybe a month. I believe that it would serve the public interest that we both care about so much."

"I'm not sure the binary is that crucial, Clark."

"Not just the binary, Mr. President. It would give our investigators, both the army and the FBI, more time to find Addams. And that's going to be easier if Addams doesn't know we're after him and if the country isn't hysterical about the gas. Once the word gets out, it's going to be a circus."

Kimball sat silent for several moments—thinking.

"You feel that the public really would panic?"

"And so would the press and the politicians," Millard predicted. "Now we have a whole new group of opportunities to catch this fellow. He's demanding money. Well, he'll have to make contact to arrange for the payment, and he'll have to collect it. He'll have to come out of his hole, Mr. President."

"It's like a kidnapping case," Kimball reasoned aloud, "and the FBI is damn good at those."

"Exactly. They'll get him. Then we can release the whole story. When you explain that we had to delay it in the national interest, nobody's going to argue—not with Addams and the gas both in federal custody."

The President shifted in his big chair as he struggled to decide.

"You'll be a hero," Millard told him.

Kimball weighed the arguments for several seconds more before he shrugged.

"I don't know, Clark. . . . I'll think about it."

"That's all I'm asking, Mr. President," Millard answered quickly. As he spoke, he made up his mind to try to move up the hearings on the binary project. Every day would count. The whole situation might explode at any time.

"You really believe they'll catch him?" Kimball asked a moment later.

"Absolutely."

"I wish I could be that sure," the chief executive said frankly. "On the basis of what he's done so far, this Addams has to be extremely clever—unless the army security screwed up. Ten MPs?"

"All carrying automatic weapons, and with a helicopter gunship flying escort. There was nothing casual about the security," Millard declared firmly.

"But he beat them all, and his own people as well. It makes you wonder, doesn't it?"

"Wonder what, Mr. President?"

"How the *hell* did he do it?"

CHAPTER 14

ERNST HENKE finished his lunch at a quarter after twelve and made his way to a phone booth in Pennsylvania Station. He had prepared for these calls; he had brought a dollar's worth of change from the jar of coins he kept in the bedroom.

There were four telephones on the wall, but seven people crowded around them. Henke didn't mind. He had to look up the number first anyway, and there could be more than one David Bloom in Manhattan. There might not be a Manhattan telephone directory here at all. People often destroyed them or stole them from public phones to take home for their own use. That was another example of the disgusting animal behavior of the swinish creatures who lived in this foul city.

He found a phone book. Someone had torn out thirty or forty pages from the back, but the B section was intact. The Blooms were there—more than two hundred of them. There were thirteen David Blooms, including two CPAs, three dentists, two doctors, one lawyer, and another who listed himself as an "attorney."

And there was no way of telling which of the others might be Lieutenant David Bloom, enemy. Yes, there was. It required studying another Manhattan directory, one that had the blue pages listing government numbers in place. It might be wiser to make this first call from a booth two or three blocks away, Henke thought. The Police Department could have the technology to trace incoming calls automatically.

Near Macy's massive, square-block department store, he found the booth, the Manhattan phone book, and the number he needed: 374–6700.

"Police Department—Public Information. Officer Feeny," a hearty voice announced.

"This is Porter at NBC Radio," Henke said glibly. "Just checking one bit on your Lieutenant David Bloom. Could you dig out where he went to college?"

"That's easy. You're the third reporter to call about him today. He got out of Columbia fourteen years ago. He's local, born in New York."

"Thanks a bunch," Henke said and hung up immediately.

Then he found the number of the Alumni Office of Columbia College up on Morningside Heights. This was probably a good time to call, he thought. It was lunch hour, so he might speak with some clerk or secretary instead of a senior person who might know Bloom's voice.

"Alumni Office, may I help you?" a young woman asked.

"I hope so," he replied in an exasperated tone. "I haven't had any copies of the magazine for almost a year. I think you've got my address wrong somewhere."

"This isn't the magazine office, Mr.—"

"Bloom. Dave Bloom. What address have you got for me?"

"Just a moment. . . . We've got two David Blooms. Are you the math professor or the other one?"

"The other one."

"Uh huh. Our records show Two Hundred West Seventy-ninth Street, New York City One-oh-oh-twenty-four. Is that right?"

Henke smiled in triumph.

"That's it," he said. "Can you transfer me to the magazine, please?"

"Sure."

Ten seconds later he heard the voice of another woman, crisper and more authoritative.

"Columbia College Today."

"Wrong number. Sorry," he told her and ended the call.

Now he had to hurry back to work. The midday traffic, both human and vehicular, was heavy in this highly commercial section of Manhattan, but he didn't mind the minor inconvenience. Everything was going well. He had mailed the note with the instructions that morning at a postbox near Times Square, and now he had found out where David Bloom lived.

It might be wise for Otto's Boy to go up there to reconnoiter the building and the neighborhood—tonight.

Otto's Boy had to take every possible precaution. As Mama had explained, these people were all against him, and they were vicious. If he weren't extremely careful, they'd kill him.

Unless Otto's Boy killed them first.

CHAPTER 15

WHAT was he doing here?

The time was 9:20 P.M., and the place was a six-storey brick building at the corner of Fifth Avenue and 103rd Street. The high-ceilinged chamber had wood-panelled walls that made Dr. O'Donnell think of an old-fashioned courtroom, but it was questions of health, not justice, that prevailed here.

This was the prestigious Academy of Medicine. Of the more than eighty men and women gathered to hear the discussion on "The Sociopathic Personality," all but one were psychiatrists. Seated alone in the last row, he was a policeman.

Why was Bloom here?

Looking out across the big room from the stage, she wanted to ask him but she couldn't. As a member of the panel, it was her job to answer questions—not to ask them. None of the others in the hall were even aware that he was present. She hadn't noticed him herself until halfway through Dr. Peyser's introductory remarks an hour earlier.

"Dr. O'Donnell?"

She recognized the Canadian accent immediately. It was Philip Weintraub, bearded and earnest and sure to ask about the new chemotherapies. That was exactly what he did.

"Perhaps Dr. Drellich is better qualified to field that," she demurred with a nod toward the graying therapist beside her.

There were four more questions before the moderator rose, drew attention to the hour, and thanked the members of the panel for "a stimulating evening." Before the applause had subsided, most of those in the audience were busy talking to each other. A determined handful started toward the panel with more questions.

Bloom remained seated, watching. Patience was a policeman's trait, she thought as the Gottleibs approached her. The portly husband and wife were aggressively intelligent, frighteningly well read and unaware that people spoke sentences of less than forty words. If this ruthless duo trapped her, she would have to endure at least ten minutes of their ponderous and doggedly Freudian conversation.

Her eyes flicked left and then right, searching urgently for an escape route. Suddenly she saw a way. Circling around the moderator, she used him as a shield as she hurried. She walked quickly, nodding and smiling to a dozen colleagues as she zigzagged toward the rear exit. She was almost there when she noticed that Bloom had left. Still wondering why he had come, she strode from the large hall.

"Good evening, Doctor."

She blinked in surprise.

"Lieutenant Bloom!"

"I didn't mean to startle you, Doctor. I hope I'm not intruding."

"It was an open session," she answered coolly. Standing a scant yard from the detective, she saw a thin scar on the left side of his neck and wondered how he got it.

"That's what my uncle said," Bloom replied. "It was very interesting."

He could see the skepticism in her face.

"Really," he assured. "I do have a question, though."

"Yes?"

"May I give you a lift? I should warn you that I have an ulterior motive. I want to talk to you some more about psychotic mass murderers."

She hesitated for several seconds. Well, at least he was honest—and there came the rotund and relentless Gottleibs. Their thick eyeglasses gleamed like truck headlights as they advanced through the rapidly thinning crowd.

"Let's go," she said.

As they walked down Fifth Avenue to where he had parked his car, Bloom told her about the many crank calls that had come in about the subway massacre. Some people blamed Soviet spy rings, others extraterrestrials or the strange people next door who chanted all the time. Ex-husbands behind on alimony payments, the Mafia and the CIA had also been accused.

"The CIA?" she asked as they crossed 101st Street.

"They're always big when something goes wrong. When there's a heavy snowstorm or a power failure, we get a whole gang of calls from people who think the CIA did it. Our phones are especially busy when there's a full moon, of course."

"A policeman's lot is not a happy one," she quoted.

Pirates of Penzance—one of my favorites. Truth is there are times when I'm not happy at all."

"Do you always tell the truth, Lieutenant?"

"I get a lot of complaints on that," he answered with a shrug.

"I didn't mean to pry."

Bloom smiled. "I don't mind questions," he said amiably. "Hell, I'm in the question business myself. See, we've got something in common."

"Are you saying we're both detectives?"

"Something like that. I'm only half serious. There's the car."

Half a minute later, he unlocked the door of a blue '83 Chrysler sedan and stepped back so she could enter.

"It doesn't look like a police car," she said.

"Isn't supposed to. I'm a plainclothes detective."

As she got in, he looked—automatically but carefully—up and down the street. Three of the corrupt cops whom he'd exposed were going on trial the day after tomorrow, and there was still the chance that there'd be another attempt on his life. That was why he checked under the hood before he entered the car and slid behind the wheel.

"Engine trouble?" she asked.

"Nothing serious. Now, if you insist, I'll drive you home."

"And if I don't?"

"Then I'll take us to a little place on Third Avenue for espresso, rum cheesecake and those questions I mentioned."

"I'm not sure that my answers will help."

"Neither am I," Bloom said. "Let's find out—*please.*"

"All right, Lieutenant."

As he drove east, Bloom glanced repeatedly at the rearview mirror. She noticed it but made no comment. This was probably a standard part of the compulsively cautious personality of a New York City policeman, the psychiatrist reasoned. Things were a lot different in her native Galway where the dangers were so much smaller that the *gardai* on patrol didn't even carry guns.

The coffeehouse that he had chosen was a small candlelit establishment with walls covered in dark red velvet. As in half the other dining establishments in Manhattan south of 96th Street, the waitresses looked as if they were unemployed actresses or dancers—and they were. Bloom guided her past two empty tables near the front window to one at the rear. As soon as they had ordered, he excused himself to make a telephone call from the booth against the back wall.

When he returned two minutes later, the detective began to ask his questions. He paused only when the lithe Eurasian waitress delivered their pastry and coffee. Then he resumed his inquiries about precisely what sort of grievances might serve as a paranoid schizophrenic's justification for mass murder.

"You're saying that it would probably be something real—like being fired from a job or losing a lawsuit," Bloom finally summarized.

"Or a dispute with a government agency or very large corporation. It becomes a power struggle. Feeling frustrated in dealing with such a huge, impersonal adversary, this kind of disturbed personality turns to big-scale retaliation."

"Like that man they called the Mad Bomber?" Bloom asked.

"A classic case of such an individual," she agreed.

Bloom looked up at the brass wall clock before he asked the next question.

"Would the same principles apply to a group of people?"

"I would think so, but I can't guarantee it."

Across the street and thirty yards south, the man who was following David Bloom was getting restless. Nothing was happening. It was a balmy night, and a warm breeze floated in through the gray Ford's open windows. Well dressed young couples, some arm in arm, strolled by in a steady stream. Three more men entered the popular single's bar beside the coffeehouse, but there was no sign of Bloom. How long was he going to stay in there?

"Freeze!"

The startled watcher turned to face the twin barrels of a sawed-off shotgun. A black man was thrusting it into the sedan's window from the sidewalk, pointing it at the driver's head.

"Hands on the wheel!" the gunman ordered. He might be twenty-eight or thirty. The weapon was a heavy twelve-gauge piece—absolutely lethal at this point-blank range.

"Jesus," the shaken driver gasped.

"Hands on the wheel or your face will be all over the windshield," the man with the shotgun promised. His eyes wide with fear and raw terror tasting coppery in his mouth, the driver moved to obey the ultimatum.

"You're making a mistake," he said hoarsely.

"No, *you* are," someone behind him contradicted. Turning his head in automatic response, the driver saw the face of an

angry Hispanic reflected in the side mirror. Then the man behind the wheel felt a cold round piece of metal at the base of
his skull. It was the muzzle of a .38-caliber pistol.

"What do you want?" the tense man behind the wheel asked.

"We want you to get out of the car, nice and slowly. Not
yet—I'll tell you when," the Hispanic announced.

Drenched with sweat, the driver nodded.

"Johnny, check the street. This creep may have friends. Cover
me with the sawed-off."

The shotgun slid back out of the window.

"Looks okay, Gabe," the black man said a few moments later.

Then the Hispanic stepped back and told the driver to come
out of the car—*carefully*. The man who had been tracking
Bloom complied.

"If you want the car, take it," he told them.

"We want *you*, wise guy. Now turn around and put your
hands on the car," Velez ordered.

"Who are you guys?"

It was at that moment that Bloom and the Irish psychiatrist
emerged from the coffeehouse. As was his custom, he looked
left and right immediately. He saw the three men across the
street; Gillespie and Velez had the watcher under control. The
two detectives nodded to Bloom, and Gillespie waved the shotgun in a short signal that meant it was safe to join them.

"Maybe you'd better wait inside, Doctor," Bloom said.

"Are those men yours?"

"The ones with the guns are," he replied.

"They're the people you telephoned?" she guessed.

"That's right. It might be more comfortable if you went back
inside. This won't take more than a few minutes."

She ignored his suggestion.

"Who's the other man?" she asked.

"That's what I intend to find out," he told her and waited
for her to reenter the coffeehouse. She looked at him for several
seconds, judging whether he really believed there might be dan-

ger or if this was some overprotective and patronizing male nonsense.

"Three minutes," she finally said and went back inside. Bloom immediately walked toward Velez, Gillespie and their captive.

"He wants to know who we are," Velez said. "Cute, huh?"

"I'll tell him," Bloom announced. "The guy with the shotgun is Detective First Grade Gillespie, and the other fellow is Sergeant Velez. As you know, I'm Lieutenant Bloom."

"Cops?"

"You read him his rights?" Bloom asked.

"Would the Supreme Court mind if I frisked him first? He may be carrying a piece."

"Okay."

Velez searched the man thoroughly, patting hips, armpits, ankles, and even the small of the back for concealed weapons. Then he flipped open the captive's jacket to check for a belly gun.

"He's clean, Dave."

"Maybe it's in the car," Gillespie suggested.

"Take a look."

As Gillespie opened the glove compartment, Velez reached into the man's jacket and pulled out his wallet. Then he opened it to search for a driver's license or other identity papers.

"You're not going to believe this," Velez said and handed Bloom the wallet. Bloom studied the car registration and plastic ID card carefully, glancing up at their captive a few seconds later.

"Turn around so I can see your face," he ordered.

The man obeyed. Bloom looked at the picture on the plastic-coated card and nodded.

"You want to explain this?" he asked.

"I want to make a phone call," the man replied defensively. "I've got a right to make a phone call."

"We'll both make phone calls. Cuff him and take him to the

office. He can call from there. I'll be along as soon as I drop off Dr. O'Donnell."

"You can't arrest me!" the man protested.

"Get him out of here," Bloom ordered and started walking toward the phone booth on the corner. As he dialed, he watched them shove the handcuffed man into his car. This was going to be a long night, Bloom thought. He was right.

CHAPTER 16

BLOOM reached his office at half-past ten. The head of the FBI's antiterrorist squad arrived twenty minutes later. It did not surprise Bloom that Inspector Fredericks had Special Agent Collery with him. FBI supervisors rarely came alone to inter-agency meetings. Wearing a dressy dark suit, white shirt, and blue silk tie, Fredericks had obviously hurried from some social event.

"Your message said it was important. What have you got?" he asked.

"Come take a look," Bloom answered and led the way into his inner office. There were three men already in the room. Fredericks and Collery recognized one as Velez. Another was black. He was holding a sawed-off shotgun. The third was in handcuffs.

"Know him, Inspector?"

Fredericks studied the prisoner for several seconds before he shook his head.

"Who is he?"

"That's the wrong question," Bloom answered. There was anger in his voice and more of it in his eyes.

"I don't understand," the FBI supervisor said.

"The right question is *what* is he. His name is Shelley. Ronald Shelley."

Then Bloom handed Fredericks the wallet.

"Don't worry. It was a nice legal search," Bloom announced sarcastically. "We had cause to believe that an attempted homicide was in progress."

The FBI executive opened the wallet and began to examine its contents. Suddenly he stopped and stared.

"I don't understand, Lieutenant."

"Neither do we. Why would an agent of the U. S. Army's Criminal Investigation Division be following me?"

Fredericks shook his head.

"I have no idea," he said.

"How about those two weapons experts who gave us the word on the gas?" Bloom challenged. "I've been thinking about that pair. You got any ideas about them?"

Three . . . four . . . five seconds ticked away before Fredericks replied.

"What do you mean?"

"Where the hell are they from?"

"Headquarters in Washington, I believe," Fredericks answered carefully.

"Army headquarters, right? They're Chemical Corps, aren't they, Inspector?"

Fredericks coughed and shrugged.

"Does it matter which branch of the government supplied the information to the task force, Lieutenant?" he reasoned. "We're all working toward the same goal."

"What's that?"

"To apprehend these criminals."

"I'm not one of them. I'm not a goddamn criminal at all. I don't even have a traffic ticket for double parking, so why the hell is the army watching me?"

"I can't speak for another branch of the government," Fredericks said coolly.

"You can't and Shelley won't. What the hell's going on?"

"This is probably just some misunderstanding," the FBI supervisor suggested. "Maybe Shelley thought you were somebody else. Mistakes happen."

Bloom shook his head.

"Or he might have misinterpreted some orders," Fredericks continued in a placating tone. "Why don't you let him go?"

"Not till somebody answers my questions."

Fredericks smiled benignly.

"I'm not sure that you've got any legal basis to hold him," he said. "Is following someone—perhaps as a result of a mistake or maybe as a joke—a crime?"

At that moment there was a knock at the door. Bloom nodded to Velez, who drew his .38 and went to see who it was. Fredericks eyed the weapon and shook his head.

The man who entered was chunky, sandy-haired, and in his late thirties. He was wearing a sport jacket, dark gray slacks and an expression of acute wariness.

"I'm Major Kieling," he said crisply.

Then he saw that Gillespie was holding a shotgun and that Velez was covering him with a .38 pistol.

"What the hell is this?" he blurted.

"You tell me. Check his ID, Gabe," Bloom ordered.

The chunky stranger showed Velez a plastic card.

"Major Michael Kieling, Army CID," he confirmed and returned the card to its indignant owner.

"I had a call that you're holding one of our personnel," Kieling announced in a rigidly official voice.

"We are. I'm Bloom—the cop your *personnel* was tailing. You want to explain that?"

Kieling glanced across the room at the handcuffed man, who shook his head—about an inch.

"That's right, Major. Shelley didn't say a word," Bloom reported harshly, "but I know you will."

"I can't imagine why he'd follow you, unless he thought you were someone else," the army officer said.

"That's what I told Lieutenant Bloom. I'm Inspector Fredericks of the FBI, and I assured him that it must have been an unfortunate case of human error."

"I'm not buying," Bloom said.

"Well, if Sergeant Shelley meant to follow you—and I doubt that—it wasn't on army orders."

"Not buying that either, Major," Bloom answered. "A CID sergeant doesn't do anything like this on his own. Right, Shelley?"

"I made a mistake and tailed the wrong car. I'm sorry, Lieutenant."

"No, you're not, but you will be. You're going to the slammer."

"Why don't we try to work this out?" Kieling appealed. "After all, Army CID has always had good relations with the New York police. If the sergeant has to be punished, why not let the military authorities take care of it? We have strict disciplinary procedures and our own penal facilities, you know."

Bloom took out a Don Diego petit corona and lit it.

"Nice try," he said and puffed, "but he's ours until he—or somebody else—comes clean. I figure that he'll do about two years."

"Two years for following you?" Fredericks erupted.

"And for resisting arrest, interfering with an officer in the performance of his duty, and a couple of other things. You've got three hours," Bloom announced.

"For what?" Kieling asked.

"To tell me the truth. If not, we'll book him."

"The major could get a court order for Shelley's release," Fredericks said.

"He wouldn't dare," Bloom answered and blew a perfect smoke ring. "If he tries—or if he does, I'll call the newspapers."

"You don't know what you're doing!"

"I don't know what *you're* doing," David Bloom corrected, "but I intend to find out—soon. You've got until . . . let's say, two-thirty. Good-bye, gentlemen."

Kieling and the two FBI men stared at him for several seconds. Then they looked at each other, and Fredericks nodded toward the door.

"You're crazy, Bloom," the army officer said bitterly.

"Two-thirty," Bloom repeated.

They left, and Bloom blew another smoke ring.

"You think I'm crazy, Gabe?" he asked.

"Always were. You never know when to stop."

Bloom tapped the ash from his cigar into a black plastic rectangle marked with the name Carnegie Deli.

"I'll stop when we've nailed those bastards with the nerve gas."

"Suppose those guys who just left don't have the answers to your questions?" Gillespie asked.

"They can phone the people who do. I'm going to the can for a minute. Keep an eye on Shelley."

Bloom walked out, and Gillespie sighed.

"Do you think he can take on the whole damn federal government, Gabe?" he asked.

"He just did."

Bloom returned in eight minutes with styrofoam cups of coffee that he had bought from a vending machine down the corridor. They sipped the barely drinkable liquid, denounced it with ritual obscenities and began to talk about the Knicks' chances in the playoffs. Gillespie took a portable radio from a desk drawer so they could listen to the last quarter of the game being played in Milwaukee. Three baskets in the final seventy seconds brought the underdog New York team victory. The Knicks would go to the NBA championships. The CID agent didn't react at all. The others talked and waited, and waited some more. The phone call finally came at 1:35 in the morning. It was not from Major Kieling or Fredericks. The voice Bloom heard was that of Terence Carty, personal aide to Police Commissioner Vincent X. Grady. The PC had telephoned the order that Shelley be released immediately.

"I'd like to discuss this," Bloom said.

"Just send him home now," Carty responded and hung up the phone.

"He walks," Bloom reported. "The Feds got to Grady. Let him go."

Shelley was out the door within sixty seconds. He didn't linger to complain or boast. As soon as the handcuffs were removed, he walked from the room without a word or a glance.

"Well, that's over." Velez sighed with a yawn.

"The hell it is," Bloom said defiantly.

The three red-eyed detectives left the building at 1:45. They were all back at 8:30 A.M., an hour before Ernst Henke's second note was delivered to City Hall.

CHAPTER 17

MAY 5.

It was exactly *two* years ago, Henke thought as he lathered his hands with the heavy-duty soap. He would be eating lunch in a few minutes, and he certainly couldn't do that with dirty hands. After lunch he would have to soap them clean again, as he did after every meal. He maintained this same before-and-after ritual for each visit to the lavatory. That was a much less ugly word than toilet, which suggested body functions and was obviously filthy.

Two years ago, he recalled happily. Ernst Henke liked anniversaries. They put the past in a restricting frame—like a picture. And they tied events to numbers, which were always good. Otto's Boy was the master of numbers—those wonderful abstractions that were so much easier to control than people. He understood that people had to be controlled too. Mama had explained that so many times.

The number was *730*. Precisely *730* days ago—*two* years—he had reported for duty at the Tooele Army Depot. As he soaped his hands a second time, he remembered every detail of that spring morning. The May sun had been shining over the mountains, and the air had been crisp and clear on the *30*-mile drive southwest from Salt Lake City to the *44,000*-acre military base.

It was a little-known but important installation. More than *3,800* people worked at the Tooele Army Depot, handling, storing, and protecting an immense amount of very powerful munitions. This included "classified ordnance" in blastproof underground bunkers. From the moment he had arrived, Henke had realized that this was no ordinary base. He remembered it all so clearly: the heavy security at the gate, the double perimeter of electrified fence, the guard dog units and mobile patrols, and the armed men ringing those special bunkers set apart from the others.

Covered by several feet of earth, they looked like Indian funeral mounds he had seen in photos in *National Geographic.* What rested beneath these mounds could cause millions of funerals, but the people assigned to Tooele did not talk about that. On the first morning of his tour there, a hard-faced captain had told Henke that he was never to discuss those bunkers or anything else about the depot with anyone who didn't work at the depot—not even other military personnel.

"And that goes after you leave here for a new assignment, Sergeant. Do your job and keep your mouth shut about this depot as long as you live. Got that?"

"Yes, sir."

There were *14,700* civilians in the nearby mining community of Tooele. They seemed to know the rules too. When people from the depot—civilian employees or Department of Defense personnel—came into town for a movie or a beer, no one asked questions about their work. Conversations focused on sports, television shows, cars, the advantages of living in the wide open spaces of Utah, the weather, and the prices of copper, lead, and silver. A good part of the population of Tooele County worked at mines or smelters.

It wasn't only the ordnance depot that people in the area didn't discuss, Henke recalled. Many local residents were Mormons. They didn't talk about dirty things such as women's bodies and sex, subjects whose popularity at other military bases had often left him sick to his stomach. Playing his role as a "good ole boy" who was just like the others, he had frequently been forced to lie about an imaginary ulcer to explain away the symptoms of his repressed rage.

Staring at his face in the washroom mirror now, Henke fought for control. There was one thing that always helped. Yes, it was easier when he thought about the numbers. Numbers were his best friends, his only ones.

Latitude $40°32'$ north . . . longitude $112°18'$ west.

Those were Tooele's numbers; 801 was the telephone area code.

He began to feel calmer. He could see the Tooele barracks clearly again. They were *one*-and *two*-storey wooden buildings, all equipped with air conditioners to cope with the 95-degree July and August heat. He'd been cautious those first months, doing his job as an electrician and starting to reconnoiter. He had to find out where key installations were and how the security system operated.

By mid-July he knew where the "classified ordnance" was stored. He also knew that it would be impossible to steal from those bunkers. Dug into the rocky earth far away from any others in a section known as Field Nine, they were so isolated that anyone approaching would be noticed and easily intercepted by armed guards. Their heavy steel doors were protected by double sets of locks and electronic alarms.

Still, there had to be a way.

Otto's Boy needed those cylinders.

He had been watching and waiting for years for an opportunity to secure a weapon of mass destruction. He might never get this close to anything like nerve gas again. He certainly hadn't in all the previous years he had been in the U. S. Army. He thought about the problem every night for months, lying awake with his eyes open and going over every possibility.

Then the answer had come to him quite suddenly. If he couldn't break in, he would take it when they brought some out for testing or destruction. It was only a matter of time until they moved some of the old containers to the Dugway Proving Grounds *forty* miles away.

He couldn't hurry.

He couldn't do it alone.

But he couldn't trust anyone else with his plan either. He would have to trick the others. It would be a *two*-part operation. First he'd shape his plan of attack, and then he'd find the fools to help him.

Somewhere in those *forty* miles there must be a place where they could strike. He had to learn how they moved the cylinders to Dugway—the route and the security procedures. He needed a vehicle for his recon run. That meant making friends with Debuskey or the other NCO at the motor pool. He had to do that slowly to avoid arousing their suspicions, but he wanted to ride the route now.

So he bought a secondhand motorcycle from a Salt Lake City dealer. He practiced driving it on various local roads, staying away from Dugway at first. Then he saw the first army convoy moving nerve gas from the special bunkers. Nobody could say that the bright blue canisters were not well protected. A jeep carrying *four* MPs with automatic weapons rode ahead of the gas truck. A truck with more armed MPs followed.

But that wasn't all.

A helicopter gunship flew overhead, ready to dump death from .50-caliber machine guns and rapid-fire 20-millimeter cannon.

That chopper was going to be a serious problem, but he would solve it. Otto's Boy was clever, superior. He would find an answer. When another gas convoy left for Dugway weeks later, he followed it at a distance on his cycle. There wasn't a moment that the convoy was out of sight of that gunship.

Until they reached the tunnel. As soon as he saw the mouth

of the passage cut through the mountain, Henke had grinned. This piece of the road could not be seen by the guards in the gunship, and they probably couldn't maintain radio contact with the convoy while it was in the tunnel either.

He had found the place.

Now he needed the men. Strangers—professional criminals— were what he required. He couldn't recruit them in Salt Lake City, for it was too near and too small for safety. Phoenix was *four* times as big, hours away in a different state and known for its large and violent underworld.

On the following weekend he bought a *.38*-caliber pistol at a Salt Lake City pawnshop and flew down to Phoenix; 645 miles, he remembered. He had been careful. The first thing that he did when he got into the city was purchase a black wig. He had immediately donned it in a booth in a public toilet. Seconds later he blew air into the small rubber pillow concealed under his brown plaid sport shirt, a garment much gaudier than his usual style. He now looked heavier, younger, coarser—different.

The men he would recruit must never see him as anyone at the Tooele Depot knew him. If one of the criminals should somehow desert or be captured, the description that he would be able to provide would not match anyone on the base. Having taken these precautions, he set out to "cruise" some of the sleazier bars. He began with a pair he'd heard soldiers gossip about as places where they'd found "action."

Action meant prostitutes.

Where you could buy them, you would have a good chance of purchasing drugs too.

And dope meant professional criminals. People who dealt in narcotics often carried guns and were not reluctant to use them. They were also familiar with local holdup men, car thieves and a wide spectrum of the Phoenix underworld. It would be dangerous. Some of these criminals were ready to kill. That was what Otto's Boy wanted them to do, but at the right time.

Step by step. He had to be extremely careful.

On that first visit to Phoenix he spent the afternoon and

evening as a scout, stopping into more than a dozen bars. In each he ordered a beer, drank part of it and got the feel of the place before departing half an hour later. He didn't ask any questions. He didn't even speak to anyone, aside from telling the bartender what he wanted to drink. He saw marijuana being smoked at two of the grubby clubs, and later watched a braless chemical blonde at Big Dude's palm a small square of folded paper to a man who had just slipped her something flat enough to hide in his fat fist.

Probably drugs—cocaine or heroin. Henke didn't know much about these things, but he was pleased. This might be a place to make his first move—next weekend. When he came back the following Saturday, he continued his reconnaissance. He first went to several other bars, including a pair in the Mexican section where he was received coolly. The Arizona capital wasn't proving to be the sin center he had expected.

But he returned to Big Dude's after dinner and chatted with a friendly and thirsty brunette named Gloria. He bought her a drink, apologized that he couldn't accept her gracious $30 "blow job" offer because he had herpes, and got Gloria to introduce him to a large bald man who sold him *four* marijuana cigarettes. Henke gave *one* to Gloria, forced himself to pat her acetate-and-rayon-sheathed thigh, and left. She wasn't there the following night when Henke returned, but the bartender remembered him and was friendly. That was exactly what Henke wanted—the role of an affable sort who was no threat to anybody.

He was making progress but much too slowly. He arranged for a fortnight's leave. He checked into a Phoenix motel the day before Thanksgiving and made his way to Big Dude's to try to start the second phase of his plan. He bought more drinks and more "joints" for a few nights before he asked for cocaine. The big curly-haired dealer looked dubious until Henke showed him the sheaf of currency.

"Outside," the beefy vendor said.

Henke followed him into the alley behind the bar and took out his money. The heavy man smiled and reached for it.

"I want a look at the stuff," Henke said.

"Take a look at *this*," the dealer replied harshly.

It was a small Beretta automatic.

"This a ripoff?" Henke asked in a voice that sounded much more nervous than he was.

The dealer nodded, smiled and waved the gun in menace.

"Just hand over the bread, stupid, and you won't get hurt," he said.

Henke took out the money and thrust it forward. The thief was grinning as he stepped closer to accept it. His expression changed abruptly seconds later when Henke kicked him in the groin. The man screamed as he doubled up in agony. Drawing his own revolver with his right hand, Henke used his left to grab the dealer's weapon. He swung it to smash the drug merchant in the face. Gasping and hurting, the fat man reeled back. Then Henke hammered his jaw again with the Beretta. The larcenous dealer's lower plate flew from his battered mouth. Henke looked at it and ground it under his boot.

"You're an idiot," Henke told him.

The man tried to answer, but only bloody bubbles emerged.

"Where's my coke?" Henke demanded.

The dealer shook his head in pain. He opened his lips and began to croak out a curse. He couldn't finish it. Henke had shoved the .38 into his mouth.

"You've got *ten* seconds, idiot."

The terrified dealer gagged, shook in pain and pointed to the pocket of his blood-spattered sport shirt. Henke reached in and removed the folded square of glossy paper. Then he took the gun from the man's mouth and retreated a few steps.

"What do I owe you?"

The dealer looked incredulous.

"You don't think I'd rob you, Fatso? I'm an honest man," Henke said.

The bleeding man hesitated, suspecting a trick and expecting more beating.

"How much, idiot?"

The dealer slowly held up *two* fingers. Henke counted out several bills and wadded them into the man's shirt pocket.

"Pure?" Henke demanded.

"G-good stuff," the dealer assured through split and swollen lips.

"If it isn't, I'll find you and break bones you never thought about. Now pick up your teeth, Fatso, and beat it."

The battered man obeyed. Henke stayed away from Big Dude's for *two* days to provide time for word to get around. When Henke returned, it was obvious that the sharp-featured bartender knew what had happened. The wary look in his eyes said it clearly.

"Sorry about the trouble you had," he announced.

Henke shrugged and ordered a beer. As he was sipping the cold Coors a minute later, he turned his head to scan the room.

"He's not here," the bartender said, "but if you're interested in buying some more stuff, Jack—"

"Call me Soldier. What's your name?"

"Tommy."

"You meet a lot of people, Tommy. Know anyone who might sell me some heavy hardware? I'm planning a big hunting trip."

"That kind of hardware? I'll ask around."

"Do that," Henke urged and drank again. "I'm paying top dollar, Tommy."

He put a *$50* bill on the bar and walked out into the starlit night. Though he had not spelled out exactly what he wanted, he was confident that his message would not be misunderstood. It wasn't. The first illegal gun vendor he met showed no surprise when Henke asked for stubby MAC-11s with "suppressors"—the silenced version of the 9-millimeter Ingram submachine gun. He sold him a pair, along with a score of *32*-round magazines. The second arms merchant had nothing better than M-*16*s, standard U. S. infantry weapons that fired a smaller bullet and were much harder to conceal because they were *21* inches longer than the Ingram.

Otto's Boy had to be back at Tooele in *six* days, and he had

less than half of the guns and none of the men the plan demanded. He forced himself to be patient. He did his exercises
every day, took his enemas each night, and waited. Then the
bartender sent him another black market weapons dealer. He
had a glass left eye that gleamed oddly, *four* more Ingrams,
and a full crate of magazines.

"Anything else you need?" he inquired as he pocketed
Henke's cash.

"Know any experienced guys who can handle this hardware?"

The gun merchant studied the stranger, trying to estimate
the possible risks and rewards.

"Good bread?" he asked.

"Better than that. There'll be a nice chunk for you too. Double what I just gave you, and you can have the pieces back."

"I'll see what I can do, Soldier. You mind Mexicans?"

Henke hesitated. Many of them were half-Indian, and mixed
breeds were inferior. Still, there was no way he could find a
squad of the tough and disciplined SS fighters he really wanted.

"I want shooters who can keep their faces shut and follow
orders. Mexicans, huh?"

"Not *all* Mexicans," the arms dealer promised.

The first pair he sent were stocky brothers, Eugenio and
Raymondo Fuentes. "Mondo" was the younger and more talkative. They had been armed escorts for a heroin importer. The
third was a muscular ex-biker known as "Wheels" who had ridden with the notorious Devil's Breed until they disbanded. He
had just done seven years for an armored car robbery. "Wheels"
Spencer had a tattoo of a naked woman on his left forearm, a
gravelly voice and a surly manner.

"It's a payroll job—a big one," Henke said. "There'll be guards
with automatic weapons."

"How much for me?" Spencer demanded bluntly.

"One hundred and fifty thousand. You'll earn it. Those
guards—you'll have to burn them all. No survivors to give de-
scriptions."

"That means a lot of heat."

"You won't be around to sweat," Henke assured him. "Each of you will have his cash and a long-distance plane ticket half an hour after it's done. You'll have to stay away, far away, for at least *six* months."

"I don't like that *six* months crap."

"It comes to twenty-five thousand a month. Are you in or out?"

The ex-biker glared hostilely and finally nodded.

"Okay, I'm in. When and where?"

"I'll let you know. Meanwhile, get some new ID. You're going to need it."

Henke was still short *three* men when his leave expired. He was on duty the next weekend, but on the Saturday after that he returned to Phoenix. With the help of the one-eyed gun dealer, he recruited a baby-faced bank robber named Mike Maltin and a crooked ex-cop named Lenny Cooke. Decorated for achievements as a Marine Corps demolition specialist in Vietnam, he had been thrown off the Phoenix police force for protecting a major gang of truck hijackers. It was Cooke who solved the last problem—vehicles—when he brought in car thief Sid Shnippa.

Now Otto's Boy was ready. He would move when the Chemical Corps did, when the next batch of bright blue cylinders was hauled to Dugway. None of the criminals knew his identity or his plan. Greedy for the big money from the imaginary payroll robbery, they were all waiting for the attack order from the leader they called Soldier.

It had to be soon. Time was his enemy. Hoodlums such as these couldn't keep their mouths shut or stay out of trouble for long. A single casual comment from any of them could ruin all his work, and there was nothing he could do to stop them. He could only continue to develop his friendship with the sergeants who assigned work at the Tooele motor pool.

Winter was near. The snows came to Utah, and ski resort operators at a score of mountain towns rejoiced. Henke waited silently, listening to his heartbeat and perspiring as if he were in some jungle. He hated many things but nothing more than those beyond his control. Weather was beyond his control, and control was *everything.*

Then the good news came on December *15.* More nerve gas would be moved to Dugway Proving Grounds *three* days later at noon. Henke was exhilarated and ready. From a pay phone halfway between Tooele and Salt Lake City, he phoned each man and told him what he was to do. No *two* of them were to stay at the same motel, and none of those motels was within *twenty* miles of the ordnance depot.

They assembled on the night of the *sixteenth* at the room he had rented for that purpose in Salt Lake City's Marriott Hotel. They eyed one another curiously. This was their first meeting. The next would be the dry run the following day, and *twenty-five* hours after that they would be fighting for their lives. Introducing them only by their first names, Henke told them that their target was an army base payroll and gave each man a sealed envelope with his individual assignment and instructions.

The only paragraph they all got concerned security: Stay out of bars and brothels. Don't drink any alcohol or smoke dope. Drive carefully and stay in the motel rooms as much as possible. And no matter what the provocation, don't get into any arguments or fights with anyone.

"And don't take candy from strangers?" the surly ex-biker jeered.

"If you do, I'll kill you," Henke promised.

None of them laughed. They could see that he meant it.

Everything went well on the rehearsal the next day. Nothing went at all on the *18*th. *Five* inches of snow tumbled down, and the convoy to Dugway was cancelled. It might be days before the shipment was rescheduled, Master Sergeant Debuskey confided. "But when it is, Ernie, it's still your deal," the Motor Pool supervisor told his recently acquired friend. "You can still drive over to collect the money that guy owes you."

"I'd go on my cycle if it wasn't busted. You're doing me a real favor, Mort."

"That's what buddies are for," Debuskey replied amiably.
December *20*.

0700.

That's when Otto's Boy heard that the roads were clear and
the gas convoy would move out at noon. He got to a pay phone,
alerted his assault force by a prearranged and innocent sounding
code phrase and then dialed for the local weather report:

Cloudy but no snow.

The convoy would roll.

He must not show his excitement. He had to be careful. His
enemies would be—every step of the way. Following Debuskey's
instructions, he drove the truck to Field *Nine* where guards
checked his ID and pass. An armed MP slid onto the seat beside
him. Only then could Otto's Boy guide the vehicle to a point
some dozen yards from Bunker M.

There were more guards at the entrance. Gesturing with
their automatic weapons, they told him to remain in the truck.
He watched a major unlock the steel door and a team of men
in coveralls enter the bunker. They emerged several minutes
later carrying a long wooden crate that looked like a small coffin.
He barely suppressed a smile. The "coffin" would go nicely with
the stolen hearse in which he would make his escape.

The crate was loaded carefully into the rear of the truck.
Then another and still another were put beside it. The military
police climbed into their jeeps as a noise like thunder sounded
overhead. The MPs looked up at the helicopter gunship, and
then a lieutenant in the first jeep spoke to the pilot by radio.
After a brief conversation, the lieutenant raised his right hand
in a thumbs-up signal.

"Let's go!" he ordered.

With his jeep in the lead and the other behind the truck to
protect the rear, the convoy left Bunker M at noon. Once it
reached the highway outside the base, it moved at a safe and
steady *35* miles an hour. Otto's Boy glanced at his wristwatch
and checked the mileage on the dashboard odometer a little

while later when the guard beside him was looking out the window.

They were right on schedule and just *four* miles from the tunnel. The MP was grumbling about how boring it was "out here in nowhere. The weather's lousy, the food sucks and nothing ever happens." He hardly noticed the perfunctory replies. Now Henke saw the intersection up ahead. *Two* miles and a few minutes from here, a great deal would happen. It would begin seconds after the convoy passed the crossroads. *One* of the assault teams would put up the Detour sign to send other vehicles away from the tunnel. Then he would circle by motorcycle to join the ambush.

One mile.

The MP was recalling a restaurant near Fort Hood in Texas that had outstanding chili and an exceedingly friendly waitress named Lorraine. Or was it Laverne? Whatever it was, there wasn't a girl in Tooele, or Salt Lake City either, who could make a soldier as happy. And that wasn't all. Playing nursemaid to these damn gas bombs was even more depressing. Just a single whiff of the stuff could rip your guts out, people said.

"Think that's true?" he asked.

There was the mouth of the tunnel.

Otto's Boy tensed in anticipation.

"Maybe more than a whiff, but it's bad all right," he replied. He saw the lieutenant in the jeep ahead raise the radio to his lips, checking in again with the helicopter.

"Be damn glad when we unload this crap at Dugway," the MP said. "Gives me the willies every run. You think they got anything worse?"

"No idea."

"I heard there's some even creepier stuff in Field *Twelve*," the MP reported and shifted the M-*16* that was lying across his lap.

The convoy entered the tunnel. It was noisy inside, making conversation almost impossible. That was good, for Otto's Boy had to concentrate. It was time. The moment that he had been waiting for for so long was at hand. In less than half a minute, the attack would begin.

He saw headlights down the tunnel moving toward him. It had to be the refrigerated truck they had taken from the meat packing plant's garage. The massive cement mixer would be following it. There would be no other vehicles entering the tunnel behind them. The attack unit had put up a Detour sign down the road on the far side too.

The meat truck was very near now. He could see the ex-biker's dour face behind the wheel moments later. Staring directly ahead, Spencer showed no interest in the military convoy. Henke guided his vehicle past the truck carrying the nerve gas, slowing just a bit. The timing and coordination were important. The meat truck had to be a few yards behind the jeep that was protecting the rear when the cement mixer reached the lead jeep carrying the lieutenant.

Another set of headlights—and Ernst Henke stiffened. He had never been in combat before. He had dreamt about it, and now it was here. Something stirred in his loins, but he could not indulge in that. There was no time. The cement mixer was only a dozen yards from the lead jeep.

It all happened very quickly, just as he had planned. The cement mixer swerved suddenly, crashing into the first jeep at *40* miles an hour and smashing it against the tunnel wall. The military vehicle and soldiers in it were crushed instantly. *Two* of the MPs died at once. The other pair were battered and squeezed unconscious with multiple fractures and critical internal injuries.

At the same moment, the rear door of the meat truck swung open and the Fuentes brothers opened fire. Handling the *700*-round-per-minute Ingrams with professional skill, they hosed the MPs in the rear jeep. Before the startled soldiers could even turn to defend themselves, each was a gory corpse. With a ruined body at the wheel, the jeep veered into the side of the tunnel and crashed.

Even before it hit the wall, the MP beside Henke was swinging his automatic weapon. He did not fire. Otto's Boy slipped out the *.32* taken from the cocaine dealer and shot him *four* times at point-blank range. As the corpse slumped forward to fall against the windshield, Otto's Boy stepped hard on the brake pedal.

The truck loaded with nerve gas shook and skidded. It was heading directly toward the cement mixer. If they collided, Ernst Henke could easily die. They might all die. The impact might rupture a gas cylinder, and that would be enough. Henke eased up on the brake, spun the wheel, and stepped down on the pedal again. The truck shuddered to a halt *five* inches from the cement mixer.

There was no time to celebrate or even curse.

The helicopter was overhead, circling and waiting for the convoy to emerge at the far end of the tunnel. The assault team had to move quickly. It must get the "coffins" out and away before the gunship crew suspected that anything was wrong and radioed for help.

"Hurry up! Get those crates!" Henke shouted.

The criminals rushed to the back of his truck, opened it and looked at the crates. There had to be a lot of money in there. Inspired by this thought, they manhandled out the first one and carried it around the cement mixer to the old school bus waiting *sixty* yards beyond. Then they came back for the other boxes.

While they were busy with that, Henke dragged the corpse beside him across the seat until it was behind the wheel. Then he put on gloves and switched dogtags with the dead man. Finally, he raised the murdered MP's automatic weapon and blew away most of the body's face. A fire would finish the obliteration, but the price was too high. He couldn't afford the smoke that might arouse the helicopter crew when it billowed from the tunnel. He couldn't risk an explosion in the tunnel either. If those fuel tanks went, he really would be dead.

Henke helped them load the last box into the bus, looked back and borrowed Eugenio Fuentes' Ingram. He walked to each jeep, and systematically pumped half a dozen bullets into every MP—even those obviously dead. He wasn't taking chances.

He returned to the bus where the others were waiting. He got behind the wheel and reminded them to get down on the floor. As soon as they did, he started the motor and drove the bus toward the far end of the tunnel. The crew in the gunship paid no attention to it when the bus emerged a few minutes later. The army men were waiting for the convoy, which should be rolling out any moment now.

The bus reached the Detour sign a few minutes later. Henke stopped, let the younger Fuentes out, and watched him move it to a place behind the school vehicle. Then the smiling Mexican got back into the bus and sprawled on the floor beside the others. Henke then drove for half an hour.

"We're here," he announced as he turned off the motor. The others stood up and saw that they were on a side road, surrounded by trees. A black hearse was parked a few yards away.

"We're switching vehicles now," the man they called Soldier told them.

"When do we get paid?" Spencer challenged.

"When we get the boxes to where I've got the cars—in about *ten* minutes."

"Any objection if I drive, Soldier?" he demanded.

"Not a bit."

They shifted the crates to the rear compartment of the hearse, talking about how easy it had been. Laughing, boasting and joking about how they would spend the money, they were in high spirits as they finished.

"I'll take the keys now," the ex-biker announced.

"Certainly," Henke replied.

Then he raised the Ingram and put *four* bullets into the man's throat. Before the body hit the ground, Henke spun and chopped down the Fuentes brothers. As he slammed in a fresh magazine, the others tried to run for the weapons they had left in the bus. They didn't make it. He shot them in the back.

When they fell face forward onto the ground, he reloaded again and systematically blew away the back of each man's head.

I did it, Mama.

After he changed into the civilian clothes he had hidden under the front seat of the hearse, he looted the corpses of watches and money. Though he still had $6,280 left of the $12,000 that he had withdrawn from his savings, there was no point in leaving cash or valuables for crooked cops to steal. He would have all sorts of expenses on the long drive east and in the months until he was settled and employed. The real ID papers, driver's licenses, and Social Security cards that he had been holding for the men might be helpful, but perhaps only temporarily. It depended on whether the army saw any point in tracking dead men, and whether the investigation focused entirely on the "missing" MP whom Henke had shot.

No time for speculation now.

The helicopter would have sounded the alarm. Army units were already in the tunnel, and other MP detachments were fanning out to establish road blocks. Soon air patrols would be up, roving even wider. Henke got into the hearse and started the engine.

Then he heard another sound. It was running water. He blinked, and he was back in the washroom in mid-Manhattan with soapy hands. Some man he didn't know was washing at the next sink. When the stranger was finished, he dried his hands with a paper towel and crumpled it. Humming, he tossed it at the waste container—and missed.

It was outrageous. The man saw the towel—damp, soiled and probably seething with germs from his grubby fingers— on the floor of a public place but made no effort to put it in the trash. Otto's Boy wanted to hit him. Instead he glared. The man was still humming as he strolled jauntily from the washroom.

"Pig!" Henke said bitterly.

He put the towel in the waste bin, considered the germs

and started to wash his hands again. People like that filthy animal should be destroyed, he thought. This rotten city was full of them. *One hundred seventeen*—that was only a sample of what O. B. could do. In his next attack he would kill a whole lot more.

CHAPTER 18

SIX MINUTES after Henke left the washroom, David Bloom entered the outer office of the police commissioner's suite. The buxom black receptionist, who was both the widow of a hero cop and one of Grady's public relations symbols, smiled in greeting. It was noon. Bloom had no idea why he had been summoned.

He smiled back politely. Then he saw Captain James Maccarelli of the 26th Precinct seated stiffly on a straight-backed chair. Bloom immediately wondered whether the Two-Six's own homicide task force had come up with something.

"How's it going, Captain?" he asked hopefully.

"It isn't," Maccarelli replied with a frown.

At that moment, Inspector Fredericks entered the room. As usual, the head of the local FBI antiterrorist unit was accompanied by Special Agent Collery. While Bloom introduced Maccarelli to the federal investigators, the receptionist picked up the telephone from her desk.

"They're all here, Sergeant," she said. "Yes. . . . Right away."

She hung up the phone and smiled again.

"The commissioner will see you now," she told them. "You know the way, don't you, Lieutenant?"

Bloom nodded and led them down the corridor. As soon as they entered Grady's private office, the dapper police commissioner gestured to them to be seated.

"Let's get to it," he said briskly. "I believe in a team effort, and that means pooling information. Captain?"

"They used a clock as a timer," Maccarelli reported. "It's a number you can buy almost anywhere in the country. The shoebox is the one used by the Florsheim chain—fifteen stores in Manhattan and Brooklyn alone. They move more than thirty-two thousand pairs a month."

"Credit card slips?" Fredericks asked.

"Most of the sales are cash."

"So there could be a phony name on the receipt," Bloom thought aloud, "or none at all."

"Go on, Captain," Grady said.

"No clear prints on the clock or the box. None on the wrapping paper either. They used Manila twine and plain brown wrapping paper—stuff on sale all over town. The FBI lab in D. C. is checking both microscopically right now."

Bloom leaned forward in his chair.

"Wasn't there anything about the package that someone in the subway that night might remember?" he asked urgently.

Maccarelli shook his head.

"It looked absolutely ordinary," he answered. "The creeps who did this were very careful."

"And very sick," Bloom said.

The veteran precinct commander shrugged.

"Every big city has plenty of those," he replied. "We'll need much more than that."

"What else do you have, Captain?" Grady asked.

"A precinct full of scared and bitter people. There's a lot of anger up there. They're saying that City Hall and the police don't give a damn, that if most of the victims were white we'd have this solved by now."

"That's utterly untrue," Vincent Grady erupted. "Haven't you explained how hard we're working on the case?"

"I told a lot of people, but I'm not sure they heard, Commissioner."

Grady's eyes clouded as he considered the situation.

Maccarelli was a first-class precinct commander, but had it been a mistake not to assign a black captain to run the 26th?

"I might go up tomorrow to meet with community leaders myself," Grady said. "There are some fine people . . . very intelligent ministers and, ah, educators . . . whom I know very well. Yes, a candid discussion might be productive."

"Don't wait too long, sir," Maccarelli advised. "They're building up one helluva head of steam. We could have a lot of trouble in a couple of days, if you know what I mean."

The commander of the Two-Six didn't use the word riot.

He didn't have to.

Everyone in the room understood his message.

"Tomorrow morning," Grady promised.

Perhaps with a press conference to follow, he thought.

Then he turned to David Bloom.

"You're on, Lieutenant."

"With the help of the FBI and CIA, we've checked on all known terrorist groups and clandestine organizations around the world. There's no record of one called O. B., no report any of them ever used nerve gas, nothing on any sale or theft of nerve gas."

"What does that leave you?" Grady asked.

"Two routes. The first—probably the best—is the blue cylinder."

Bloom turned to Fredericks who would report on what the federal experts had found.

Seven . . . eight . . . nine . . . ten.

The seconds ticked away. The FBI inspector said nothing.

"Yeah, what's it made of?" Maccarelli demanded bluntly. "Where did it come from?"

These were direct questions. They had to be answered.

Fredericks sat up straighter in his chair before he spoke.

"I believe that the Department of Defense people are looking into that," he replied.

"With all their experts and sophisticated equipment they don't know yet?" Bloom asked.

There was something unpleasant about the silence that followed.

"I can't understand that, Inspector," Bloom announced in a calm but rock-hard voice.

Now David Bloom waited for the federal agents to acknowledge his implicit challenge. They ignored it. Solemn-faced and cold-eyed, they looked directly at the police commissioner—and no one else.

Something was wrong.

"I'll check on it," Fredericks finally said.

"Let us know as soon as you can," Grady told him. "What's your other route, Lieutenant?"

Though he was annoyed, Bloom, as in a chess match, automatically computed and analyzed the situation before him. It didn't add up right. Between the Army Chemical Corps and the CIA, they should have identified that cylinder in hours, not days. Grady had to know that. Why was he holding back?

"The second route, Lieutenant?" Grady prodded.

"When I said to Captain Maccarelli that the people who did this were very sick, I had something specific in mind. I meant a special kind of very sick."

Grady nodded.

"You've consulted a psychiatrist?" he guessed.

"An exceptional one, Commissioner—an expert on the terrorist mind."

"What does your expert tell you?" Grady questioned.

"That O. B.'s leader is likely to be a paranoid schizophrenic with a bitter grudge—someone who might seem quite normal outside but burning with rage inside."

Maccarelli frowned. He didn't trust psychiatrists. He remembered the two who had signed Oscar Poe's release papers last year. Poe had gone directly from the asylum to his grandmother's house where he hacked the old woman to pieces.

"This shrink—what's his name?" the cautious captain asked.

"*Her* name is O'Donnell."

Maccarelli looked startled. There was something quite different in the commissioner's eyes. For just a moment Vincent X. Grady permitted himself the luxury of a guarded smile. It was probably her Irish name, Bloom guessed. He wondered whether to mention that his uncle had mentioned Galway as her birthplace. That might please the commissioner.

Bloom decided not to, for it might seem like currying favor. He didn't care whether the commissioner liked him. He certainly didn't like Grady. Right now he didn't owe the PC anything, and Bloom had no desire to change that.

"There's more," Bloom said. "Dr. O'Donnell believes that the leader is almost surely male . . . probably between twenty-five and forty . . . with at least a high school education."

"If she's right and he is a paranoid schizophrenic," Grady reasoned, "shouldn't we be checking on mental patients?"

"We are. We're phoning every hospital, asylum, and prison within fifty miles. We're calling psychiatrists too. There are many hundreds of them—maybe more than a thousand."

Grady turned to the FBI supervisor.

"What do you think, Inspector?"

"I don't mean to criticize," Fredericks replied, "but fifty miles may not be enough."

"You're right," Bloom agreed. "This whole route's a gamble anyway. The man may not even have a psychiatric record—not in this country. O. B. could well be a foreign outfit. Since '82 we've had repeated warnings that terrorists from any of seven or eight countries might hit New York or Washington."

Fredericks nodded solemnly.

"The Bureau has issued several alerts," he confirmed. "I'd suggest that we expand the ring to one hundred fifty miles for a start. I can bring in a dozen of our people to speed up your telephoning. Two dozen, if you need them."

"Thanks," Bloom replied.

"We certainly appreciate your help," Grady announced in his best public executive voice.

"It's our job by law," Fredericks reminded him. "The Bureau has primary responsibility for dealing with spies . . . terrorists . . . subversives of every kind."

And it wasn't about to let a local police force get all the credit for solving such a major case, Bloom thought. Well, the FBI was good at this sort of thing. It was sometimes ponderous and bureaucratic, but damn good.

Grady decided that it was time to tell them.

"Now I have something to report," he said. "We've heard from O. B. again."

He opened a drawer in his desk and took out a folder.

"There's been a second note to the mayor," he announced as he placed the folder on the large leather-framed blotter directly in front of him. "It contains instructions for delivery of the money."

It would be something tricky, Bloom calculated.

It had to be.

"We're to run an ad in the classifieds of the Monday edition of the *Times*," Grady continued. "It is to include the words Furth Flower Company."

"F-u-r-t-h? Like the playwright?" Bloom asked.

"Right. So far as we can tell, the firm doesn't exist. It isn't incorporated in New York, New Jersey, or Connecticut," Grady said. "There are twenty-four Furths in the Manhattan phone book and about forty-six more in the rest of the city. My guess is that none of them have any connection with this and that O. B. just selected the name randomly for the code phrase."

Bloom hesitated. Grady was wrong, but it would be better to have proof before saying so.

"That code phrase will confirm the city's agreement to pay the five million dollars the next afternoon," Grady explained. "A million in used one-hundred-dollar bills with nonconsecutive serial numbers, the rest in top-quality uncut diamonds."

That division of forms of payment meant something too. Bloom *knew* it—beyond any doubt.

"Where's the drop?" Maccarelli demanded.

"The main information booth in Grand Central station—at half-past five."

That would be the heart of the evening rush hour for commuters heading home. The rail terminal would be jammed with hordes of hurrying people—thousands. In that situation, surveillance would be difficult. Almost anything could happen.

"How do we deliver?" Bloom asked.

"A blonde woman in the uniform of a TWA stewardess is to bring it there in a large airline bag. End of message."

"There has to be more, Commissioner," Bloom said.

Grady shook his head.

"I assume that they'll contact her by telephone or by messenger," he replied. "Whatever they do, we'll have to be ready. I'll get the court order for taps on every phone line into that information booth, and I want complete coverage of the entire terminal. No uniforms. All plainclothes."

"Whatever personnel you need, we'll deliver," Fredericks promised enthusiastically.

"Good, and we'll require cars outside too," Grady said.

"Cars, vans, motorcycles—an assortment of vehicles," the FBI supervisor suggested. "And a mix of agents for surveillance: men and women . . . young and old . . . white, black, Hispanic, and Oriental. We'll cover every exit and every street for five blocks around."

Now Grady was smiling broadly.

"That should do it," he exulted.

"Do *what?*" Bloom asked.

"The job, Lieutenant," Vincent Grady answered vigorously. "I've talked with the mayor, and he's decided that we've got to stop these monsters. We're going to follow whoever picks up the bags, find the gang's headquarters, and trap them all."

But it couldn't be that sure or that simple.

"Wait a minute," Bloom appealed.

"They'll never blackmail this or any other city again," the commissioner announced confidently.

He was obviously convinced that he was right. If it succeeded, he'd be something of a hero. If it didn't, the mayor had made the decision, hadn't he? Maybe Fredericks could be reasoned with, Bloom speculated.

"Inspector, you've had a lot of experience," he said. "As a professional, can you guarantee that we'll nail them all? Every damn one?"

The FBI supervisor hesitated for only a moment.

"I think we can do it," he answered, "and we'll commit three hundred agents—or double that—to make sure."

Unconvinced, Bloom shook his head.

"What if one of them gets away—*just one?* With a cylinder?" he asked.

"The decision has been made," Grady said firmly. "If you find your paranoid schizophrenic before Tuesday at five-thirty or the cylinder leads us to them by then, fine. If not, we go with this operation. That's an order."

Bloom nodded.

"I expect your complete cooperation, your best shot. Is that clear, Lieutenant?"

"Yes, Commissioner."

The meeting ended a few minutes later. While Grady and Fredericks were discussing how they would set up liaison with the Midtown South Precinct where the rail terminal was, Bloom glanced at his wristwatch.

It was 12:18 P.M. on Friday.

He had 101 hours and 12 minutes to identify and seize the

entire O. B. group. The odds against doing that by tracking mental patients were enormous—almost impossible to compute. Was that why the FBI supervisor had been so eager to ratify the risky plan to capture the terrorists? Or was there some other reason?

After shaking hands with Grady, Fredericks started for the door. Bloom stopped him.

"I want to talk to you, Inspector."

"Don't worry, Lieutenant," Fredericks said. "We'll have those two dozen agents phoning your psychiatrists within ninety minutes."

Bloom stepped closer.

"That's good, but it's not what I want to talk about. I want some answers. I want the truth about why the CID was tailing me—the whole truth."

"Lieutenant, I don't really know—"

"Find out," Bloom broke in harshly. "You know whom to ask. Do it now. Today."

"I'll try," Fredericks said in his most conciliatory tone.

"Trying's not good enough. And there's the question of that cylinder. I want answers on that too—all the answers. You've got until six o'clock tomorrow night."

"These things are out of the Bureau's control. I can understand why you're so deeply concerned, Lieutenant—"

"Six o'clock," Bloom interrupted. "That's when I go public. And don't bother to have somebody phone the commissioner or the mayor either. It won't help. *Six o'clock* is when I blow the whistle."

"There's no need for any confrontation," Fredericks said earnestly. "We've always worked well together in the past, haven't we?"

David Bloom did not answer the question. He hadn't heard it. He was already out the door, striding swiftly away from Grady's office. The conversation was over and Bloom was gone. The threat remained.

CHAPTER 19

AT SEVEN P.M. Dr. M. C. O'Donnell got into her white Triumph convertible. Three or four nights a year she drove up to the northern Bronx to have dinner with her father's widowed sister. It was usually a pleasant experience. Aunt Mary was an excellent cook and always provided news of various relatives on both sides of the Atlantic. This was one of those nights.

Everything went well until ten minutes after nine when Mary Heggerty asked her favorite niece what she'd been doing recently. The eruption came two minutes later. That was when the psychiatrist reported that the police had asked for her help with the terrible subway massacre, and mentioned that she had been consulted by the head of the antiterrorist unit—a Lieutenant David Bloom.

The pleasantness ended immediately. Mary Heggerty exploded in anger. "He's a devil," she raged, "working hand in glove with the bloody Brits. Your cousin, Sheila, is crying her eyes out now because of him. It was Bloom who led the F.B.I. to arrest Johnny Kelleher, the man Sheila's to marry. For what?

For buying guns to free the North . . . to drive out the Brits. He's a terrible man, that Bloom. Even his own wife left him. Don't have anything to do with that devil."

The fierce defense of the I.R.A. and bitter denunciation of Bloom went on for nearly half an hour. It was 10:22 when the weary psychiatrist finally got home to her apartment on East 87th Street in Manhattan. There was no way to discuss the shipment of arms to the I.R.A. rationally, she thought gloomily as she turned on the hot water for her bath. All those centuries of oppression and violence had put the whole question on the list of things that neither reason nor psychiatry could help. Such deep rooted mass hatred was beyond the reach of doctors, she reflected as she stepped into the tub.

For fifteen minutes she managed to escape into the therapeutic warmth and silence. It wasn't until she began to get out of the tub that she thought again about what her aunt had said. Mary Heggerty's last admonition had been that Bloom was not to be trusted. Like a lot of other men in New York and Galway and elsewhere, the psychiatrist recalled. Then she sighed, reached for a large bath towel and began to dry herself.

When she was finished, she put on a robe and checked her answering machine. She usually did that automatically as soon as she returned and was annoyed that she had forgotten this basic Manhattan ritual.

For a few seconds she wondered why.

There had to be a reason.

It was one of the fundamental psychoanalytic tenets that people did or didn't do things for some inner cause, but she couldn't think of any. Perhaps she was too weary. No, that was a cop-out. Whatever the motivation, it couldn't have anything to do with Bloom. She hardly knew him. He meant nothing to her.

There were three messages on the tape. One was a call from a patient seeking to change an appointment . . . another an invitation to the birthday party of a very rich and boring lawyer whom she had met in Barbados. The third was heavy breathing and a highly graphic sexual solicitation. It was the same sick man who had phoned in similar obscene litanies before. As a psychiatrist, she understood that there was nothing personal in his calls. As a woman, she found herself wishing that he would migrate to Australia.

Now she settled down in a comfortable, well padded armchair to read the latest bulky issue of the *Journal of the American Psychiatric Association*. The prose was pompous, dense and almost solid jargon. She accepted the fact that it was her duty to read such periodicals and reminded herself that there was usually an idea or two buried under the thick quilting of pretentious language. The authors of these "studies" meant no harm. Getting published was necessary for their professional advancement; each article was equivalent to a stuffed animal mounted on the wall of a hunter's living room.

After thirty-five minutes she had managed to burrow through only four pages. Her mind turned to what her aunt had said about Bloom. The entire harangue about the detective had been completely unnecessary. Maeve O'Donnell's contact with him had been correct and professional. It was ridiculous to think that she would have anything else to do with an obsessive, righteous, and aggressive policeman. She wasn't a snob, but doctors didn't get involved with detectives, not even those elected to Phi Beta Kappa at a top Ivy League college.

She rose, got one of the glittering glasses of Waterford cut crystal and poured herself a drink of Strega. After two sips of the fiery Italian liqueur, a reassuring glow began to warm her. She returned to the journal. She drank and read, somehow forcing her way through another page. After a while she found herself thinking about Bloom again. Aunt Mary had told her that Bloom had once been married. Marriages failed for many reasons, but why had his wife left him? Was there a secret, dark side to David Bloom?

Standard Freudian theory about why a man might choose a career hunting criminals would suggest one, she recalled. Then she refilled her glass and decided that there was something about

Bloom that didn't seem standard. Sipping more Strega, she real-ized that she had no idea what it was.

Now she felt tired. It was time to go to sleep. Tomorrow was Saturday, thank God. She made her way to the bedroom, took off her robe, and yawned. Glancing at her nude figure in the full-length mirror on the closet door, she thought about the imminent effects of the ample dinner that she had eaten earlier.

"Too late now," she sighed.

As she pulled back the covers a moment later, she remem-bered something that she had forgotten to tell Bloom. It was a small thing, but it might be helpful. She yawned again as she turned out the lights. Perhaps she would call him in the morning.

CHAPTER 20

"LIEUTENANT BLOOM, please. It's Dr. O'Donnell."

"Good morning, Doctor," a strong and definitely New York voice replied. "This is Sergeant Velez. Actually, it's a bad morning down here, and last night was lousy too."

"I'm sorry."

"This afternoon's gonna be worse," he predicted. "About the lieutenant, he's not in right now."

"Can you tell me when you expect him?"

Twisting the wrist on the hand that held the telephone, Gabriel squinted at his watch through red-rimmed eyes. It seemed to be 10:25 A.M.—probably a nice morning outside. He didn't know. Busy telephoning endlessly in an office that stank of cigarette smoke, he hadn't looked out a window in hours. He was tired, and the noise of the others on four adjacent phones didn't help.

"Hold it down, will you?" he appealed. "Doc, I think Lieutenant Bloom should be back soon. Any message?"

"If he returns before eleven o'clock, would you please ask him to call me?"

"You got it," Velez told her.

Now Maeve O'Donnell stared at the telephone impatiently. Saturday was the only time she could do her chores. She was fully occupied on weekdays from eight A.M. through seven P.M., and very few stores were open on Sunday. As soon as Bloom phoned, she could leave to buy the food and other items on her list.

She glanced at the wall clock, checked her shopping list, scanned the clock again. Maybe what she had to tell him wasn't that significant. She could phone him back later. When there was no call by 11:20, she flicked on her answering machine and started for the door. She had it open when the telephone rang.

"I was just going out to buy groceries," she said. "I'm glad you caught me."

"So am I."

"Lieutenant, I remembered something else last night. It may not be important, but I wanted to tell you."

"Tell me in five minutes. I'm just up on Ninety-sixth Street. I'll pick you up in front of your house."

He hung up before she could say anything more. When she emerged from the apartment building, Bloom was waiting in his blue Chrysler. She got in and sat beside him.

"I'll make it brief," she said. "There's another aspect of paranoid schizophrenics that I should have mentioned."

The detective nodded and pressed down on the accelerator. The sedan began to roll.

"Where are we going?" she blurted.

"To buy your groceries. We can talk on the way."

"This isn't necessary."

"Yes, it is," Bloom answered. "Sorry I didn't get back to you since that incident on Third Avenue, but we've been busy."

Now the light turned green, and he swung the Chrysler down Fifth Avenue.

"Would you please drop me at Gristede's on Madison at Eighty-fifth?" she asked.

"Sure. Now what did you want to tell me?"

"These paranoid schizophrenics are often ritualistic," the psychiatrist reported. "They tend to go by rigid schedules, to do things in the same sequence. Small details are important to them."

"There are some older people like that too."

"Mostly the ones who live alone," she said. "It gives them something to hang on to. The syndrome may be related to loneliness, but I suspect that there's also a reaching out for security."

The detective slowed his car to avoid bumping a sleek green Maserati convertible.

"In today's world where so little is predictable," he reasoned, "rituals and schedules could give a sense of security and control. Control means safety, right?"

"You could put it that way."

"So there's a fear component? The paranoid schizophrenic may be scared as well as angry?"

"They're acutely insecure," she agreed. Then she went on to give examples of other terrorists' rituals in earlier cases. She was speaking about the Italian Red Brigade group when the Chrysler reached the supermarket.

"Thanks for the ride. I hope that what I've mentioned may be useful."

"How long will you be?" Bloom asked.

"About fifteen minutes. Please, there's no reason to wait."

"See you in fifteen minutes," he replied cheerfully.

As soon as she got out, he drove up Madison Avenue until he saw an empty phone booth. After hesitating a few moments, he double-parked beside it in flagrant violation of the traffic regulations. Some twenty seconds later, he dialed swiftly.

"Sergeant Velez."

"Listen, Gabe, I've got work for Andy," Bloom said.

Policewoman Andrea Chu specialized in installing and detecting electronic bugs and wiretaps.

"Where?" Velez asked.

"The office. Don't interrupt what you're doing. Call her on your lunch break."

Gabriel Velez stiffened in silent surprise. The unspoken message was clear. If Andy's assignment was in the antiterrorist unit's office and Bloom didn't want him to phone from there, it meant one thing: The lieutenant suspected that their own headquarters telephones were being tapped.

"I'll give her a buzz. By the way, you get anything from that head case on Ninety-sixth Street?"

"Not much. He died last month. I'll be in touch."

When the redheaded psychiatrist came out of the supermarket with her purchases, Bloom was waiting. He loaded the two bags into the Chrysler carefully.

"This is really very kind," she said as he started the motor.

"I have an ulterior motive," he confessed. "I thought you might have something else to tell me. We've been phoning hundreds of your colleagues . . . mental institutions . . . police departments . . . and getting nowhere. We've been checking on dangerous paranoid schizophrenics all over the place."

"That's a good idea," she replied as the car moved north.

"Not so far. Any other suggestions?"

"Lieutenant, I'm just a working psychiatrist, not an encyclopedia. I don't have all the answers. I probably don't even have all the questions."

Bloom stopped the sedan at a red light.

"*Anything* at all," he urged.

She stared ahead, concentrating and feeling almost defensive.

"It's desperation time, Doctor," Bloom pleaded. "And we don't even have much of that."

Then she remembered.

"There's one thing you might consider. The word in the O. B. note—attack?"

"Military and naval hospitals?" Bloom guessed immediately. "You're terrific!"

Now the traffic light turned green.

"Another thing that you might keep in mind," she said as the Chrysler picked up speed, "is that this type of terrorist, being deeply afraid in his subconscious, does nothing casually. He pays enormous attention to detail and makes very few mistakes. Like some other irritating people you've met, they're obsessive perfectionists."

She'd been facing him. Now she turned her head and looked up Madison Avenue.

"Like me?" Bloom asked.

"I didn't say that," she snapped. "I'm not your therapist, and I don't intend to be."

Even as she spoke, she wondered why she was being so righteous and wary with him.

"I'm not sure I need one," he answered pleasantly as he turned the car left at her corner. "To quote a song that a friend of mine wrote, what's wrong with doing things right? I mean decent things, of course."

He stopped the car in front of her building. They both got out. Bloom stood on the sidewalk a yard away from her, holding the two bags.

"Thank you," she said.

"You're welcome. And if you should think of anything else, Doctor—"

"You always want more, don't you?" she demanded sharply.

"A lot more. I'll see you."

He was smiling now, and it was more than the look of a man seeking only a professional exchange of information. He meant her. She had met a whole gamut of confident, achieving New York princes—Jewish, Italian, Irish, New England WASPs and Texas tycoons. Stockbrokers, advertising wizards, television network executives, best-selling novelists, politicians and famous doctors who appeared on talk shows—she had known them all . . . briefly. That look was nothing new or magical. It hadn't been for some years.

"Good-bye, Lieutenant," she said and walked into the building.

Bloom started to drive downtown. On many Saturday afternoons he would go to the chess club and a battlefield made of
sixty-four black-and-white squares inlaid in a precious old gaming
table—but not today. This afternoon he was on his way to a
living battlefield, where a life-and-death war would be fought
in a little more than seventy-seven hours. He had gone over
the situation a hundred times. Attack was a military term. Nerve
gas was a military weapon, not a terrorist's tool. The subway
slaughter had been carried out with military precision.

Military—that was the key word.

The O. B. leader almost had to have some military back-
ground. He would plan the next operation like a soldier too.
There was no way to guess which country had trained him,
but the armed forces of most nations thought a great deal alike.
They were orderly, analytical, methodical. They chose where
and when to strike carefully. They studied the place thoroughly.
They evaluated the enemy's numbers, equipment, order of battle and defensive positions in meticulous detail.

Why had O. B. chosen Grand Central for the drop? In this
strange war of wits, why had the terminal been selected for
the battleground? Why a railroad station? Why this one? There
had to be a reason.

Maybe Bloom could find it at the terminal, he thought as
he entered the historic landmark sixteen minutes later. He
walked through the doorway on Lexington Avenue, looking
around carefully every step of the way. There were steps on
the right to the Graybar Building and shops on the left. He
had to consider every possibility, every detail. He had to think
like a military planner too. Maybe that way he could figure out
what the terrorists meant to do.

FBI teams had probably been over every foot of this station
already—twice. They were thorough and practical, a lot smarter
than their critics understood. They were often disturbingly naive
politically, Bloom thought, but they were competent cops. Yes,
they had checked out all of Grand Central, but David Bloom
still wanted to inspect the battlefield himself.

He had to.

He was just as compulsive as the criminals he stalked. David Bloom had known this for a long time. He had been aware of his need for control and perfection for years before he spoke to this beautiful redhaired psychiatrist. After a good deal of reflection, he had decided that he had no reason for concern or guilt. He was reasonably confident that life wasn't a psychology textbook. He was on the side of right, and that made a crucial difference.

Now he was in the main chamber, a huge area with a very high ceiling. At the far end were two sets of stone steps leading up to the Vanderbilt Avenue entrance. His reaction and judgment were immediate—instant reflex.

The high ground.

The military theories of every nation called for seizing the high ground. From there you could watch and dominate the enemy. Whoever held the high ground had a clear view—intelligence—and a superior position for firing every kind of weapon. Control again.

Bloom turned his head to look at the circular information booth where the city's courier was to bring the ransom. Even on a Saturday afternoon, the four clerks on duty were occupied with lines of questioning travelers. There would be many more milling about this part of the terminal on a busy weekday in the evening rush hour.

Bloom had no suspicion that he was being watched.

The detective had no idea that Ernst Henke already held the high ground.

Otto's Boy had also come to Grand Central this sunny May afternoon to check out the battlefield again. He had been over the terminal half a dozen times in April, but he was taking no chances on missing anything. Up-to-date intelligence and scouting reports on possible enemy infiltration were simply sound infantry practice. The maniac wasn't surprised that his foes were also reconnoitering this sector. He had expected it.

132

But to find the man he hated most was a bonus. Henke had studied Bloom's photo long and carefully. He had recognized the detective almost immediately. This was wonderful, exciting. He was less than fifty yards from his worst enemy, and the stupid Jew didn't know it.

Looking down, Henke savored the thought that he could kill David Bloom right now—one shot. No, that would spoil the wonderful plan. It would ruin everything. Striking down one inferior foe wasn't worth it. Otto's Boy was going to wipe out thousands. It would be in the history books. The SS martyrs would be avenged.

He turned his head. It could be risky to look at the detective too long. Eye contact, even for a second, might later help Bloom to remember Henke's face. When the cunning murderer glanced down again, he saw Bloom walking toward the bottom of the stairway. He watched his enemy mount the first step.

Danger.

Bloom was coming up. In twenty or thirty seconds they might be within a few yards of each other. He might even brush against the so-called Super Cop as he passed, hurrying by rudely as so many New Yorkers did.

Knife or gun? He had both. At this range he could easily kill Bloom with either.

Henke sighed. It was really too bad, but this wasn't the time or the place. He had no escape route set, no plan. He couldn't attack without a plan and a timetable, both tested in dry runs. He could kill Bloom later.

Aware that he might be noticed if he lingered here any longer, Henke started down the steps. He was one-third of the way when he passed David Bloom ascending. Henke's heart beat faster for a moment. The stupid detective stopped a moment later, turned to look down thoughtfully. He would have a different expression when the gas got him.

Henke walked past the information booth to make his way south up a wide corridor, through another room with a large newsstand and out onto 42nd Street. He wasn't ready to go back to New Jersey yet. If Bloom was thinking about O. B., O. B. was thinking about Bloom. Henke had already made a plan. Now it was time to do the reconnaissance, to work out the timing, the exits, the train schedules.

It was pleasant and sunny as Henke walked west toward Vanderbilt Avenue. Too bad he had to waste this balmy May afternoon, he thought when he reached the bus stop. There was no choice. He had to secure accurate intelligence information. He must be sure of every detail.

A bus numbered 104 arrived, and Henke joined the trio who boarded it. The traffic was heavy as the bus moved toward the Hudson River. The maniac watched and hated everything he saw: the big headquarters of the public library . . . the park beside it where drug dealers and homosexual prostitutes plied their trades . . . the porno movie houses . . . the live sex shows . . . fast-food joints . . . theaters showing horror and "action" films—Henke loathed them all.

At Eighth Avenue, the 104 bus turned north. He glared at more of the disgusting sex movie houses . . . cheap restaurants . . . bars . . . young sluts in doorways . . . hotels. Columbus Circle. He smiled. This was where he had gotten off the subway on the day of his first attack.

The second would be much bigger, Mama.

The neighborhood changed instantly above Columbus Circle. The Upper West Side was visibly middle class and residential, stocked with apartment houses, boutiques, and Japanese restaurants instead of harlots, bars, and sex-film theaters. The people on the sidewalks looked better dressed and less sleazy than the rabble of Times Square and Eighth Avenue, Henke noticed.

His destination was 83rd Street, but he left the bus at the north corner of Broadway and 79th. It might be safer to walk the last four blocks, timing how long it would take to return to the subway station. He would get the feel of the area, scout ways to leave swiftly if that became necessary. Walking up Broadway in the stream of strolling Saturday shoppers, he recalled reading in some newspaper that this was becoming an "in" neighborhood. That must have been a lie, he decided. It didn't seem the least bit unusual.

There was the movie theater—the Loew's 83rd Street. Once a single unit, it was now a "quad" showing four different films in small, separate chambers. And it was David Bloom's neighborhood movie house, the nearest to the apartment building where the detective lived.

Otto's Boy glanced at the showcards touting the four films, picked one and announced his choice to the bored ticket clerk. Henke didn't care a bit about which film he saw. He would only look at it briefly anyway. It was the layout and size—the number of seats—of the theater he had picked that mattered. The number and location of exits were also important.

He sat down in a half-empty row in the back and waited for his eyes to adjust to the darkness. Then he began to count . . . the number of seats per row . . . the number of rows. A precise number was difficult. That was irritating but not really essential. All he had to know was that there were more than two hundred fifty seats. This unit of the quad theater had more than four hundred. That was good.

After twenty minutes of Clint Eastwood's hard-boiled heroics, Henke left the chamber and walked upstairs to the men's lounge. He hoped that he wouldn't be approached at the urinal by a sex deviate. That had happened once in a Washington, D. C., movie house. It had enraged Henke, who had barely controlled his impulse to smash the filthy seducer to the floor. He had never mentioned the terrible incident to anyone, lest they tease him. He still remembered the sweet scent of the man's aftershave.

After he emerged and checked the exits from the building, Henke left to walk back to the subway station at 79th Street and Broadway. Moving at an inconspicuous pace, it took almost six minutes, including the wait for the light to turn green so he could cross Broadway. Then there was a seven-minute delay in the station before the train arrived. It was 2:20 before he got on the bus that would take him home to New Jersey.

Even with the cooperation of the Grand Central security chief, Bloom didn't complete his careful walking tour of the terminal until a quarter to three. He went directly to his office in the main police headquarters. Four men and a woman—all plainclothes detectives of the antiterrorist unit—were busy telephoning.

"Uh huh . . . yeah . . . thank you very much, Dr. Mandelstam," Gabriel Velez said and hung up. Then he sighed something in Spanish. It was brief and obscene.

"I checked with the Feds about fifteen minutes ago," he reported. "As of then, adding our numbers to theirs, we're batting oh for seven hundred and two. It's a new world's record for strikeouts."

"We've got to stick with it," David Bloom answered.

"Only game in town, right?"

"For the moment, Gabe. I'm sorry."

The door to Bloom's private office opened. Policewoman Andrea Chu came out carrying her satchel of electronic gear. The five-foot two-inch eavesdropping specialist saw Bloom and stopped abruptly.

"You ought to get the janitors in here," the bright-eyed Chinese-American expert said. "This place is filthy."

She patted her small valise, and he understood.

Filthy meant *dirty,* the trade word for a place that was bugged.

Bloom pointed at the nearest telephone. She nodded.

There were taps too.

"I'll tell the maintenance people on Monday," Bloom said.

He couldn't even thank her. Whoever was listening might wonder why, and Bloom didn't want to run that risk.

Velez understood too. He opened his mouth to swear, realized the danger and said nothing. He watched Bloom step forward to shake her hand in silent appreciation.

David Bloom was a very attractive man, she thought as their flesh touched. But it was most unlikely that a lieutenant would go out with a policewoman so far below him in rank. There were probably departmental regulations against it. Still, you couldn't be sure about Bloom. That was another thing that she found appealing.

"See you, Lieutenant," she said with her best smile and left.

Thinking about what she had found, Bloom stood there for several seconds. He wondered who had the boldness and ability to do this. Then he turned to Velez.

"Any calls for me, Gabe?"

"Several. The message slips are on your desk."

The Associated Press, CBS Radio, *New York Daily News,* Reuters, *Los Angeles Times, Tokyo Shimbun, Amsterdam News,* Tass, NBC News, *Toronto Globe,* and an Arkansas minister whose entire congregation was praying for Christ to help Bloom defeat the Red atheists.

Bloom pushed the message slips aside to concentrate on the immediate issues he faced. Should he have the bug and taps ripped out? Or should he pretend that he didn't know about the eavesdropping equipment? Could he use it against the listeners?

He weighed the alternatives, warily projecting his moves and each one's consequences as he did at the chess board. He had to think several moves ahead, computing how the listeners might react and what their moves might be. It would be a lot easier if he knew whom he was playing against—and why. That would help him define what his friends at the Marshall Club—those intense chess players—called "the matrix of possibilities."

Not knowing put him at a definite disadvantage.

At 4:10 the telephone rang.

"For you—personally," Velez said. "He won't give his name."

"I'll take it. . . . This is Lieutenant Bloom."

"You wanted some answers by six o'clock tonight," an unfamiliar male voice—hard and staccato—said.

The FBI inspector had passed on his ultimatum.

137

"That's right," Bloom confirmed.

"You'll get them, but not till tomorrow morning. Where will you be at ten?"

"My apartment."

"There'll be a phone call at ten."

"The number's unlisted. It's—"

"We know the number," the stranger said irritably and hung up.

Bloom wondered who would call the next morning. Then he walked out and told Velez about the brief conversation. When Velez pointed to the telephone on his desk, Bloom nodded in agreement. Whoever was listening had heard, and there was no way to guess what they might do. Even a grand master of chess couldn't predict that.

But David Bloom knew what he would do. Ten o'clock on Sunday morning was more than seventeen hours away. There was no time to waste. O. B. was out there—not far away and almost surely armed with more nerve gas.

"Give me a couple of pages of your list," he said.

Lieutenants didn't do that kind of drudge work, Gabriel Velez thought. Well, no other NYPD lieutenant whom he knew would.

"You gonna start phoning shrinks yourself?" Velez asked uncertainly.

"Unless you've got a better idea."

Velez handed over two pages of the list. Bloom returned to his private office and began to dial.

CHAPTER 21

BLOOM had his Sunday morning routine. He would sleep later than usual—until nine. Then he would bring in the three pound *New York Times* left outside his door, make a special breakfast and read the paper for two hours. After that he would shower and dress and walk through his neighborhood.

He liked this part of the city. He had lived here long before the fashionable boutiques, sushi restaurants and chic shops made the area popular in the last five years. It hadn't been trendy or appealing to movie stars or foreign tourists when he was growing up here. No cute shops, no dining spots whose nouvelle cuisine was touted by the most "with it" food critics, no ultra-modern clothing stores offering the latest creations of Italian and Japanese designers—not then. There had been good delica-tessens and shoe repair shops, not sushi bars and places selling $200 boots.

Bloom liked the new Upper West Side too. He hadn't asked for the changes, but he didn't mind. He could handle it all—even the visitors who came from New Jersey, Long Island, and

Paris to enjoy the "exotic" delights of his neighborhood. He had to walk blocks now to a hardware store, thanks to soaring rents, but he coped. And he still enjoyed walking around his neighborhood on Sundays.

But this one was different. O. B. had done that. Bloom had set the clock for eight. He got out of bed immediately, brought in the massive paper, showered, shaved and dressed swiftly. His custom was to buy food for Sunday's breakfast on Saturday afternoon at Zabar's. The big gourmet emporium on Broadway was dedicated to elegant excess—the best of everything in awesome variety.

Vigorously New York and earthily Jewish, the bustling bazaar had a high energy level—one you could almost touch. It was usually noisy and crowded with serious eaters, Bloom thought as he double-locked his apartment door in the regular Manhattan manner. He didn't have time to wait on line today, but there might be fewer shoppers so early in the morning.

His estimate was correct. When he entered the store at 8:35, he found only a handful of other customers. Aware that this would change very soon, he acquired his purchases quickly. In fifteen minutes he was out the door with freshly ground Colombian coffee, Eastern cure smoked salmon, Zabar's own cream cheese and dark Westphalian bread.

He hurried home. He was finishing his breakfast when he paused to look at his watch. It was 9:30—thirty minutes before they would call. Of course, they might not telephone at all. He had to plan for that too. As he considered what he would do, he poured another cup of the black Colombian brew. The beautiful Japanese photographer he had gone out with last year had complained that his coffee was much too strong. Bloom found himself wondering what Dr. M. C. O'Donnell would say about it.

At 9:45 he phoned his office to check on progress. When Gillespie reported that there wasn't any, Bloom told the black detective that he would be down later. Then he rinsed off the dishes in the kitchen sink and glanced at his watch again. It was 9:49—eleven minutes to go.

His mind was racing now. He was getting ready. He returned to the living room and stared at the phone. It could be tapped. There might be a bug in his apartment—maybe several. For a few moments he was angry with himself. He should have thought of that yesterday. He would have to get Andy Chu up here to "sweep" as soon as possible.

He had been careless. He had made a mistake . . . and O. B. probably wouldn't make any. They hadn't so far, damnit.

9:53—too early to smoke a cigar. David Bloom had that habit under control. Three Don Diego petit coronas a day—never before noon. He shrugged, took out a cigar, and lit it. Seated by an open window, he looked out at the bright spring morning and waited. Puffing on the cigar, he thought about the questions he would ask.

At 10:01 the telephone rang.

It was the same man who had called him at the office yesterday.

"Bloom?"

"Yes."

"About your answers—not on the phone. He wants to see you."

So he—whoever he was—was concerned about taps too.

"When?" Bloom asked.

"There's a car and driver waiting in front of your building right now."

The car was a dark gray Ford. The man behind the wheel was tanned, lean, about thirty. He was wearing sunglasses, a checked shirt, and a light brown sport jacket that almost matched his slacks.

"You waiting for me? My name's Bloom."

"Get in."

The Ford moved east to Columbus Avenue and then south. The driver did not speak. The Sunday morning traffic was light as they rolled downtown. They turned onto Ninth Avenue at Lincoln Center, and Bloom wondered how far they were going. Was it the FBI office near Foley Square?

"You work with Fredericks?" the detective asked.

"No."

Hell's Kitchen . . . Chelsea . . . the West Village. Now Bloom saw the huge twin towers of the World Trade Center jutting up ahead. They were nearing the financial district. The streets were almost deserted. They couldn't go much further, for this was the bottom end of Manhattan island.

"Is it far?" Bloom questioned.

"Not very."

Six blocks later the driver turned right, and a minute after that he stopped the car. They were at the World Trade Center Heliport on the edge of the Hudson River. The man behind the wheel pointed at an olive-drab Black Hawk helicopter. Bloom had seen one on a television news broadcast last week. It was new . . . fast . . . army.

"Where to?" the detective asked.

The driver didn't answer. Something defiant and uncomfortable in his eyes made Bloom think that the man didn't know. Bloom left the sedan and walked to the Black Hawk. Inside were two men in coveralls and hard, plastic, flying helmets. One of the men was black, the other white. The white crewman gave the detective a helmet and showed him how to fasten his seat belt. The black pilot nodded in greeting and started the rotor.

The unpleasant screech of the turbine grew louder and louder. Then the helicopter rose and flew south. Bloom looked down from time to time, trying to estimate where they were and where they might be going. An hour and twenty-eight minutes after takeoff, he saw a large city on the shore of a wide river. As the Black Hawk circled, he noticed several big white buildings and one with a familiar dome. It was the Capitol of the United States. They were approaching Washington.

The helicopter did not land in the city or at National Airport nearby. At two minutes before noon the Black Hawk set down on a large open field on the Virginia side of the Potomac. As Bloom got out he noticed, off to the left some one hundred twenty yards, a big American flag fluttering atop a tall white pole.

It was hot in the midday sun. A sedan painted in the same muddy olive-drab color as the Black Hawk was parked thirty yards away. Bloom saw a uniformed figure emerge from the car and stride toward him. As the man neared, the detective noticed the twin pairs of silver bars on each epaulet.

Military.

"What's the name of this base?" Bloom asked.

The young captain seemed surprised.

"Fort Myer," he replied stiffly. "Would you please come with me?"

It was a very short ride. The view down the grassy hill was the Potomac, but Bloom was looking the other way. He saw houses—none new or small—and a tree-lined street, but nothing that resembled a laboratory complex or an office building. This could hardly be a Chemical Corps installation.

The captain stopped the car in front of a handsome two-storey home of Victorian brick. The flowers that flanked the path to the white front door reflected years of care. This wasn't the residence of a junior officer. Someone important lived here.

A minute later Bloom was ushered into the comfortably furnished den at the rear of the house. A tall man wearing chino pants, a light brown sport shirt, and loafers stepped forward to greet him.

"Please come in. . . . Thank you, Captain," he said, dismissing the young escort officer in a tone of quiet authority. There was steel in that soft southern voice.

After the captain left, the tall man turned to the detective and thrust out his hand. He had a firm grip, Bloom noticed. Was he the man with the answers?

"I'm General Younts."

"Chemical Corps?"

"I'm the army chief of staff. Would you like some coffee?"

Controlling his surprise, David Bloom nodded and followed him to an electric percolator on a low bookcase against the wall.

"Black?"

"Sugar, if you've got it."

Some forty seconds later, they sat facing each other in armchairs. Each of them swallowed a sip of the hot dark liquid.

"Coffee all right?" Younts asked. Bloom shook his head and put down the mug.

"No offense, General."

"That's okay. They said you always told the truth."

"It's a birth defect," Bloom said. "Can we talk about the blue canister?"

"We have to. There's a serious problem, Lieutenant. It concerns national security. There are some extremely sensitive matters involved."

He paused, watching and waiting for the detective's reaction.

Bloom took out a cigar from his jacket.

"What about the canister?" he asked and lit the petit corona.

"I'm afraid that this situation has aspects that are highly classified. In fact, they're Top Secret."

Bloom puffed on the cigar.

"Tell me about the nerve gas, General."

"I'm appealing to you—as a responsible public servant yourself—to leave this alone."

The detective shook his head.

"I *can't* discuss it with you," Younts said. "You're not cleared for Top Secret, are you?"

"No, but I'm cleared for the *New York Times*, CBS News and the Associated Press."

"Is that a threat?" Younts demanded angrily.

"It's a promise."

And David Bloom was a man of his word. That had been in the report too.

"It would be a very serious mistake."

"As bad as bugging my office and tapping the phones of the New York Police Department?" Bloom challenged.

"I don't know anything about that."

"You can read the whole story in every paper in the country tomorrow, if you like."

James Raleigh Younts was sixty-one years old. He had learned a great deal about people on his way up the ladder to chief of staff. It had taken a lot of reading character and a fair amount of politics to get those four stars. Looking at the detective, he saw total determination. The son of a bitch would do it.

"Let me think about it," the chief of staff said.

"There's no time. For God's sake, General, I'm not out to hurt the army. I'm not one of those righteous fools who despises the armed forces and the government as the enemy, damn it. I'm trying to stop a gang of terrorists from killing another one hundred seventeen people next week! You want that on your conscience?"

Younts shook his head slowly.

"I guess I'll have to trust you," the soldier said. "What do you want to know?"

"The truth—all of it. Whose nerve gas is it?"

Younts stiffened in his chair. He couldn't help it.

"Ours," he said.

David Bloom nodded. Now it made sense.

"You don't seem that startled," the chief of staff noted.

"General, I'm an experienced professional detective and a chess player. I've considered many different possibilities—in a whole assortment of scenarios. This was one of them."

Cool . . . analytical . . . logical . . . just as the dossier described him.

"How did they get it?" Bloom asked.

"They ambushed a convoy moving the cylinders between two of our bases in Utah."

"Tooele to Dugway?"

"How the hell did you know that?" Younts demanded.

"Educated guess—and some homework at the public library. The fact that nerve gas is stored at Tooele and tested or destroyed at Dugway has been in the papers more than once."

Bloom puffed on the cigar before he spoke again.

"Please tell me how they did it."

"The convoy had armed escort units front and rear. A helicopter gunship was flying shotgun overhead. Our security was good," Younts insisted.

But the terrorists were *better*, Bloom thought. He wasn't going to say that to the chief of staff, though. It wasn't the kind of thing that a general wanted to hear from any lieutenant, military or civilian police.

"One of our own men in the convoy sold us out," Younts continued bitterly. "They'd never have pulled it off without him—*never*."

"Why don't we start from the top? It might help if you explained exactly what happened."

In short, angry sentences, the chief of staff told him about the ambush in the tunnel, the slaughter of the escorts and the discovery of the bodies of six armed civilians beside the stolen school bus.

"You're sure they were the ones who did it?"

"Ballistics proved that," Younts replied. "Their guns killed our men in the tunnel."

"Who were these men?"

"Professional criminals—all from the Phoenix area. Not one of them had any record of political activity. Neither did that son of a bitch Addams. He didn't belong to any clubs or organizations, didn't read any radical publications. Never discussed politics at all. He'd been in the army eight years. Never in any trouble. Everyone who knew him said he was a nice guy who never complained . . . didn't get into fights . . . got along well."

"Any money problems?" Bloom asked.

"Not that we could find. He had no unpaid bills, no history as a gambler. Had twenty-nine hundred dollars in a money fund."

"Family trouble?"

"Divorced two years before. No alimony—she remarried."
Bloom tapped his cigar end over the ashtray.

"Psychiatric history?"

The chief of staff shook his head.

"Nothing—and they checked him back to kindergarten. No
record of mental problems in his family either. They're all clean
politically too."

"There's got to be something," Bloom said. "Drugs? Alcohol
dependency? Unusual sexual activity?"

Younts sipped more coffee. "I didn't read the file on him
myself," he replied, "but I was told that the CID couldn't find
anything like that, and even his ex-wife said he was a decent,
ordinary guy."

"Ordinary guys don't mastermind a job like this. It wasn't
any ordinary mind that found the one weak spot in your security.
And it certainly wasn't any ordinary MP who carried out that
gas attack in the subway."

"Are you saying Arthur Addams planned all this?"

"Either he did or he knows the planner," Bloom said. "When
did they grab the gas?"

"About twenty months ago—before I became chief of staff.
I can assure you that there's been a massive and continuing
search for Addams and the nerve agent. It's been a maximum-
security operation."

"That's the understatement of the decade," the detective
told him. "Keeping the murders of sixteen men and a massive
U. S. Army search for stolen poison gas secret for twenty months
is a remarkable achievement."

"It wasn't easy."

"General, why in the world did you do it?"

Younts crossed his long legs and looked directly into Bloom's
eyes.

"Not *in* the world," the chief of staff said. "*For* the world.
General Joel, my predecessor, was worried that news of this
incident could cause a panic. It might trigger hysteria all across

the country. That would have a negative impact on our defense posture."

"What does that mean in non-Pentagon talk?"

The senior commander glared.

"Certain rabble-rousing politicians and sensational press types might start an emotional crusade to have all our stocks of nerve agents destroyed. It isn't that difficult to manipulate the public, you know. There's already a large antinuclear movement."

"Let's stick to nerve gas."

"Very well. If our stockpiles were destroyed, we'd have no counter-deterrent to discourage the Soviets from a possible nerve agent attack. They'd still have their huge supplies, but we'd be naked."

"You're saying Joel did this for world peace?" Bloom asked.

"Exactly."

Bloom puffed on the cigar and leaned forward.

"And why are *you* doing it?"

"To avoid the panic and buy more time to locate those cylinders. Once we've got them and the thieves, it's less likely there'll be any mass hysteria."

"I think you just ran out of time—in the subway," Bloom said.

"Just the opposite," Younts argued. "What happened was terrible, but it was our first big break. They've finally shown themselves. They'll do that again when they collect the ransom. That's only three days from now. When they come for the money, we'll nail them."

"What if you don't?"

"We will. Trust me—for three days."

David Bloom thought for several seconds and shook his head.

"Sorry, but I can't. The stakes are too high. Besides that, I can't trust anyone who doesn't trust me," he announced.

"I thought you'd have a sense of responsibility to the national interest."

"You know what *I* think?" Bloom asked harshly. "I think

that your people have been tapping our phones and spying on me so you could find the terrorists first. I think you meant to send in some kind of assault team—army or FBI—to blow them all away. You'd have the gas, and there'd be no survivors to tell anyone about what happened in Utah!"

"That's preposterous!"

"Maybe—but how do I know? Sure, I could be getting paranoid," the detective admitted. "It doesn't really matter. I think you really do care about defending the country and avoiding war. So do I, and that doesn't matter right now either. What counts is that you're willing to risk the lives of hundreds, perhaps thousands, of people in my city, and I'm not."

"I've answered your questions, damn it. Why can't you wait three more days?"

"Because I'm scared. I'm afraid that you're lying . . . or you're wrong . . . or O. B. may not wait three days before the next slaughter. We're dealing with homicidal maniacs. Well, the leader is anyway. This isn't one of those make-believe war games you guys are so good at," Bloom warned. "This is the real thing."

"Watch your mouth, mister. You don't talk to the chief of staff of the U. S. Army that way. I don't have to put up with lectures from some smart-ass New York—"

Younts stopped himself just in time.

"Don't say it," Bloom advised. "I could be wired."

The general tensed. Then the detective stood up and opened his jacket. Younts saw a .38-caliber Police Special in a shoulder holster. There was no tape recorder.

"I don't play those games," Bloom said. "Now I have a proposition for you. I've got something you want—three days. And you've got something I want."

"I'm listening."

"You've got all the information on Arthur Addams and the ambush. I want it—*now*. Complete access to the complete file."

"But it's classified," Younts blurted.

"That's your problem, and you've got about twenty seconds to solve it."

After several moments of silence, Younts frowned.

"Ten seconds," the detective told him. "Look at it this way. I may spot something your people overlooked. If I don't, you're still three days ahead."

Younts' eyes glowed with naked hostility.

Bloom waited for several seconds, but the general did not answer.

"Nice to meet you," Bloom announced and started for the door.

"*Okay,*" Younts said. "You can read the reports, but you aren't to discuss the contents with anyone. Is that clear?"

"Absolutely."

"No one is to know of the Utah incident. Do I have your word on that?"

Bloom thought of the problems ahead. It might be extremely difficult to direct an investigation under this restriction.

"All right," he agreed. "I don't like it, but you've got my word."

The chief of staff finished his coffee, walked to the desk and picked up the telephone.

CHAPTER 22

SOME THREE-QUARTERS of an hour later, four men approached Suite 5D22 in the Pentagon. Three were in the uniform of the U. S. Army—a full colonel and two first lieutenants. The junior officers wore MP insignia and holstered sidearms. The fourth member of the group was David Bloom.

The colonel took a key from his jacket and unlocked the door. Inside, a pair of enlisted men, each with a rapid-fire M-16 rifle across his lap, was seated facing the entrance. The guards rose immediately in instant reflex, weapons pointed and fingers on the triggers.

"Avalanche," the colonel said.

"Yes, sir," one sentry acknowledged. "May I see your ID, please?"

The senior officer showed them a plastic card with his photograph on it, and they checked a list of names on a clipboard. Then the guards sat down again.

The colonel carefully locked the door through which he had just led Bloom and the others from the D ring corridor. Then he walked straight ahead a dozen steps to another door. This one was metal-sheathed, and there was a small slot in the wall beside it. He drew from his pocket another plastic rectangle, slid it into the opening, and waited. After a brief whirring noise, the armored door opened.

Inside was a room twenty-four feet long and sixteen feet wide, one wall lined with olive green file cabinets. These were "security" models, each protected by a built-in combination lock. There was a small table with four chairs in the middle of the room. The chamber had no window. Overhead fluorescent tubes provided the only light.

"You can read," the colonel said, "but you may not copy or remove any documents. And under no circumstances are you to discuss with anyone what you read in this room."

He nodded toward the two lieutenants. Bloom understood. They were security personnel who knew nothing about the theft of the nerve gas.

"Fine," the detective agreed. "I'd like to start with the report on what happened."

The colonel dialed the combination of the first cabinet, opened it, and took out an inch-thick folder which he placed on the table. The security officers moved two chairs to the far end of the room. Bloom realized that they had orders not to look at any of the documents. They sat down, loosened the flaps of their holsters, and sighed.

The message was clear: If he violated the rules, they had authority to use force to stop him.

Bloom took off his jacket and draped it over a chair. The colonel pointed at the .38 in his shoulder holster.

"May I have that weapon?" he asked.

Bloom gave it to him, sat down and opened the folder. The colonel handed the pistol to one of the security men. Then he turned to the detective.

"When you finish that file, put it back in the drawer before you take out another," he instructed. "I'll be back in an hour."

He left, and David Bloom began to read. He went through

the report slowly and carefully—twice. He found many bits of information that Younts hadn't mentioned but none that seemed important. Maybe they would be useful later after he had studied more folders.

The next file that he examined bulged with typed transcripts of taped interviews with Tooele personnel about the day of the attack and the preceding seventy-two hours. The third and fourth contained the same men's comments on the soldiers who had gone out with the doomed convoy. Bloom was just starting the fourth when the colonel returned with three cartons of hot coffee.

"Thanks," Bloom told him.

"Uh huh," the man with the gold eagles on his shoulders answered. He glanced at the security officers who shook their heads. The civilian had done nothing wrong so far.

After the colonel left, Bloom finished the file and went on to others that provided the complete military records of every man in the convoy. Then he started on the second drawer—dossiers of the professional criminals who had killed the soldiers. These included police records, reports from prisons where they had served time, interviews with friends and ex-cellmates, wives, teachers, ex-girlfriends, and even doctors who had treated the hoodlums for venereal diseases and other medical problems. Neighbors, landlords, stool pigeons, and underworld enemies had been interrogated at length. The army's CID had apparently done a thorough job.

In the mass of facts, one thing was missing:

Why?

There didn't seem to be any logical reason for these criminals to steal nerve gas. The market for it was tiny and the risks huge. Why would men whose entire careers had been devoted to illegal profit strike an army convoy? Not one of them was political. What the hell were they?

As Bloom read on, he began to feel the first pangs of hunger. They got a lot worse before the colonel returned at four o'clock. The detective explained that he hadn't eaten since half-past nine in the morning, and he also needed to get to a toilet. They led him out to a nearby men's room, with the security officers entering to maintain their surveillance. Then they proceeded to a nearby bank of vending machines. Not one of the Pentagon cafeterias was open on Sunday, so these devices were the sole source of food.

"I want to phone my office," Bloom said as they started back.

"What for?" the colonel asked.

"My people may have come up with something."

They returned to the Avalanche chamber behind the armored door, and the colonel opened another locked cabinet. He took out a telephone and listened as the detective spoke to Velez.

"Anything new, Gabe?"

"Not on the head case, but we've still got a big bunch of calls to make."

"Is that all?"

"Not exactly," Velez replied. "Some guy phoned in at noon to say he's gonna kill you."

"Did he leave a number?"

"For chrissakes, this could be serious. There are lots of people, including some cops, who'd like you dead. I called your apartment, but you were out. We've got two plainclothes guys in an unmarked car in front of your house right now."

"I get these threats twice a month," Bloom reminded him.

"This creep sounded different. He wasn't drunk or raving or spitting political slogans. He was cold as goddamn ice. Where the hell are you?"

"Down in the Pentagon—with plenty of security."

Velez barely resisted asking what he was doing there. With the bug and taps, it wouldn't be wise.

"When will you be back?" he asked.

Bloom considered all the files he still had to read.

"Tomorrow, I think," he answered. "Meanwhile, tell Andy I've changed my mind. I want the place *clean* by six tonight. She's to save the garbage. She's got to handle it carefully. I may ask the DA to go for a felony indictment, so she better not mess up any prints."

Let the eavesdroppers sweat that, Bloom thought. Then he wondered who had phoned in the death threat.

"You got it," Velez promised.

The conversation ended, and Bloom went back to studying the CID reports. He stopped at nine, endured more vending machine food with his armed escorts and returned once more to the windowless Avalanche room. He read and thought and read some more until he was exhausted. His eyes were tired, his body was stiff and his mind was so weary he could barely concentrate. At ten minutes after midnight he stood up and yawned. He put the file he had been eying glassily back in the cabinet and yawned again.

"Could you fellows recommend a motel around here?" he asked the security officers.

"That won't be necessary," the taller of the pair replied.

Some twenty minutes later the detective was in a bed in a room on the second floor of a house six miles from the Pentagon. It looked like a private residence, but it wasn't. This was a "safe house" used by Military Intelligence to hide people engaged in covert operations.

Bloom turned off the lamp on the bed table, leaned back onto the pillow, and closed his sore eyes. There had to be *some- thing* in those files, he thought. All his instincts told him that the deep and extensive CID investigation must have turned up one or two clues. He just hadn't recognized them, but they were there. In the morning when he was fresher, he would reread the reports on Addams and the criminals again.

He could not allow himself to be intimidated by the enormous amount of information that the CID had collected. He had to keep control, to stay analytical and logical. That was his only hope of finding the answer—if there was an answer in the Avalanche room. But if it wasn't there, where the hell would it be?

Then his mind drifted to the threatening telephone call.

Velez could be right. After so many of these promises of death, it really was possible that one of them could be serious. Was this the sort of thing that a paranoid schizophrenic would do? Bloom decided that he would ask the Irish psychiatrist when he returned to New York. Where was she now? He was still thinking about her when he fell asleep.

CHAPTER 23

AT 8:10 the next morning David Bloom was back in the windowless room in the Pentagon. Now there was a different pair of armed lieutenants watching him—a change that he barely noticed. Bloom was completely focused on the file he was rereading: the dossier on Arthur Addams.

The detective went over it twice. Then he tried to think and plan as Addams must have. Addams surely anticipated that there would be an intense, coast-to-coast, no-holds-barred hunt for him. He must have known that hundreds of investigators and the complete arsenal of modern technology—everything from taps on relatives' phones to computers checking banks and credit card firms—would be used. He must have expected that the homes of his friends, male and female, would be under twenty-four-hour surveillance.

He would have planned to defeat all that. He would have prepared a hideout where he could lie low, and he would have put aside cash to live there for at least six months. But there was no sign that he had drawn out any significant amount of money for half a year before the raid, and after twenty months there was no trace of the fugitive.

The O. B. organization must be hiding him. Addams had to have such help. Bloom recalled the radical Weatherman bombers of the 1970s who had escaped the FBI for years and lived underground with the assistance of networks of ultra-Left sympathizers. That had involved many people. But how could O. B. be that large and still be totally unknown?

Dead end.

Back to square one.

Bloom started all over, searching for another route. There had to be some other way to find Arthur Addams. He wasn't a ghost or even an actor expert in disguise. He had to be somewhere. Somebody must have seen him. He wasn't the Invisible Man in some Hollywood fantasy.

Then Bloom suddenly sat up straight in his chair.

Yes, that could be it.

Maybe the answer lay not in anything that was in the dossier but in something that wasn't.

He quickly took from the cabinet another file, the one filled with interviews covering what Tooele personnel recalled about the day of the attack and the previous seventy-two hours. His eyes raced across the pages searching for anything that might confirm his theory.

And there it was.

Buried in a narrative, one casual remark now stood out as if the words were typed in letters a foot tall.

"Son of a bitch!" Bloom whispered.

The two lieutenants looked at him.

"I want to see the colonel—*now*," the detective said.

Ten minutes later the senior officer arrived.

"I think I know where he is," Bloom said. "It's right here in the file."

"Hold it."

The man with the gold eagles turned to the junior officers across the room.

"Please wait outside," he told them.

Bloom understood. They were CID security men but not specifically cleared for ultrasensitive Avalanche. The detective watched them leave the room.

"I'm listening," the colonel announced as the armored door clicked shut behind them.

"First, I want to say your investigators did a good job. They collected an enormous amount of information, and the manhunt for Addams was both thorough and professional."

"Would you get to the point?"

"Sure. Point one: You never found Addams because he wasn't out there to be found," Bloom said. "Point two: Arthur Addams isn't the man you want anyway."

"What the hell are you talking about?"

"Incongruities . . . differences . . . abnormalities. Those are the first things a cop looks for. They're like red flags. Let's take the dead soldiers in the tunnel. They were all shot to death, but only one had his face blown away. Why Letherby and nobody else?"

"Because he got it at point-blank range from that traitor sitting next to him."

Bloom shook his head.

"I don't think so, Colonel. Why half a clip when a couple of rounds would have done it?"

"Maybe Addams hated him."

"Or maybe the man who pulled that trigger wanted to obliterate the corpse's face and dental work to screw up identification. How was that body identified?"

The colonel's eyes narrowed in sudden concern.

"Dog tags, I think. Maybe prints too."

"There is no reference to any fingerprints in any of the reports on the dead soldiers," Bloom said. "I just noticed that this morning—the third time I read the file. Would you mind phoning Tooele right away to check again on this one identification?"

"No harm in that, though I'm not clear why."

"I'll explain that in a minute," Bloom promised. "Now let's

get to the second abnormality. There was one man in that escort force who wasn't really scheduled to go. According to the sergeant who ran the motor pool, that man *asked* to go because he had personal business at Dugway."

"And the poor bastard was killed with the others. That's lousy luck, isn't it?"

Bloom shook his head.

"I can't buy that, Colonel. There was no element of luck in this operation. It was carefully planned and meticulously executed by a perfectionist. And there's another point where we don't agree: I'm not sure he was killed with the others."

"What are you trying to tell me?"

"I think that the faceless corpse wasn't Ernest Letherby. I believe that he's probably still alive."

"That's crazy!"

"There's more, Colonel. I said I'd tell you where Addams is. He's not far from here, just a couple of miles. It's right near General Younts' house, and there's no rush. He's been there for more than nineteen months, if I'm right. Six feet down . . . in an army coffin."

"Arlington?" the colonel asked incredulously.

"Exactly. I think that Arthur Addams' corpse is buried in Arlington National Cemetery in the box that's supposed to contain Letherby."

"Jesus!"

"And I believe that Letherby switched ID with him after he shot his face off. It's just a theory, but it's the only scenario that I can come up with that deals with both incongruities. Please don't ask me why Letherby—who also has no record of radical interests or psychiatric trouble—did this. I don't have any idea," Bloom admitted.

"You're telling me this *nothing* Letherby is some kind of Marxist mastermind?" the colonel challenged.

Bloom shrugged.

"I don't know what his politics are," the detective said, "but if he wasn't the brain behind this, he knows who was."

"He was a career soldier, damn it. Regular Army. I think his father was too."

"Stepfather," Bloom corrected. "Look, I could be wrong. Why don't we find out by exhuming the body?"

"It would be a waste of time. After nineteen months in the ground, there won't be any flesh left for us to take prints."

"Try blood types."

"They're just broad categories," the colonel reminded Bloom. "They can't tell us who the corpse was."

"I'll settle for who it *wasn't*. Blood typing can do that all right."

"I don't know about this. Arlington's a national shrine. Nobody digs up bodies there on a theory. If you had something more—"

Bloom glanced at his wristwatch.

"What I have is no more time," he said. "I'd better talk to Younts now."

The colonel flinched. He didn't like pushy civilians going over his head.

"General Younts is out of the building," he replied stiffly. "I'll take your idea up with him as soon as he gets back."

"When?"

"Around noon. Is there anything else that I can do for you?"

"Wheels to the airport. I'm catching the next shuttle to LaGuardia."

Bloom and the colonel left the Avalanche chamber together. In the anteroom outside, the detective saw the security officers and flipped open his jacket to expose the empty shoulder holster.

"My piece," he said.

His weapon was returned. Some thirty-five minutes later he was reading the *Washington Post* as the Eastern jet climbed into the sky. A front-page article explained why the army's chief was out of the Pentagon. He was across the Potomac in the "new" Senate Office Building testifying on the controversial bill to authorize production of binary nerve gas. A difficult congressional battle was expected.

Bloom browsed on restlessly through the rest of the paper. When he reached the sports section, he remembered that the Knicks had played the previous night. He found the story and smiled. They had won by a single point. Their hopes for the National Basketball Association championship were still alive.

Then he closed his eyes and thought about tomorrow's ransom payment at Grand Central. The perfectionist who led O. B. was as cunning as he was deranged. The man who had masterminded the Utah raid would never simply walk into a trap. He would be expecting just such a move. He would have some ingenious scheme to thwart the FBI and police who would be waiting for his messenger. It would be something tricky and shocking—like the theft of the gas itself.

In his mind's eye, Bloom visualized the main floor of the railroad terminal. He could see it all clearly—everything except the complex escape route that O. B. would have prepared so carefully. There had to be some way that the terrorists' courier would defeat the dragnet.

It could be some form of stunning diversion:

An incendiary device.

Tear gas bombs to pour out blinding fumes.

Maybe even one of the deadly blue cylinders.

O. B.'s righteous leader would have no compunction about killing more scores of people—or hundreds.

And David Bloom couldn't think of any way to stop him. Tense and troubled, the detective opened his eyes. He was still breathing hard when the plane touched down at LaGuardia.

CHAPTER 24

As THE TAXI rolled toward Manhattan, David Bloom thought about what he might do if the army refused to exhume the corpse. There was always more than one solution, he reasoned, and if he applied his experience and intelligence, he would find it. He analyzed the situation carefully again and again. Then he shook his head in frustration.

There was no significant alternative.

The army had to examine that body.

It was the only way that they would know for sure.

At 11:35 A.M. the cab reached police headquarters, and Bloom hurried up to the antiterrorist unit. Sour cigarette smoke and the sounds of four detectives speaking urgently into telephones greeted him. Bloom gestured to Velez, who followed him back into the private office.

"Where do we stand, Gabe?"

"There are about three thousand psychiatrists and analysts in the city alone. Our crew and the Feds have managed to contact just over one thousand nine hundred."

"Go on."

"That's what the shrinks did," Velez grumbled. "Some of them weren't sure we were cops, and others were real edgy about the confidentiality of the doctor-patient relationship."

Bloom nodded in understanding. He'd been fifteen when his uncle first explained that sanctity at a cousin's Bar Mitzvah party.

"A gang of them were leery about telling us anything over the phone," Velez continued. "We pleaded with some and had to remind a couple about the penalties for obstructing justice in section 1103 of the Penal Code."

"What does 1103 say?"

"I have no idea, Lieutenant, but they didn't either. Most of the shrinks—maybe ninety percent—were very cooperative. Hell, we ran into nearly a dozen who gave us five-minute lectures on paranoia. There are some big talkers in that crowd."

"Did any mention patients who fit our profile?" Bloom asked as he sat down behind his desk.

Velez nodded.

"We got seven possibles," he replied. "One killed himself last month, three are in the funny house, and the Feds are checking out the others."

"So there are still eleven hundred therapists you haven't reached."

"At least eleven hundred in the city alone. How did you make out at the Pentagon?"

"The security was good and the food was rotten."

"I'm talking blue cylinders, Lieutenant."

"And I'm not. I can't. They told me where O. B. got the gas, but I had to promise not to discuss it with anyone."

"Sounds weird."

"It wasn't my idea," Bloom explained. "The man who told me is very powerful and very scared—a difficult combination."

"Who the hell is he?"

"I can't say—not yet. Anyway, that's not half as important

as all the information I got. . . . I learned some very interesting things."

He paused to light a cigar. Now there was a distinctive gleam in his eyes. After a few seconds, Gabriel Velez recognized it.

"You know!"

"Know what?" Bloom asked.

"You know what O. B. is!" Velez insisted.

Bloom puffed on the petit corona and shrugged.

"I have an idea about one member—completely unproven," he admitted.

"You know!" the sergeant accused exuberantly.

"It's still only a theory. I've asked the Pentagon people to run a test that might confirm it."

"When will they do it?" Velez pressed.

The issue was *if* and not *when,* but Bloom couldn't explain that without going into facts he'd promised to keep secret.

"I'm hoping for news soon, Gabe. Meanwhile, don't mention a word of this to anyone."

Velez smiled as he flashed a thumbs-up gesture.

"One more thing. Andy says a Baltimore outfit named Gunton-Lovearn made that bug she took out. Should we check it for prints, Lieutenant?"

Grady wouldn't like it if the fingerprints pointed to the army or the FBI, but David Bloom had to know—for two reasons: A law had been broken. And Bloom might need ammunition if his negotiated peace with the Pentagon collapsed. With the prints off the bug in his possession, they might *have* to exhume the body at Arlington.

"Do it—right away," Bloom ordered.

Velez left the room, and David Bloom turned to the reports on his desk. A passionately anti-Castro group of Cuban exiles was talking about a kidnapping when "Enrique" arrived from Miami. The Black Revolutionary Brigade which had robbed two midwestern banks was probably heading for the East Coast. A National Security Agency listening post abroad had heard that three Arab terrorists were about to leave Frankfurt to attack the Israeli mission to the United Nations. Much closer to home, an IRA sympathizer in Brooklyn was trying to buy a dozen hunting rifles with powerful scopes.

Business as usual.

These were typical of the problems that the antiterrorist unit faced week in and week out. They were less urgent threats than the imminent danger posed by O. B., Bloom thought, but they had to be taken seriously. That meant preparing plans and diverting manpower at a time he could barely afford to do either.

But he couldn't afford not to.

New York was among the world centers of diplomacy, finance and media activity. That made it an inevitable target for all kinds of terrorists who knew they would grab global attention with an attack here. Even if O. B. was stopped, the dark and dirty little war would go on and on.

For the moment, Bloom didn't mind that. It gave him something to do while he waited for the message from the Pentagon. He gave instructions for surveillance of the Cubans to be increased and drafted a Flash Alert on the heavily armed Black Revolutionary Brigade. Within the hour it would move by teletype to every precinct in the city and the headquarters of the New York State Police. Copies would go to the major security firms protecting local banks.

Two o'clock.

No call from the Pentagon.

Bloom forced himself to focus on the other reports that he had just read. There wasn't much that he could do now about the NSA warning from West Germany. The global U. S. eavesdropping and code-cracking organization would have already notified the FBI, which must have relayed the news to both Immigration and the Washington liaison officer of Israel's energetic Mossad.

But he couldn't be certain. There was always the chance of a slip-up somewhere . . . somehow. David Bloom had to be sure about this as with everything else. So he telephoned the Israeli

166

mission to the U.N. up on Second Avenue and spoke to an inexorably cheerful man named Josef Tsur who ran the security team.

"Have you heard about the visitors coming from Frankfurt?" Bloom asked.

"Not to worry, David," the affable Mossad executive answered. "They've stopped off in Madrid en route. My cousin there reports they're having a wonderful time."

"When does your cousin think they'll get to New York?"

"Hard to predict. They might stay there for quite a while."

It could be forever, Bloom thought. Mossad methods for dealing with terrorists were often terminal.

"If you hear anything else from your cousin—"

"I'll let you know," Tsur assured.

Bloom hung up the phone and immediately wondered why Younts hadn't called. He was frowning as Velez entered the office carrying a bulletproof vest.

"That's for you—until further notice," he announced.

"Who says so?"

Velez pointed at the ceiling.

"Upstairs—the Chief of Detectives. He heard about the guy who swore he'd kill you."

"How could he?"

"I reported it."

Bloom looked at him for several seconds.

"I suppose you didn't want me to get killed," he said slowly.

"Something like that. . . . Do you mind?"

Bloom shook his head. Then they talked about tactical plans for tomorrow's operation at Grand Central. Bloom drew a chart of what he had seen during his own inspection of the terminal, and they went over every escape route that seemed even remotely practical. O. B. had to have a way out—maybe two.

Again and again, Bloom's eyes moved to the telephone. What the hell was taking so long? The delay had to mean trouble. They didn't believe him. They weren't going to do it. Now the tension knotting his stomach began to turn to anger.

The call came at 4:20.

Yes.

The grave diggers would start work within a few hours.

A team of forensic specialists was standing by at Walter Reed Hospital to do the test.

Barring unforeseen problems, they would have the results by 1:00 P.M. tomorrow.

CHAPTER 25

IT WAS an excellent model.

Three feet wide and about twice as long, it completely covered the table.

Bloom had been impressed by the meticulous reproduction of Grand Central's main floor from the moment he had entered Fredericks' office. Now it was 11:50 A.M., five hours and forty minutes before the ransom was to be paid.

The FBI supervisor and Midtown South's precinct commander were going over the assignments for their men again. Each held a slim wooden pointer, using it as a football coach might to explain a new play. They spoke confidently with an air of professional authority.

Bloom could see no doubt in their eyes. They had been trained for such operations, and they had run them successfully before. Their methods were proven. Their planning was careful and detailed. They had applied their experience and intelligence to provide for any contingency.

It was to be a defense in depth. To assure complete visual coverage, there would be five hidden observation teams above the main floor. To cope with the risk of radio failure, there would be two complete communications units. Three separate rings of armed men and women would circulate as unobtrusively as possible within forty yards of the information booth. Outside that perimeter another 112 city and federal detectives would patrol all routes to the station's exits.

Outside the building there would be dozens of unmarked radio-equipped vehicles on adjacent streets. If a single O. B. courier came for the money, he or she would be followed by rotating units of the fleet of assorted cars, vans, motorcycles, and trucks. If more than one gang member showed up and they separated, each would be tracked by a different surveillance team. Three helicopters would be circling to help track the terrorists to their hideout.

Radio frequencies had been assigned.

Communications equipment and vehicles had been double-checked.

In case O. B. tried to use smoke bombs or tear gas, all personnel stationed inside the terminal had been equipped with respirators that they'd concealed in attaché cases, shopping bags, knapsacks, and various packages.

"Any questions or suggestions?" Fredericks asked.

"How about the platforms?" Bloom answered.

"Of course," the FBI supervisor agreed. "We should have thought of that. The obvious way to leave a railroad station is on a train. Right—we'll cover every platform on both the main floor and downstairs."

The meeting broke up a few minutes later. Bloom got back to his office at 12:15. There was no call at 1:00 . . . or 2:00 . . . or 3:00. Had the test failed? Bloom wondered. Or was it something else? What could it be?

At 4:10, Bloom left police headquarters with Velez and Gillespie. Bloom was dressed in a blazer with light gray slacks and carried his gas mask in a black leather briefcase. Swinging the attaché case that held his respirator and a shotgun, Gillespie looked properly executive in a blue pinstripe suit. Velez was attired in banker's gray, complete with vest and a cardboard Brooks Brothers box that held a walkie-talkie, his mask and a short-barrelled M-10 submachine gun.

It was 4:30 when they entered the Vanderbilt Avenue doors of the rail terminal. At the head of the stairs leading down to the main floor, Bloom paused to study the panorama below.

Everything looked normal.

He hoped that it still would when the scores of federal agents and plainclothes city detectives began drifting into position at 5:15. The observation teams and communications units had been in place for two hours. The main force had to arrive with the nightly flood of homeward-bound commuters. Before that, so many people loitering would be noticed.

"Let's take a walk," Bloom said.

Chatting energetically about the Knicks' play-off chances, they descended and circled in a wide arc around the information booth before they took the escalator up to the Pan American Building. When they got off the moving stairs, they turned left to enter the Ticketron company office. They walked past the clerks selling seats for sports, stage, and concert events to the back room. Two other members of their unit were already manning the observation post there.

"We're all set," the detective beside the videotape camera reported.

"Radio's fine," announced the chunky man beside him.

Bloom nodded and unpacked his briefcase as Velez and Gillespie took out their gas masks and weapons. Then they looked down through the peepholes at the rapidly increasing flow of humanity below. By 5:10 it had swollen to a torrent. Perspiring in their bulletproof vests, the men in the hidden observation post said little as they watched it grow.

"Here they come," Bloom said a few minutes later.

He had recognized one of Fredericks' agents. He was slowly pushing a wheelchair that held a gray-haired woman.

171

"Hey, there's Bernie!" Velez called out softly.

Some thirty yards beyond the information booth, two young men in U. S. Navy uniforms lounged beside bulging duffel bags. One of the "sailors" was a baby-faced detective named Bernbaum whose fluent Hebrew had helped nail the trio that torched the Soviet consul's car last year. Off to the left there was something familiar about the broad-shouldered man with the battered suitcase. A dozen seconds ticked away before David Bloom recognized him as a crack marksman attached to Midtown South.

Hundreds of people were hurrying into the terminal every minute. Bloom's eyes roved over the eddying crowd. He knew that seventy more undercover operatives were moving into position, but in this seething mass of humanity he couldn't spot any who looked like police. He hoped that no one else could either.

There were terrorists down there right now.

There had to be.

The cunning butcher who had planned the Utah ambush and the subway massacre would reconnoiter the terminal carefully before the pickup. Those bloody assaults had each reflected detailed planning and up-to-the-minute information. This operation would be no different.

O. B. was already here.

As David Bloom continued to scan the churning throng of people below, Henke entered the station from 42nd Street carrying a collapsible brown overnight case. His whole body was tingling with excitement. He moved along in the hurrying crowd to the main floor of the terminal and started toward the east end of the noisy station.

It was thrilling to think that there were police nearby—probably only yards away. At this moment he was almost surely surrounded by dozens of them—all waiting for him. There was danger here, he exulted. The very idea made his heart beat faster.

Henke zigzagged slowly through the crowd toward the passage to Lexington Avenue. Halfway down the corridor he noticed a curly-haired black man wearing a headset attached to a miniature cassette player. Something was wrong.

His head wasn't bobbing to the music. His feet were still. The man was smiling, but his eyes weren't. He was studying the people who passed. As the man raised his hand to look at his watch, Henke caught a glimpse of the butt of a pistol.

He was one of *them*.

Henke looked down so the detective wouldn't see the sudden glow of recognition in his eyes. Then Henke walked on to Lexington Avenue, turned left, and started north through the bustling crowd. After forty steps he noticed a pair of men in the front seat of a parked sedan, both looking steadily toward the rail terminal. Across Lexington on the next block, a motorcyclist was doing the same thing.

At 46th Street he turned west. Henke walked a dozen steps before he stopped, looking up thoughtfully as if trying to remember something. His face showed no reaction when he saw the spot in the sky. It had to be a helicopter. He had expected that.

He continued on to the Roosevelt Hotel, found a public lavatory for men and entered a cubicle. He took off the gray nylon windbreaker and baseball cap, and put on a blue sport jacket and sunglasses that had been in the brown overnight case. It had also held a large Macy's shopping bag. He folded up the windbreaker, collapsed the case, and put both in the shopping bag with the cap. Then he washed his hands—for Mama.

They might be watching for anyone who passed through the terminal more than once, Henke thought as he left the hotel. These simple changes in appearance would make it harder for them to spot him when he returned. Henke still had business in Grand Central.

He was calm until he reached Vanderbilt Avenue. But the excitement surged in him again as he approached the station. They would be all over the place—on every side. That Jew bastard Bloom was bound to be among them. Henke entered the massive Pan American Building, walked south through the lobby, and got on the down escalator.

There she was.

He could see her clearly on the terminal's main floor. The blonde woman in a TWA uniform was standing five yards from the information booth. There was a large airline bag at her feet. For a moment Henke wondered whether it might actually contain the $5,000,000. No, that wasn't possible. It probably held a few hundred dollars and a radio beacon. Perhaps even a bomb.

Yes, that was the kind of thing a tricky mongrel such as Bloom would try. They never intended to give him the money for the martyrs' memorial, Henke thought angrily. They meant to kill him. The armed undercover men were proof of that.

Well, Ernst Henke was much too smart for their stupid traps. He had only sent instructions for the ransom to see what they would do, and they hadn't disappointed him. He had meant to attack again anyway. Their vicious attempt to destroy him only strengthened his determination. No one could blame him now. They had brought it on themselves.

I'll teach them a lesson, Mama.

He stepped off the escalator, made his way to the subway entrance, and started the journey home. The scores of plainclothes detectives waited. They were patient for a while. By 6:15 they began to grow restless. Half an hour later, they were worried. The crowds were starting to thin out as the main rush of commuters dwindled rapidly. The watchers' concealment would soon be gone.

"I think it's over," Bloom said into the walkie-talkie.

"Let's give it another twenty minutes," Fredericks' voice crackled in electronic reply.

The vigil ended at 7:15. Weary and uncertain, the small legion of plainclothes detectives dispersed. As they retreated like some beaten army, David Bloom met with Fredericks and the commander of Midtown South in the stationmaster's office. After a brief discussion of what had happened, they agreed that O. B. would send another message soon.

They were right.

He was preparing it at that moment. Seated in his kitchen with the blinds drawn, he was about to attach the timer to one of the blue cylinders. He was wearing the white cotton gloves, and an open newspaper covered the surface of the table. As he picked up the pliers, Henke noticed a department store's advertisement. One pair of high-heeled shoes caught his eye.

They were the same kind that the slut had worn.

He remembered it all quite vividly. After he had shot down the criminals, he drove the hearse eighty miles north and transferred the cylinders to the trailer he had parked there. He saw it all again, as if on television. He hooked the trailer to a car he had bought the previous week and headed east. Moving in careful compliance with speed limits, he reached the outskirts of Scranton, Pennsylvania five days later.

He parked at a scruffy trailer camp nine miles from the city. That night he drove into the downtown area to find where the local prostitutes congregated. Once he had done that, he returned to his trailer for a good night's sleep. He paid his bill at eleven the next morning, drove to the other side of Scranton, and wandered back roads for two hours until he found a suitably remote spot in some woods.

Just before midnight he returned to Scranton and waited near a bar where he had seen the whores. His opportunity came forty minutes later. One of the painted sluts left with a customer. It was when she was returning at ten minutes to one that Henke approached her. When he showed her $50, she agreed to drive out to his "place" for some "fun."

She asked for her money as soon as they entered the trailer, and he paid her immediately. Her grumbling about the long journey ended. She smiled as she stripped. Henke couldn't quite recall her face, but he still remembered the scar on her abdomen clearly.

"You're gonna have a great time, baby," she promised as she caressed her heavy breasts to arouse him.

Henke excused himself to "get a bottle from the car." After he furtively triggered the timer on the way out, he double-locked the door behind him. He got in his car, drove some two hundred yards, and waited. He listened carefully.

No screams. No sounds of her trying to break out. All he heard were the seconds ticking away inside his head. After five minutes he took from the car trunk a gas mask and protective suit he had stolen from Tooele and put them on. Then he walked back to the trailer. Making sure not to touch it, he peered inside.

She hadn't been pretty in life. She looked a lot worse dead in her own vomit. Of course, that wasn't important. All that counted was the success of the test. He had the weapons he needed. The cylinders in the trunk of his sedan would do the job.

Henke walked back to his car, got the can of gasoline and the timer, and carried them to the trailer. After he sloshed the inflammable liquid over its sides, he set the incendiary device for fifteen minutes.

Otto's Boy was six miles away when he stopped the sedan to look back. In a little while he saw the distant ball of yellow flame glow suddenly in the blackness. Then he heard the blast as the propane tank that fed the trailer's stove exploded.

No one had seen him pick her up, and the disappearance of a cheap whore wasn't likely to get much attention. The trailer that was her coffin would soon be destroyed. Confident that there would be only cinders by the time any fire truck reached that remote place, he drove north through the winter night.

Suddenly the pictures vanished. It was as if he had turned off a television set. Now he was back in his kitchen staring at the beautiful blue cylinder that he would use next. The memory of that test outside Scranton had been good, Otto's Boy thought. Tomorrow would be even better.

CHAPTER 26

COFFINS.

There were six of them. Some of the eighty men and women marching in front of police headquarters were carrying the grim wooden boxes. Others held up signs denouncing the failure to catch the "subway killers." Most of the demonstrators were black. Led by a female member of the City Council who was using a bullhorn, all of them were chanting angry slogans.

Uniformed patrolmen formed a silent security line across the brick building's main entrance, while television news crews and other journalists nearby were trying to earn their salaries. This public protest was only the beginning, David Bloom thought as he observed from fifty yards away. This one was loud but not violent. Not yet.

Now Bloom saw four burly "uniforms" approaching and used them as a shield to slip into the front door unnoticed. He looked at his watch, saw that it was 8:32 A.M., and wondered why there was still no word from the Pentagon on the blood tests. It had been on his mind half the night. Bloom hadn't fallen asleep until nearly three in the morning. He was tired, tense, and half raw with impatience. Awareness that the continuing phone poll of therapists and clinics probably hadn't produced anything didn't help either.

"*Nothing,* right?" he asked harshly as he entered the antiterrorist unit's suite.

"No, but there are over two hundred shrinks we haven't reached," Velez answered.

Bloom shook his head, the bitter frustration clearly visible in his frown.

"Something wrong?"

"Almost everything," Bloom replied and disappeared into his private office.

The army was playing games with him, he thought. They must have had the results for at least twenty-four hours. Now they were stalling for some reason. Yes, the bastards were stringing him along. Why?

He had to stay calm, analytical. He couldn't afford to let loose the reins of anger. That corpse in that cemetery—both under Pentagon control—was his only lead. It was his only hope to prevent another attack. The O. B. madmen had nine more of the blue cylinders, including two big ones. That was enough nerve gas to massacre tens of thousands. In a confined space such as the 5,874-seat Radio City Music Hall, a single cylinder could kill everyone in six minutes.

How many minutes did New York have before the next slaughter? Younts might be buying time for his binary gas project, but the terrorists wouldn't wait. O. B. could attack at any moment. After yesterday's fiasco at Grand Central, who could predict what they'd do? Or when?

Suddenly he thought of Red O'Donnell, and he sighed. It wasn't just that he found her attractive, Bloom told himself as he reached for the telephone. No, it was time to consult her again—professionally.

"I've got a patient arriving in three minutes," she announced, "and at noon I'm flying up to Harvard. Could we speak tomorrow afternoon?"

"This can't wait. I'll make it fast. O. B. sent a note that they'd pick up the ransom yesterday at Grand Central. My boss and the FBI set up a trap. Either the terrorists didn't show, or they came and saw the trap. Now what do you think O. B. might do next? I'll settle for an educated guess."

Ten seconds passed before she replied in a slow, cautious voice.

"The possibilities of another dramatic act of violence have increased—a lot. If they saw the trap, that kind of mind can hardly resist some retaliation—something big to punish those who dared to plot against them."

Another gas attack.

"Soon?" Bloom asked

"Maybe, but not until they've prepared every detail. They might have done that already. Paranoid schizophrenics often plan ahead very carefully. . . . Well, some of them do. Is there anything else?"

"Just one item. Do you think that the head of O. B. would try to kill me?"

He heard her gasp.

"You?" she asked in a suddenly intense voice.

"I've had a threatening phone call. The chief of detectives seems to take it seriously, so I'm wearing a bulletproof vest and traveling with bodyguards."

"You call a death threat an *item?*" she demanded. "All right, I'll answer your question. Yes, they might attempt to kill you or the police commissioner or the mayor. Listen, Bloom, I don't like this whole conversation."

"I didn't mean to—"

"My business is saving, not killing. I despise all this casual talk about murder. I don't cope that well with killing people— even in conversation. I don't like it. I don't need it."

179

"Neither do I," Bloom said.

"Are you *sure?*"

Then she told him that her patient had arrived and hung up before Bloom could say anything else. That was it, he thought. She hadn't said good-bye, but her message was clear. He reminded himself that she wasn't the first woman who wouldn't or couldn't understand what it was like to be a policeman. That didn't help very much. After this case was over, he might try to explain it to her . . . if she would listen.

During the next half hour, he avoided calls from four journalists and someone who claimed to be a Hopi Indian shaman. Then he telephoned Younts.

"The general's in a meeting. May I give him a message?" Specialist Fifth Class T. T. Shea offered.

"Tell him that his three days are up. He just ran out of time. Have you got that?"

"Sure do. Bloom? Is that B-l-o-o-m?"

"Exactly. He has the phone number—and ninety minutes to use it."

Younts was on the phone twenty-eight minutes later.

"Why do you keep threatening people, damn it?" he asked indignantly.

"Don't try to butter me up. What about the tests?"

"Is this line secure?"

"Unless your friends put in a new set of taps. The tests?"

"We ran 'em twice," the general replied cautiously, "and it looks like the man in the box isn't the fellow he's supposed to be. That came as quite a shock to a number of folks down here."

"Anything else?"

"Quite a bit. Once it looked like your idea wasn't entirely impossible, I decided to check it out some more. Let's take a good look at the dental records, I said. Never know what you can turn up. What do you think we found?"

"No dental records?"

"He wasn't that crude. The son of a bitch had gone and switched them. We only found that out when we tracked down the dentist who'd done Addams' upper plate four years ago. I had this hunch that anybody tricky enough to pull off the deal in the tunnel would have other stunts up his sleeve, so we ought to double-check everything. It sure looks as if you figured it right."

"When do we start looking for Letherby?" Bloom asked.

"Right away. I'm sending Colonel Mills up to New York with the Letherby files tonight. With Letherby operating in your area, it makes sense to run the search from the FBI bureau there. Mills will coordinate the operation."

"Mills? Are you expecting me to walk away?"

"Take it easy," Younts said.

"I won't walk."

"Would you hear me out? Lord, you're touchy. Tell me, you play any poker?"

"Now and again."

"Then you know there are versions of poker where one card or another is wild. A wild card can do most anything," the general reminded. "Well, you're our wild card. Excuse me—I'm *asking* you to be our wild card."

Bloom hesitated. It could be a ploy to ease him out of the way.

"I'll put it another way," Younts continued. "You can rove all over the field like a free safety in football."

"Why me?"

"Set a thief to catch a thief. I'm not calling you a thief," Younts explained quickly. "Just spelling out my rough idea. Now the only thing we know about the O. B. gang is that one of them—maybe the top man—is a real tricky son of a bitch. No offense meant, but the fact is you are—"

"The trickiest son of a bitch you know. Is that it?"

"Somethin' like that," Younts admitted without a trace of embarrassment. "You know, I was sure you'd see the logic in it. You'll have complete freedom and all the support facilities you want: cars, helicopters, communications gear, weapons, lab back-up . . . you name it."

There was a sound in Younts' voice that Bloom recognized.

"But there's one more thing you want from me, right?" he asked.

"Course. There's always one more thing in any kind of a deal," the Tennessean answered in a knowing man-to-man tone. "Since there'd be no benefit for you or your city to let it out yet whose gas it was and who we're tracking, I think it might be best to go public later. The other way, you'd panic everybody and you might provoke these terrorists into another attack even sooner."

"There could be one tomorrow anyway. After that abortion in Grand Central—"

"It's a crap shoot," Younts broke in, "but the odds are a little better my way. Now I can get your boss to cut you loose for detached duty if I have your word."

Bloom calculated swiftly.

"Me—and two detectives named Gabriel Velez and John Gillespie," he said.

"Who are they?"

"The best I know."

"Why not use our people?" the general suggested.

"Take it or leave it."

"Shit," the army chief of staff exploded, "you've got no damn human relations skills at all. You'll *never* get to be police commissioner talking to folks like that."

"You can be police commissioner. Velez and Gillespie—yes or no?"

"You gonna tell them?"

"Yes, but they won't talk. I guarantee it."

"All right," Younts yielded. "Okay, the three of you. Mills wants a meeting at your local FBI bureau at eight-thirty tonight."

"We'll be there."

Half an hour after Bloom put down the phone, Gillespie and Velez walked into his office. They looked puzzled, uneasy.

"The Chief of Detectives' office just called to say we're on some kind of special assignment," Gillespie reported.

David Bloom nodded.

"What kind?" Velez asked.

Bloom told them. He went over everything slowly and carefully . . . the theft of the gas . . . Letherby . . . the army's ground rules on absolute secrecy . . . the very limited time there was to find a cunning paranoid who had almost surely changed his appearance . . . the real risk of another massacre if they failed. The three men spoke about it for more than an hour, talking in the shorthand phrases and half-finished sentences of people who know each other well.

At 8:30 P.M. they entered Fredericks' office. Colonel Mills was waiting with two army majors, a carton of documents, and an air of impatient concern. Bloom glanced at the FBI inspector and for a moment wondered whether *he* knew whose gas it was. Then Mills began the briefing.

"The man who may well lead us to the O. B. organization is Ernest Letherby, a sergeant in the U. S. Army with some twenty years of active service. We're going to pass out folders containing his records and the only pictures we have. Please notice that the folders are stamped Top Secret."

One of the majors distributed the envelopes. Ernest Letherby didn't look menacing. He didn't appear to be the least bit unusual. He seemed strong and fit, and one photo showed a wide smile with good teeth.

"Five feet ten . . . one hundred and eighty pounds . . . brown hair . . . no special scars or other distinguishing characteristics," Mills continued. "You can read the whole list by yourselves. I think that we ought to start by going over our division of responsibilities and organization. As the coordinator—"

At that moment the telephone rang.

"Sorry," Fredericks said. "I told them to hold my calls."

It rang and rang. The FBI inspector shrugged and picked up the instrument.

"Yes, this is Fredericks. . . . What? . . . Are you sure?"

For a few seconds he seemed stunned. Then he recovered quickly.

"He's here. . . . I'll tell him. . . . We'll be rolling in a few minutes. . . . By the way, do you have any numbers? . . . I understand. Good-bye."

He turned to the men in his office.

"I believe—I believe that there's been another gas attack," he said in a stiff, controlled voice. "Heavy casualties, they think."

"Where?" Bloom asked.

"Movie theater at Eighty-third and Broadway."

Five blocks from where David Bloom lived.

Over the years he had seen more than a hundred films in that Loew's "quad" complex.

Bloom stood up abruptly.

"You coming?" he said to Mills.

Unwilling to risk being noticed at the scene of a nerve gas attack, the cautious colonel shook his head. The meeting was adjourned until eight o'clock the next morning. As they emerged from the federal office building a few minutes later, Fredericks stopped suddenly as if to catch his breath.

"They say the smell is terrible," he told Bloom.

Then the FBI agents walked off to their car, and Gillespie and Velez followed Bloom to his sedan. Both groups made their way through the turbulent crowds and police lines ringing the Loew's 83rd Street Theater some twenty minutes later.

Even from the street outside, the smell was terrible.

CHAPTER 27

DOZENS of police cars and emergency trucks, their rotating lights flashing in the night.

Scores of uniformed patrolmen diverting civilian vehicles and holding back crowds of pedestrians.

A small army of print and broadcast reporters.

The police commissioner and the mayor, with his press secretary hovering nearby.

The scene in front of the Loew's 83rd Street Theater looked like any major disaster in any great city, the sort of thing that runs on TV news shows three times a week.

But there was also something different here.

Hundreds of men and women lined the far side of Broadway for two blocks north and south of the movie house, and many others stared across the legendary artery from windows above the street. There were Caucasians and blacks, Hispanics, and Asians—a mixture typical of the polyglot Upper West Side.

They were all very *quiet*.

Even the police and journalists who had dealt with many

other disasters were oddly subdued. No one was shouting or pushing. There was no uproar or impatient anger. These professionals who knew tragedy and death so well stood silent, tight-lipped and stunned by the enormity of the horror. From the youngest patrolman to the precinct's bull necked commander who paced near the empty box office, they all looked shaken.

"Unbelievable," Captain Michael Callahan sighed as Bloom approached. "Twenty-nine years on the force. First time I've ever seen cops scared."

"They have good reason to be," Bloom said.

"It was bad in the sixties with the riots and the anti-Nam bombers, the LSD explosion and militants shooting cops as political statements," the captain remembered aloud. "But we didn't have animals using nerve gas in the middle of Manhattan. That's the lowest."

"Captain, it isn't over."

"Can't get any worse," Callahan insisted. "Shit, of course it can. It always does, doesn't it? Well, I suppose you want a body count."

"I'll take any information you've got."

"I've asked the theater manager for numbers on ticket sales. Here he comes now."

His face glistening with perspiration, a pale man in a three-piece suit approached. He gulped in air and shook his head in distress before he spoke.

"This is just a neighborhood theater. I really can't understand why they did it here. Could it have been a mistake?"

The precinct commander looked at Bloom for an answer.

"I don't think that these people make that kind of mistake," David Bloom replied.

"But why us? Loew's is a class chain. Passes for senior citizens—the whole bit. We never hurt anybody."

"Please, Mr. Marks, we need those ticket figures," Callahan reminded.

The troubled manager nodded and took a slip of paper from the pocket of his wrinkled jacket.

"Paid admissions for the eight o'clock show in Theater Four tonight—two hundred fifty-three. That's two hundred thirty-nine adults and fourteen children. *Children?*" he repeated hoarsely. "What kind of monsters would gas *children?*"

Tears were coursing down his cheeks. Suddenly his whole body began to shake. He was still shuddering a minute later when two patrolmen guided him to the ambulance thirty yards away.

"Used to be awful when some guy went crazy and chopped up his wife and two kids with a cleaver," Callahan recalled. "Now we're up to nerve gas. Could be atom bombs next month. My son, who's a senior at Fordham, tells me it'll be germs after that."

"Almost anything's possible, thanks to the cooperation of certain governments," Bloom acknowledged.

"This deal tonight? Could it be the Iranians or some Arab outfit?"

"I don't think so. Captain, would you please tell me anything you know about what happened in Theater Four?"

"Picture started at eight," the commander of the 20th Precinct began in a singsong voice. "We got the squeal about nineteen minutes later. By then it was panic time. Hundreds of people in the other three parts of this quad theater were pouring out. They were literally running for their lives. A few got trampled. It wasn't nice."

"The person who set the bomb must have left between the time the lights went down at eight and ten after eight. Did any of the theater staff notice someone going out then?"

Callahan shook his head.

"A woman taking tickets and a security guard in the lobby saw a dozen or so people exit in that period, but they didn't *notice* anyone."

At that moment Bloom saw the mayor's press secretary gesture. It was a summons—a command. Bloom excused himself and started toward him. Rosenthal didn't wait. Walking briskly, he met David Bloom halfway.

"Want to talk to you," Rosenthal announced. "No bullshit. You understand?"

Bloom nodded. Charlie Rosenthal's blunt manner didn't surprise him. They had met last year at a breakfast of the Shomrim Society, the organization of New York's Jewish police.

"What have you got?" Rosenthal asked.

"A lot of bodies. Captain Callahan thinks there may be as many as two hundred fifty-three dead inside."

Rosenthal flinched but plowed ahead.

"That's terrible," he said, "but it doesn't answer my question. Callahan's got two hundred fifty-three bodies, and the PC can tell that to the reporters."

Rosenthal was leaving that messy job to Vincent Grady, deftly distancing Mayor Warner from the horror.

"Lieutenant, I want to know what *you've* got. Do you have any solid leads? Any real suspects?"

"One—very real."

"Why hasn't Grady informed the mayor?" Rosenthal demanded.

"Because I haven't told Grady yet. It wasn't definite until a few hours ago."

"Bottom line: How close are you to grabbing these terrorists?"

"Much closer than we were yesterday. We know the identity of the man who supplied the gas. We'll find him," Bloom vowed.

"Three days? Three weeks? What can I say to the mayor?"

"Say that he mustn't tell anyone that we know who one of the terrorists is. They've got more gas. If we do anything to spook them, Mr. Rosenthal, they'll use it."

"Why do you think they used it here tonight?"

There was no point in debating the wisdom of yesterday's obvious trap at the rail terminal. It was too late for that now.

"I'm not really sure," Bloom replied carefully.

"Was that operation at Grand Central a mistake? Could that have spooked them?"

"Who knows what goes on in terrorists' minds?" Bloom answered with a shrug.

To his total surprise, there was his reply. Some twenty yards away, Maeve O'Donnell was standing at the barrier, showing her ID to a tall black patrolman. Bloom urged Rosenthal to bring Callahan over to brief the mayor and then hurried to her.

"Dr. O'Donnell's with me—official business," he told the patrolman and brought her inside the perimeter. For the first time since he had met her, she looked agitated.

"Are you all right, Doctor?"

"Don't be cute," she replied sharply. "How bad is it?"

"Worse than the subway. We were expecting a message from O. B., but not this."

"That's why I'm here," she said. "I was driving in from the airport on my way back from Boston when I heard the news on my car radio. I came to make sure you understood the message."

"I'm glad you did," he replied warmly.

"Lieutenant, this is no time for pleasantries. The message was addressed to *you*. O. B.'s choosing your neighborhood movie theater as the target was no accident."

"I didn't think it was. Last week an Irish psychiatrist explained to me how paranoid schizophrenics plan everything with immense care. She's a brilliant person. I take her very seriously."

"You'd better take this death threat seriously," she warned urgently. "That's what it is—a death threat from a fanatical group that kills with considerable skill and no apparent hesitation. Somehow this has become a personal thing between you and O. B. That's what I came to tell you."

There seemed to be more than professional concern in her tone.

"Thank you, Doctor. I'll be careful."

Now she saw the thoughtful male look in his eyes, and suddenly she felt oddly uneasy.

"Well, I'd better go," she announced.

Across her shoulder he saw Vincent Grady speaking earnestly to a throng of reporters.

"I'll walk you to your car," Bloom said.

"Don't they need you here now?"

"Not for the moment. I can't get inside the theater, and the commissioner seems to be taking care of the press outside quite well."

Her Triumph was parked on West End Avenue just above 84th Street. She didn't notice Gillespie and Velez trailing them, and Bloom saw no reason to add to her tension by mentioning his bodyguards. When she reached the car, she unlocked a door and turned to say good-bye. Bloom spoke first.

"Your name. What do the letters M. C. stand for?" he said.

"Maeve Cathleen. Why do you ask?"

"Maeve? That's Gaelic?"

"For Mab."

"Mab, Shakespeare's fairy queen," Bloom remembered. "It suits you."

Then he stepped forward, took her in his arms, and kissed her.

"Why did you do that?" she asked a moment later.

He kissed her again. Now all of her was pressing against him, and she couldn't stop it. It was several seconds before she pulled back.

"That was a mistake," she said.

He watched her enter the car and drive down West End Avenue, leaving him and the movie theater horror behind. She had been right about one thing, he decided as Velez and Gillespie came up to join him.

"It's personal, all right," Bloom thought aloud as they started back toward the theater.

"She's very attractive," Velez approved.

"I'm not talking about her, Gabe. It's personal between me and the O. B. leader," Bloom announced, "and I don't mind."

Both Velez and Gillespie looked puzzled.

"He just blinked," Bloom announced. "He just made his first mistake. Now we know he has emotions that he can't control. He hates me personally. That's why he picked my neighborhood movie house."

"What do you figure he'll do next?" Velez asked.

"It's my turn next," Bloom said. "I'm going to use that hatred against him. I owe it to those dead people in the Loew's Eighty-third Street. They'd be alive if it weren't for his war with me."

"What will you do?"

"I'm going to maneuver that bitter bastard into making an even bigger mistake. We haven't had any luck finding him, have we?"

Gillespie and Velez shook their heads.

"Well," Bloom said, "I'm going to make him come to me."

CHAPTER 28

THEY FOUND Fredericks at the theater. Three of his aides stood beside him.

"Can you reach those army officers?" Bloom asked.

"I think so," the FBI inspector replied.

"Good. Please tell them to meet us at your office in forty-five minutes. There's nothing we can do here now, so let's get back to work."

"Shouldn't we stay a bit longer?"

"Not unless you want to count body bags when the decontamination units carry them out," Bloom said. "I'd rather catch terrorists myself. Forty-five minutes?"

Fredericks looked at him coldly for several seconds before he nodded. Then the city and federal policemen separated, each heading for their own vehicles. As Bloom's car rolled downtown, he thought about his plan to make the O. B. leader come after him. David Bloom knew how he would do it. The question was when.

Not just yet.

This wasn't the right moment. He couldn't wait too long though. The time factor was critical now. Everything had changed in the past few hours. What had been a systematic search was now an urgent race. They had only a few days to find Letherby, their sole lead to the vicious O. B. organization.

He analyzed the situation carefully. There were three players in this bizarre and bloody game: the terrorists, the investigators, and the politicians. When details of tonight's massacre exploded on broadcasts and in newspapers, the entire nation would flinch. Millions of people—even those who despised or envied New York—would recoil in shock.

And raw fear.

It would be worst here—the target city. The horrible weapon used and the greatest mass murder in U. S. history could sweep some local residents into panic. Even if others of that stubborn breed didn't yield to the terror, it would overwhelm the politicians who ran the municipal government. It would sweep them before it like a tidal wave.

They were responsible for the safety of these 7 million people. They wouldn't dare risk another nerve gas slaughter and the blame that could destroy their political careers. After the massacre at the movie theater, even those as well meaning as Mayor Warner might pay the next ransom demand without delay or question.

With millions of dollars and their skill in clandestine survival, the O. B. butchers would escape. They might never be found. Of the entire gang, only Letherby had been identified and he might have a new face by now. The terrorists could get away to kill hundreds more—perhaps thousands—somewhere else.

They had the canisters to do it, Bloom thought as the car moved down Broadway past the dramatically lit buildings of Lincoln Center. They had to be stopped before they could use them again. The next ransom letter might already be in the mail. O. B. had to be smashed here and now.

Bloom turned on the radio at Columbus Circle, dialed to the "all news" CBS station, and listened to an almost constant series of reports on the gas attack until they reached the federal office tower. The meeting began at 10:05 when the army officers arrived.

"I'll start by telling you what we've done already. Take a look at the photo of Letherby in your folders," Colonel Mills said. "We're mass-copying it for immediate distribution to every police department, state and federal law enforcement agency within five hundred miles."

"What are you telling them?" Bloom asked.

"That he's wanted for the murder of two armored car guards. We're announcing a reward of twenty-five thousand dollars. That's not all. With the help of the Bureau, we've started a full field investigation of this guy to the day he was born."

"Our liaison man at the embassy in Bonn has already been in touch with the BKA," Fredericks reported.

"BKA?" Velez repeated.

"*Bundeskriminalamt*," the FBI inspector explained. "That's the West German national police. Both his parents were born there, and the BKA is checking out the whole family."

"He was born there too," Bloom reminded Fredericks.

"Naturalized after his mother—let's see—Anna Benke . . . married an American GI named Letherby. She became a U. S. citizen then too. Letherby died of a heart attack a couple of years ago," the colonel said. "According to our pension records, his widow's living in Longwood, Florida. That's about twenty miles north of Orlando."

"What about her first husband?" Bloom wondered.

"German—a soldier like Letherby. Guess she goes for military types. He seems to have died about a year and a half before she met Letherby. What are you looking for?"

"I'm not sure. Anything that can give me more of a picture of Ernest Letherby," David Bloom said. "Anything that might give us some clues to his character . . . some hint as to why an apparently unimaginative and nonpolitical NCO who never even received a traffic ticket in his whole life might get involved with this gang of homicidal maniacs."

"What about Ernest Letherby's brothers and sisters?" Fredericks questioned. "Any mental illness or radical history there?"

The colonel shook his head.

"He's an only child."

"And his mother?"

"We've run her name through the FBI computer and the CIA one too," Mills answered. "Goose egg. Clean as a whistle. She's never had any trouble with the IRS either."

"It doesn't add up," Bloom reasoned. "What about his other relatives or friends?"

"According to the guys who knew him at Tooele, he wasn't that close with anyone. Pleasant, but not friendly. We've got CID agents checking on men who served with him at previous posts too. As for relatives, the only blood kin we can find is his mother. They were close. Men in his unit at Tooele say he wrote her every week."

"Maybe we ought to watch that lady," Velez suggested.

"We have been doing that since six o'clock tonight," Fredericks said.

"We've got a team checking all her long-distance phone calls for the past year, and by noon tomorrow we should have a wiretap in operation and an electronic surveillance unit working full blast."

"Let's hope they get something fast," Bloom declared. "As of now, she's the only connection to Letherby we know about, and we don't have a damn thing on her."

"Just copies of the pension papers and her naturalization forms, which aren't much, but there'll be a great deal more within forty-eight hours. We're giving it our best shot," the FBI supervisor assured, "and we've asked the West Germans to do the same."

Then Mills said it.

"I certainly hope we're after the right guy and that he's still alive. The terrorists could have killed him after he delivered the gas, you know."

"Pray that he's the one and that he's alive, Colonel," Bloom advised grimly. "Burn candles and sing psalms. If it wasn't Ernest Letherby or he's not alive, we're dead."

Bloom was right, the FBI supervisor thought, but why did he have to be so damn confrontational?

"Time will tell," Fredericks soothed swiftly in a voice as bland as a funeral director's. "Now why don't we get to work on the files that Colonel Mills brought up from Washington?"

The top document in each folder was a photocopy of Ernest Letherby's birth certificate. Beneath it was a heap of reports from every post where he had served. There were his enlistment papers, periodic medical reports, certificates covering training courses, annual EERs—enlisted efficiency reports—records of completion of the NCO academy program, and his yearly "qualification" in firing the M-16 and .45-caliber automatic pistol. He was rated "expert" with both weapons.

Letherby had worked his way up to E-7, Sergeant First Class. He was an electrical specialist. Again and again he had been judged "outstanding." All of his commanders had found him reliable, cooperative and hard working. The photos—each dated with military precision—showed a lean, fit man with a crew cut and a serious expression. There were six pictures, and he wasn't smiling in any of them.

He had never been arrested, caught a venereal disease or paid his taxes a penny short or a day late. In all his years in the army he hadn't been sick a day or received a single reprimand. In fact, he had been commended for two years of volunteer service as leader of a Boy Scout troup while stationed at Fort Bragg, North Carolina.

"And look at this," Mills said as he pointed to Letherby's financial record. "Not only did this man have an unblemished military career, but he sent three hundred dollars a month to his mother. That doesn't sound like a terrorist to me."

Unwilling to debate this sentimental approach, Bloom turned to the next document in the file. It was Anna Benke Letherby's naturalization certificate. Facing Bloom across the table, Fredericks saw the sudden gleam in the city detective's eyes.

"*Bingo,*" Bloom said and tapped the document.

"What is it?" the FBI inspector asked.

"His mother's citizenship paper. Check it out."

Fredericks began to scan the form. After twenty seconds he stopped abruptly.

"Place of birth?" he questioned.

Bloom nodded.

"What's this all about?" Mills asked.

"She was born in the Bavarian city of Furth," Fredericks told him. "The second message that O. B. sent the mayor instructed him to signal that he'd pay the ransom by running a newspaper ad containing the words Furth Flower Company."

"That could be a coincidence," the colonel argued.

It was then that Fredericks sighed, looked at his watch, and saw that it was 10:45.

"We should have more information from both Germany and Tooele by nine tomorrow morning—maybe even something from Florida," the FBI inspector said. "Why don't we knock it off till then? Tomorrow's going to be rough, so why don't we all get a good night's sleep?"

David Bloom didn't. When he entered his apartment, he hung his jacket on a doorknob and poured an inch of the excellent Martell Cordon Bleu cognac into a balloon-shaped snifter. Then he settled into his favorite leather armchair and closed his eyes for fifteen seconds. When he opened them, he took two luxurious sips of the fine brandy and clicked on his TV set with the remote control.

NBC was carrying a half-hour special report on the massacre. So were the other networks.

All three had live segments from outside the theater. Each showed the army unit carrying out the body bags in an endless and frightening parade. This time the army was better prepared to handle the media. A public information officer had been sent with the decontamination team.

"How many bodies are there inside?" one reporter asked.

"A lot. We don't have an exact number," the soldier answered. "I've counted eighty-two bags brought out so far, and I'm told that there are more than a hundred additional corpses."

"How would you describe the scene in the theater, Major?"

"I haven't been inside. Two of our men who have both used the same word: horrible. Captain Bart said it was like a slaughterhouse, only worse. We may have a full statement in a few hours."

Each network had taped Vincent Brady's comments, and ABC had managed to get a very brief interview with the mayor as he entered his car. "This is a terrible affair that shocks me and every New Yorker," Warner announced. "I'm glad that we have such a fine police commissioner and force. It's completely in their hands, and I have great confidence in them."

Charlie Rosenthal had done his job well, Bloom thought as he sipped more of the elegant Martell. It was Grady whom the public and press could crucify if anything went wrong. Bloom turned back to CBS and saw a familiar face: Professor Robert Geller of Columbia University's chemistry faculty was speaking on nerve gas and how it worked. Bob Geller had gained weight and lost hair since he'd been the saber star on the fencing team that Bloom had led to an Ivy League championship.

ABC had an "expert on terrorism" speculating that the gas might be either Iraqi or Iranian, since Iraq had made and used poison gas against Iran, and Iran's fanatical leaders hated the United States as the "Great Satan." On NBC a retired two-star general was summarizing the most sensational terrorist acts of the past three years.

Bloom drank more of the Martell, hoping that it might ease his tension. It helped, but not enough to permit him to escape in sleep. Otto's Boy was watching these special reports too, but he wasn't sipping alcohol. He didn't drink intoxicating beverages or smoke. Mama had warned how dangerous these filthy things were when he was only ten, even before she had spoken to him about the dirtiness of sex.

The whole news broadcast was fascinating. Ernst Henke realized that half of what they showed on television was a vile lie because Jews and Communists dominated the networks, but he still couldn't take his eyes off the screen. And all across the country, millions of others were staring—awed and afraid.

He couldn't help smiling. Why shouldn't he? He had every reason to be proud. He had done this—alone. The son of an SS hero could accomplish anything, as Mama had said so many times. Mama was always right, he thought, and he wondered whether she might be watching this broadcast too. He wanted so much for her to see . . . to know. He got up and walked to the telephone to call her. He lifted the instrument, dialed her area code, and paused.

No, he couldn't risk it. Maximum security came first.

Even though they thought he was dead, he shouldn't take the chance. He would tell her later. She was entitled to know that Otto's Boy had kept his promise.

He hung up the phone and went back to enjoying his success. They were bringing out more of those plastic sacks now. He hardly heard what the network correspondent was saying. The words didn't matter that much anyway. It was those bags that really counted.

They were exciting. This was somehow even more thrilling than last time. From what he had heard, he had killed even more of them tonight, but that wasn't the only reason he felt so good. He was seeing it *live*. At this very moment they were actually bringing out the corpses of his enemies. After the subway attack he had only watched tape the next morning.

Something began to happen in his loins. He attempted to ignore it. He had to. He mustn't give in to this swelling pressure. He had to concentrate on the numbers. He was always safe with them. He had to stop this immediately.

He changed the channel. More bags. What was the ABC reporter saying? One hundred and nine? They had sent for more of the wonderful bags? Running out? He couldn't watch any more. He shouldn't. He might lose control. His body might do something bad. No, he had to stop.

Panting, he turned off the set. It was time to go to bed. He could get away from it there. The swelling and throbbing would disappear in the void of sleep. He washed his hands and face carefully. Then he undressed, making sure to face away from the mirror. He didn't want to see the shameful state of his private parts.

The embarrassment would be over soon. He knew what to do. He turned out the light, got into bed, and forced himself to think about other things: the rewiring that he had to do at work tomorrow morning, the monthly report due the next day, the packing that he had to start. Otto's Boy had already made a list of exactly what he would take and had chosen which suitcase to use. One was all he would need. He was going far, moving fast, and traveling light. He had planned every detail.

As he went over them in his mind, he began to feel weary. But the electric currents that harassed his loins still lingered. The tingling that came with seeing those body bags wasn't all gone yet. He remembered so clearly how angry Mama had been when she had seen those sinful stains on the sheets, how she had beaten him with the strap. She had been right. A decent Aryan boy didn't have such disgusting dreams.

It won't happen tonight, Mama, he vowed sleepily. *I'll try my very best.*

He did.

He failed.

CHAPTER 29

IT WAS 1:40 A.M. when they carried out the last body bag. The number of dead was 252, not 253.

Barbara Howe, an assistant editor at *Working Woman,* had been with the victims until a few minutes after the film began. Then she felt nauseous as a result of tainted seafood eaten at a local restaurant and hurried to the toilet to throw up. With her body wracked by waves of hot and cold chills, she decided to go home. She was leaving the building when the slaughter was discovered and hordes of shaken people poured out onto the street.

A dozen hours later, sandy-haired Barbara Howe was known around the world. Satellites flashed her eyewitness account to television stations in nineteen countries, and some 60 million Americans saw it on the U. S. networks' morning news programs. Thousands of newspapers on five continents ran the Associated Press photo of her captioned "the luckiest woman alive."

That picture was on the front page of the *Washington Post, U.S.A. Today,* and both of New York's morning papers. Those publications were on the conference room table when Bloom arrived at the local FBI headquarters at 9:00 on Thursday morning. The *Times* gave the story a five-column headline and a quarter of the front page. The *Daily News* account included the entire front page and four more inside. The afternoon tabloid would double that, Bloom thought.

"Have you heard anything from Florida?" he asked.

"Mrs. Letherby left her house at eight this morning to drive to work," Fredericks replied. "She's got a three-day-a-week job as a cashier at Disney World. Our agents are watching her right now as part of the round-the-clock surveillance."

"I've heard from Washington," Mills volunteered. "General Younts is extremely disturbed about what happened last night. He's most anxious for the task force to put these terrorists out of business as soon as possible."

"Did he have any suggestions?" Bloom asked icily.

"He mentioned swift and aggressive action to avert public panic," the colonel answered.

"Tell him this city isn't panicking," Bloom said as he took off his jacket and hung it on a chair. "Lots of people shook up . . . some scared . . . others puzzled . . . and most angry."

"Sore as hell," Velez confirmed.

"I'll pass that along," Mills promised. "I have one more thing to report. The decontamination unit found another blue cylinder with a timer. They're on their way to the FBI lab in Washington for a complete check at this very moment."

"We don't have too many moments. We can expect another ultimatum from these bastards any minute," Bloom predicted, "and we'd better be ready for it. The mayor's going to be under tremendous pressure to pay the ransom, you know."

Silence.

"We're the experts," Bloom reminded them. "What do we tell him?"

Ten seconds ticked away before the FBI inspector replied.

"I'll have to consult with my superiors," he said.

"What do you think, Colonel?" Bloom asked.

"Personally or officially?"

"Both or either."

"I'm a soldier," Mills said. "I'm not as clever as you two about terrorists. Personally, I hate them. I wouldn't pay a cent. Officially, I'm not sure that the military would want to intervene in a civilian policy matter."

"Going to consult your superiors?" David Bloom questioned.

The colonel nodded.

Then the telephone rang. For the next five hours, calls and telex messages came in swift succession from FBI teams and Army CID units around the world. They had found and interrogated men who had served with Ernest Letherby at Tooele and five previous posts. They had located his former commanders too. They had tracked down retired army personnel in a score of towns and three foreign countries.

None of them were friends of Ernie. Not close friends anyway. Ernie was a good guy—didn't have an enemy in the world. But no close friends. Easy to get along with. Never one for fights or trouble. He sure knew a lot about sports and star athletes. Practically a walking encyclopedia on baseball and football. "Really into physical fitness. Never drank or smoked or fooled with women. Seemed to be shy with girls. Hell, he wasn't a fag or anything like that. No, Ernie sort of kept to himself. Pumping iron and writing to his mother were his main recreation."

Absolutely GI. Spit and polish all the way. Everything by the manual. Not one for joking. He would laugh if somebody else got off a wisecrack, so long as it was clean. Ernie didn't appreciate dirty talk at all. Even routine cusswords put that cool, negative look in his eyes. "He was hooked on the clean thing. Hell, ol' Ernie washed more than anyone else I ever met."

Corporal Letherby was a model soldier. Sergeant Letherby was reliable, diligent, and resourceful. Sergeant Letherby never complained or shirked. "Within a month after Corporal Letherby joined my unit, I knew he'd move up in grade." Even as a recruit, Private Letherby demonstrated unusual commitment. "When you gave a job to Sergeant Letherby, you knew it would be done right." Letherby maintained excellent discipline in his unit. "No, I don't recall anything special about him as a person. I think he was sort of dull, at least in conversation."

Then the reports began to trickle in from federal agents assigned to question members of his stepfather's family: Ernie was a good boy; did well at school; always polite to elders; never got into scrapes; played first base on his high school team; sang in the church choir; never caused his daddy a moment's concern; seemed closer to his mother. "No, he never talked politics at all. More into hunting and fishing." "That boy was a damn good shot from the time he was fourteen." "Sorry, we haven't heard from him in years. Even before his daddy died we didn't have regular contact. Was kind of a shy boy, you know."

"He deserted from the army, you say? That's hard to believe. That kid was raised real strict. Lord, he must have been talked into it. Maybe some woman fooled him." "Poor Ernie in trouble with the government? The army was his home. You say it could be amnesia? He needs help? Ernie'll be okay if he goes back, huh? Sure, we'll let you know if we hear anything."

While the men in the FBI conference room in New York listened and took notes on yellow legal pads, another public servant some fifty-five hundred miles to the east frowned as he studied a report. Wilhelm Gansenbein, an assistant *komisar* in the West German BKA and a police executive in the Federal Republic, took his work seriously. Tall, bespectacled Wilhelm Gansenbein had the pride and standards of a professional. As anyone in BKA's headquarters here in Wiesbaden could tell you, he was a perfectionist.

This was just sloppy.

Not that unusual for the Americans, he thought with a mixture of annoyance and satisfaction.

For all their high-powered talk and technology, the often patronizing Americans made quite a few mistakes. So other people had to clean up after them, which was both wasteful and irritating. Wilhelm Gansenbein was a senior law enforcement specialist, not a janitor. He would tell that to the FBI liaison officer at the U. S. embassy in Bonn.

Gansenbein could not tolerate waste, and the incorrect spelling the Americans had provided had caused many hours of useless effort. The father's name was Henke, not Benke. Having no idea that Otto Henke's widow had deliberately erred to wipe out the trail, Gansenbein righteously assumed that the FBI had garbled the spelling. The efficient BKA had discovered the mistake, of course.

Otto Kurt Henke, born 3 October 1919 in Munich. Second of the four offspring of Herman and Karla Henke . . . vocational high school . . . Hitler Jugend . . . Party membership . . . SS service record . . . convicted by U. S. military tribunal for war crimes at some place called Malmedy. Gansenbein's brow furrowed as he tried to recall where that might be. Wherever and whatever Henke's crime had been, it was done five years before Assistant *Komisar* Gansenbein was born. The death certificate said suicide. According to a note attached to that document by the doctor who signed it, Henke's father was then in a mental institution himself.

The report on Otto Henke's widow was much thinner. Anna Lutz, born 8 April 1923 in Furth, had two sisters . . . After high school, trained as physiotherapist . . . married at nineteen . . . gave birth to a son seven months later . . . no other children . . . widowed in 1947 . . . rewed U. S. Army Specialist-Fourth Class Jerry Bob Letherby in Heidelberg, 11 June 1949 . . . left Germany 6 December 1950.

TOP SECRET—URGENT.

That's what the Americans had marked their request. They were probably wrong about that too, Gansenbein reflected, but he would get the information to them right away. After all, the BKA had its reputation as one of the most efficient governmental organizations in the Federal Republic. Gansenbein buzzed for his assistant and told him to send the documents in the pouch that would reach the Federal Republic's embassy in Washington tomorrow.

For a few moments after his aide left, Assistant *Komisar* Gansenbein wondered why the Americans were so interested in a couple of nobodies such as the Henkes. Even when both were alive, they had never been of the slightest importance. Otto Henke had been in the ground for nearly four decades, Gansenbein thought as he straightened the papers on his desk, and by now his widow was either dead herself or a fat grandma of no interest to anyone.

The BKA supervisor was wrong. Dozens of tough and highly competent men and women were very much concerned about Anna Henke Letherby. Some were taking pictures of her with expensive cameras equipped with telephoto lenses. Others were monitoring the tap on her home telephone and the bugs that had been concealed in every room. A dozen more were poring over copies of her canceled checks and phone bills for the past twenty months.

Operating in rotation to avoid being noticed, four FBI vehicles followed her home when she left Disney World just after five o'clock. When she parked her car beside her white, four-room, one-storey house, FBI videotape cameras across the street whirred in the late afternoon sun.

Other videotape machines were rolling one thousand miles north in lower Manhattan. In a screening room twenty yards from Fredericks' office, Detective John Gillespie and two FBI agents were studying the tapes made at Grand Central forty-eight hours earlier. Their eyes hurt, and after so many hours of peering, it was difficult to maintain absolute concentration.

"Would you roll that back?" the black detective asked for the fiftieth or sixtieth time.

"Sure thing," replied the FBI woman running the machine.

The federal agents seemed to have infinite patience, Gillespie thought. This long and dreary routine didn't appear to bother them a bit.

"Just a little more," Gillespie told her. "Okay, let her go again."

There were hundreds of people—taped from different angles. There were slow, steady "pans" as the cameras swept methodically across the surging sea of commuters. There were sudden close-ups for no apparent reason. Probably random, Gillespie guessed.

"Okay . . . okay . . . FREEZE. Take a look. . . . What do you think?" he asked.

The three federal agents stared, considered, and stared some more.

"It could be," the woman said.

They summoned the others from the conference room and ran the tape for them.

"We're almost there . . . just a bit more . . . NOW!" Gillespie called out.

"The guy on the right. See him, Lieutenant?"

"Doesn't look much like the army photo," Fredericks said warily.

"He's dyed his hair black and grown a mustache," Bloom thought aloud, "but it's him. You did it, John."

"It's Letherby," the colonel admitted grimly.

Now they could be sure whom they were seeking.

"That could be a disguise," Fredericks pointed out.

David Bloom nodded in agreement.

They still didn't know what Ernest Letherby really looked like now. They had no idea where he might be or what he might do next.

Only one thing was certain: He would do it *soon*, while he still had the initiative—the control—that was so important. They probably had forty-eight hours to stop Letherby and the O. B. group. Seventy-two at the most.

It was time for Bloom to make his move.

CHAPTER 30

OTTO'S BOY moved first.

Press your advantage while the enemy is still groggy from your surprise attack. That was basic military strategy.

As Bloom and the others left the screening room, Ernst Henke entered a telephone booth on West 42nd Street. He looked at his watch again. He was on schedule. In six minutes his bus would leave the nearby Port Authority terminal. He had rehearsed and timed precisely what he would say. It ran less than twenty seconds. They couldn't trace a call that brief.

He felt so good as he dialed the number. Everyone had been talking about what he had done. This was much more important than the thing that happened in his sleep. Passengers on the morning bus into the city, people at work, senators and cardinals and even the President had spoken of his daring deed.

The President of the United States.

The most powerful man in the world, was "gravely concerned."

Otto's Boy wasn't just another sergeant anymore. They

wouldn't admit that he had won a great victory, but it was obvious that they were all impressed. He had shaken them up, smashed their complacency. Hundreds of millions of people were holding their breath, waiting to see what Otto's Boy would do next.

"Mayor Warner's office . . . Miss Sturdivant speaking."

"I'll only say it once. There's a message for him taped under the second phone off the lobby of the Milford Plaza Hotel on Eighth Avenue."

"Who is this?"

"O. B.," he answered and hung up the phone.

He was boarding his bus when two plainclothes police arrived at the hotel in an unmarked car. Following orders, they removed the envelope surreptitiously and brought it directly to City Hall. Grady and Rosenthal waited tensely as Warner opened it.

"No more tricks," the mayor read aloud. "Railroad station trap cost two hundred and fifty-two. . . . Next time one thousand or more. . . . You must pay for your sin. . . . Price now ten million . . . one million in used hundreds . . . rest in diamonds. . . . Delivery Saturday night at nine. . . . Will phone instructions. . . . Signal agreement with words *full cooperation* in public statement before noon Friday. O. B."

Then Thomas Warner put the note down on his desk.

"Same stationery. Letters cut from a newspaper," he announced.

"Can we be sure it's them?" Grady said worriedly.

Now the mayor saw that there were two other things in the envelope: One was a piece of string, the kind used to tie up the shoebox; the other was a Polaroid color photo. It was a clear picture of four metal cylinders in a row, all of them bright blue. Two were like the subway cylinder, the size of tennis ball cans. The others were bigger—like large, sinister scuba tanks. The mayor turned pale.

Without saying a word, he gave the Polaroid to Grady. After a few seconds the police commissioner silently passed the photo to Rosenthal.

"Was any picture of the nerve gas cylinders ever released?" the graying press secretary asked slowly.

"I don't think so," Grady answered.

"So this couldn't be a fake?"

"That's most unlikely," Grady admitted. "We'd better send all this to the task force right away."

"That's the easy part, Vince," Mayor Thomas Warner said as he buzzed for his secretary.

They got to the hard part as soon as she had departed with the envelope and its contents.

"A thousand lives or more," Warner said.

"And they have the weapons. Even if this picture was taken before the attack on the subway," Vincent Grady pointed out, "they've got two cylinders left—monsters."

"At least two," Warner agreed. "What do you think, Charlie?"

"I wouldn't worry about the press, Tom. They're just as scared and confused as we are," Rosenthal told him. "I can handle the packaging of whatever you finally decide to do. I can wrap it up so it'll do you the most good. Well, the least harm anyway. But that's not the issue, is it?"

Warner sighed and nodded.

"What is he saying?" Grady asked.

"He's telling me to act like a mayor, not like a candidate for reelection."

Rosenthal shook his head.

"I'm *asking*, Tom," he corrected. "You're not the mayor of the media. You're the mayor of more than seven million people, and you're a damn good one."

"You have my full support too," Grady volunteered quickly. "It's going to be a tough decision, Tom. Don't you think we should get some advice on this from the task force? Their input could be valuable."

It was blame, not input, that the canny commissioner had in mind, Rosenthal told himself. Grady wanted the members of the task force to share the responsibility for this risky decision.

"You're right, Vince," Warner agreed. "We can use all the help we can get."

"I'll call them right now," Grady said and reached for the phone on the end table beside him. Half a minute later he told Fredericks about the package en route to the task force and asked for a recommendation as soon as possible.

"By ten tomorrow morning? We'll get on it immediately," the FBI inspector said. "We have some news for you. It looks very much as if we've identified one member of the O. B. group. . . . No, we don't know where he is. . . . Yes, it could take days to find him. . . . I understand the problem. . . . Good night, Commissioner."

Then Fredericks told Bloom, Mills, and the others what Grady had said.

"He's worried about the time factor," the FBI supervisor reported, "and I can't disagree. There's almost no chance we'll locate Letherby before the O. B. deadline."

"Are you saying the city should pay?" Bloom asked.

"It may be necessary."

"We're dealing with mental cases—seriously disturbed people. There's a definite possibility that they'll use the goddamn gas again even if they get the ransom," Bloom warned.

"And an even better chance if they don't," Fredericks replied. "Look, there's no point in arguing. This is a very complicated question that requires a great deal of thinking."

"I've done that," Bloom answered, "and so have you. What the hell are you going to tell Grady?"

"An FBI inspector doesn't tell the police commissioner of the biggest city in the country what to do," Fredericks said.

"Are you bailing out?" Bloom challenged.

Fredericks shook his head.

"No, I'm going to talk to the head of this office and to our senior experts on terrorism in Washington," he explained patiently.

"How long will that take?"

"I'll let you know tomorrow morning at eight, right here," Fredericks answered. Then he rose to his feet.

His message was clear. He wouldn't discuss it any further now.

The meeting of the Joint Task Force was over.

David Bloom said nothing as the elevator carried him and his aides down to the street. There was something in his eyes that said a great deal though. Velez had seen it before.

"What are you going to do?" he asked as they left the federal tower.

"Make a phone call. Don't ask me to whom or why."

"Can I make a suggestion, Lieutenant?"

"Sure."

"Please don't do anything crazy."

Bloom stopped walking and smiled.

"What makes you think I would, Gabe?"

"I recognize that look," Velez replied. "It's that fucking knight-on-the-white-horse look—pure trouble. Whatever it is, don't do it."

Bloom thought of the photo of the gas cylinders.

"I'm afraid I have to," he replied.

It really didn't matter whether they paid or not, Bloom reasoned as he drove home. Catching Letherby and the rest of the O. B. group before they killed more people was all that counted. Making this call might speed that up.

When he entered his apartment, Bloom considered what he would say. He had to tell the right person. It must be a journalist who wouldn't break the story until after eleven tomorrow morning. The timing was important.

Arnold Shain.

He was the energetic young reporter on the *Post* who had dubbed Bloom Super Cop.

The *Post* was an afternoon paper and a sensational one. Yes, that would be perfect.

Bloom telephoned the paper, found that Shain was out, and left word for the reporter to call him. Then the detective poured himself some of the Cordon Bleu cognac and waited. He had nearly finished the Martell when the phone rang.

"Lieutenant Bloom?"

"Speaking."

"This is Arnold Shain. Uh . . . did you call me?"

"Yes. I've got something for you. It'll be exclusive, if you play it my way."

"What's that?" the journalist asked warily.

"It can't run in your early editions. I don't want it in print until after eleven o'clock. Is that a deal?"

"Deal. What is it?"

"A statement of my personal views about the nerve gas gang. You ready to take it?"

"I'm always ready, Lieutenant."

"You can say that I'm convinced that this group of thugs . . . group of thugs . . . is led by a very sick person. . . . I believe that he's a mental case who should be in an asylum."

"Just a second," Shain pleaded. "Okay, *go.*"

"He's a man of no real principles—just a psychotic. . . . Because he's so crazy, it's only a matter of time until we hunt him down. . . . He belongs in a cage . . . in a zoo. He's a sick animal."

"You hate this guy, huh?"

"No, I *despise* him."

"You think you'll nail him soon?"

"I know it. He doesn't have a chance. You got that?"

"I certainly do. Thanks a lot, Lieutenant. This is quite a surprise. I'd heard that you were kind of annoyed with me about that Super Cop thing."

"I am, Arnie," Bloom replied truthfully. "Now please keep in mind our deal. If this runs before eleven o'clock, I'm going to say you made the whole thing up, that I never spoke to you."

"You'd do it, wouldn't you?"

"Bet on it. Good night, Arnie."

"Good night, Lieutenant."

Bloom drained the last of the fine cognac and thought about

dinner. He decided to walk up Amsterdam Avenue to the Left Bank for some of that excellent swordfish. There wasn't anything else he could do about the terrorists tonight.

He had made his move.

Now all he could do was wait.

No, there was one thing more.

He would do that tomorrow.

CHAPTER 31

THE COFFEE was terrible.

Bloom didn't complain. It was 8:05 A.M., and he didn't want to offend Fredericks any further. Bloom put down the cardboard carton and concentrated on what the FBI inspector was saying.

"We can start with the reports from Florida. The team going over her bank records found nothing that seems relevant to our case. No unusual checks to anyone. Just routine stuff to pay her water and gas bills, a few to food merchants and a clothing store, and a couple for taxes. In case you're interested, she doesn't owe a cent in taxes. She doesn't have any bank loans and doesn't use credit cards. This woman doesn't owe a cent to anybody."

Bloom rubbed his eyes. He hadn't been able to fall asleep until nearly three, and they were tired.

"Income?" he asked.

"Salary checks from her job . . . pension checks as the widow of an army warrant officer . . . dividend payments on some IBM and phone company stock worth a total of nineteen thousand dollars. The house is appraised at forty-six thousand dollars—

nothing fancy. She's got seven more years of mortgage payments to go."

"Any unusual income in the past twenty months?"

"A thirty-thousand-dollar lump-sum payment on her son's GI insurance. I guess she'll have to return that," Fredericks reflected.

"Unless we kill him," Bloom said.

The FBI inspector shook his head and continued. "Her phone calls don't tell us much either. She isn't a very talkative lady. Her bills run less than fifteen dollars a month. In the past year she made only one out-of-state call. That was to a number in northern New Jersey. The computer may have goofed, though. We've checked the number out, and it's a pay phone about twenty-five miles north of the George Washington Bridge."

"Any sign of foreign contacts?" Mills questioned.

"None that we can find. She hasn't called outside the country. Mailman says she doesn't get any letters or magazines from abroad. We've talked to her supervisor at the Disney park, and he gives her a clean bill of health. Always on time, hard worker, never sick a day, and completely honest. Two of her previous employers said the same thing."

Bloom rubbed his weary eyes again.

"Any pet causes or prejudices?" he asked.

"Well, one boss mentioned that she didn't seem too fond of black people, but there was never any trouble. We've got a medical rundown too. No record of any kind of emotional difficulties, and physically she's as strong as the proverbial horse. Big into exercise. Works out with weights—the whole number."

"Sounds like her son," Colonel Mills commented.

"You're right. She's a large woman. Five feet six and one hundred forty pounds, most of it muscle. No diseases. No record of serious illness. And she's like her son in another way: She doesn't drink alcohol or smoke."

"And she's a perfect neighbor," Bloom guessed.

Fredericks sipped the terrible coffee and nodded.

"Has she ever been up to Arlington?" Bloom asked.

"I don't know. Why do you ask?"

"Trying to figure out if she knows that her homicidal son is still alive. After all, he's her only child. Most mothers might come to the cemetery to see the grave . . . maybe put down some flowers."

"That could be hard to check," the FBI inspector said.

"Try. Find out if this hardworking perfect neighbor has bought an airline ticket from Orlando to Washington since the coffin was put in the ground. Can't be more than two or three airlines on that run, and they might have something in their computer records."

Fredericks turned to Collery.

"Would you please call the Orlando office on that immediately?"

"Yes, sir."

As Collery left the room, Fredericks put several eight-by-ten-inch photos on the conference table.

"These were taken yesterday," he announced.

The pictures were handed around one by one. Anna Henke Letherby had gray hair cut somewhat short, a plump but strong face, and no makeup.

"Any comments?" Fredericks asked.

"I've got a question," Bloom answered.

"Yes?"

"What are you going to advise Grady to do?"

Fredericks sucked in a deep breath before he replied.

"As I told you I would, I've discussed the matter with the Special Agent in Charge of the Bureau here and with our senior experts on terrorism in Washington. They're very experienced men, you know. We analyzed the situation and the risks at great length, and consulted with the director himself."

"Bottom line," Bloom said coldly.

"I was trying to explain how much serious effort—"

"Don't bother. What is the Bureau recommending?"

"Well, the decision is really up to Mayor Warner. He has the primary responsibility for the safety of the citizens of New

217

York City. Now the Bureau is also very concerned, as our years of work on this Joint Task Force confirm."

"Are you going to tell the city to pay?" Bloom demanded.

"The general policy of the Bureau is to oppose the payment of ransom to terrorists if at all possible," Fredericks answered. He spoke stiffly in a flat, "official" voice. "I think it's clear that the current situation is quite an unusual one. This O. B. organization has already killed three hundred and sixty-nine people and has the weapons to murder many more. The Bureau does not believe that it would be appropriate to subject the people of New York to that risk."

"Pay?"

"Only to end the immediate threat of another massacre," Fredericks explained quickly.

"It won't end anything. We're dealing with a gang of thugs who've got the morals of a barracuda and a leader who's a paranoid animal. They could use that goddamn gas again an hour after they're paid."

"There is that possibility," Fredericks admitted, "and I can assure you that the Bureau considered it. However, we feel that the prudent thing to do is to deliver the ransom and continue our search for O. B. later. We've already identified one member of the terrorist apparatus, so it should only be a matter of time before we find him and his associates."

Bloom swung his eyes to the colonel.

"What's the army position?" the detective asked.

"We see as the primary mission the complete elimination of the O. B. organization," Mills said.

"How about the ransom?"

"That's a policy matter for the civilian authorities. It would be improper—probably illegal—for the military to interfere. Of course, we will continue to play an active role in hunting down these criminals."

"You'll cooperate with the Joint Task Force in every way?" Bloom tested.

"Absolutely."

"Good. I'd like you to get me some army ID, Colonel. I need papers that say I'm a CID agent, and I need them immediately."

Mills looked startled.

"Would you mind explaining what you intend to do with them?" he asked.

"I'm going to deceive and intimidate that perfect neighbor down in Longwood, Florida. If it works, we may get a little closer to her tricky son—the one who murders people."

Mills considered what Bloom had just said.

"Any objections?" Bloom asked. "The army told me that I could have almost anything I wanted. I'm supposed to be General Younts' 'wild card.' Those were his words. Are you canceling the deal?"

Mills shook his head.

"You'll have your papers this afternoon," he promised reluctantly.

"By eleven this morning," Bloom corrected. "Hate to be pushy, but that's when I need them at the Eastern counter at Kennedy."

Now he turned to Fredericks.

"Who's running the surveillance operation in Florida?"

"The head of our Orlando office—Ted Seigenthaler."

"You'd better tell him I'll be arriving there on the Eastern flight that gets in at two this afternoon. I'd like to talk to him before I see the lady."

"She'll be working at Disney World."

"I don't mind," Bloom replied. "I'm just a kid at heart."

The FBI supervisor opened his mouth, closed it as he reconsidered, and finally opened it again.

"I'm not sure that this is a good idea," he said.

"I knew we'd agree on something. I'm not sure it is either," Bloom said, "but I think I've got to try it."

"Would you spell that out?" Mills asked uncertainly.

"If she's as clean as she seems, then there's no real harm I can do. The worst that can happen is she'll threaten to sue the army, and you'll tell her that the guy who shook her up has no connection with CID or the Pentagon. You can be honest. Say he must have been using phony ID papers."

"What if she's not clean?" Fredericks questioned. "You could arouse her suspicions and negate the surveillance. She might get very careful on the phone. She might start checking for bugs or strangers following her."

"That's possible."

"She might try to warn him," Fredericks said.

"I certainly hope so. That way we'd have a chance of finding the son of a bitch a lot faster."

"You've got it all figured out, huh?"

"About half, Inspector. You're right to think it's a gamble," Bloom told him, "but we don't have the time to play it safe."

"You could wait until the BKA reports arrive from Wiesbaden this afternoon. I hear they're on their way."

"*You* could wait. *I* couldn't. I'll call you from Florida," Bloom said as he stood up and retrieved his jacket. "Come on, Gabe."

Velez left with him.

"Lieutenant, is that the . . . the crazy thing you had in mind?"

Bloom shook his head as they stepped into the elevator.

"No, and I don't think it's crazy. It's unorthodox and it could bother a few people, but it doesn't seem crazy to me."

When they reached the antiterrorist unit's offices in police headquarters, Bloom drafted a two-page memorandum to Grady spelling out why he believed that paying the ransom would not solve the O. B. threat. After it was typed in triplicate, he gave a copy to Velez.

"Please deliver it to him at a quarter to ten," he requested.

"Right. I hate to pry, Lieutenant, but has he authorized this Florida thing?"

"A quarter to ten should be just about right," Bloom said.

"What do I tell the Chief of Detectives if he asks what the hell is going on?" Velez appealed.

"I should be back tomorrow afternoon. Watch the store."

The army courier who delivered the fake ID at the airport

was the same tight-mouthed man who had driven Bloom to the heliport for the flight to Fort Myer. He was just as taciturn as he had been that Sunday morning. In fact, he didn't utter a word. He found Bloom at the Eastern Airlines ticket counter at five minutes before eleven, handed him the sealed envelope and walked away.

Bloom boarded Flight 861 a quarter of an hour later. The wide-bodied A-300 Airbus was taxiing for takeoff when the telephones began to ring at the antiterrorist unit's offices. The United Press, BBC, *New York Daily News, Time, Washington Post,* NBC Radio, ABC-TV, somebody from the *Times*—he didn't say which—a female reporter for WCBS News, and the Chief of Detectives of the New York City Police Department all wanted to speak with David Bloom.

Now.

It was both important and urgent.

They all mentioned a statement that had appeared in the most recent edition of the *Post*. A few of them seemed to be irate. The driven journalists were openly disappointed that Lieutenant Bloom was out of the office, and all promised to call back soon. The Chief of Detectives, who had a B. S. degree in Public Administration and a reputation for coolness, was abusive. His demand that Bloom call him as soon as he got back was delivered in a voice loaded with threat and anger.

"You tell him that he's got one hour to explain this crap," the chief ordered. "*One hour.*"

Then he slammed down the phone. Velez turned to Gillespie.

"Sounds like our boy really stepped into deep shit this time," Velez said. "We'd better find out what the hell's got everyone steaming."

He took three dimes from his pocket and gave them to Gillespie. The black detective returned with a copy of the *Post* ten minutes later.

"He did it all right," Gillespie reported.

"Something crazy?"

"Strange, anyway. Take a look, Gabe."

The story was on page two, under a three-column headline: *Super Cop Rips Gas Killer as Sick Animal!*

And there was a big picture of Bloom. Velez read the article carefully, shaking his head. Then he reread it. The chief probably figured that David Bloom was grandstanding, playing to the media. He didn't understand that Bloom had a reason, Velez thought. David Bloom always had a reason for whatever he did, one he had considered carefully.

Vincent Grady's personal assistant called next. After that, it was an audibly tense Dr. Maeve O'Donnell. The damn telephones kept jingling off and on for hours. They were still ringing steadily when Eastern Airlines Flight 861 touched down at Orlando.

CHAPTER 32

THE TWO FBI MEN waiting for David Bloom in the air terminal weren't that hard to spot. They might have passed for businessmen in their dark suits, white shirts, and forgettable ties, but the way they looked at people gave them away. Their eyes scanned the arriving passengers in a way that Bloom recognized at once. It was definitely a police look.

For a long moment Bloom wondered whether this entire trip was a mistake—a dangerous one. Then he thought of the photos taken by the army decontamination unit inside the movie theater: rows of bodies . . . heaps of bodies . . . tangles of bodies—some hardly recognizable as human under the coatings of vomit. For some reason he suddenly remembered those masses of corpses in the historic pictures taken when U. S. and British troops smashed into the Nazi death camps in 1945.

He couldn't dwell on those horrors now. He had to suppress the anger that those memories always sent flooding through his entire being. He had to concentrate on now: Orlando, Florida; Mrs. Anna Henke Letherby. Pushing away the bitterness, he walked directly to the older of the two men—sharp-featured, tanned, and in his early forties.

"Mr. Seigenthaler?" the New Yorker asked.

"What did you say?"

"My name is David Bloom."

"I'm Seigenthaler," the wary head of the FBI's Orlando office admitted." This is Frank Tutherland. Have you got a bag?"

"No. I'm not staying that long."

"Car's outside," Seigenthaler announced and led the way out of the terminal. It was warm in the bright afternoon sun as they walked through the parking lot to a gray Dodge. The FBI executive didn't speak again until they were in the car.

"I suppose you've got some ID," Seigenthaler said in a matter-of-fact tone.

Bloom handed him his NYPD identification and driver's license. The FBI executive examined both carefully before he returned them.

"Hope you don't mind," he said as he started the engine.

"Not a bit. Mind if I check *your* ID now?"

Both agents showed their plastic-sheathed FBI cards. Bloom studied the photos, nodded, and gave them back.

"Thanks," he said as the Dodge began to roll. "How's the surveillance going?"

"Full blast. We've got twenty-seven agents on this one," Seigenthaler reported. "Brought in people from Miami and Atlanta for round-the-clock coverage. Her son must be a major offender."

They hadn't told him about O. B. and the nerve gas.

"Did your New York office explain why I'm here?" Bloom asked.

"They said you wanted to talk to her," Seigenthaler replied and shook his head.

"Don't you think I should?"

"No. You could blow the whole deal. I'm not telling you how to run your business, Lieutenant, but you sure could mess up mine."

"I wouldn't risk it if we had more time," Bloom said.

The FBI supervisor shrugged in silent disagreement.

"How far is it to Disney World?" Bloom questioned.

"We aren't going there. She's not working today. She's home, according to our one o'clock surveillance report. Went out to buy food; came back around noon. We're heading for her house now. It's about forty minutes from here."

Bloom looked at his watch.

It was more than two hours past the deadline O. B. had set.

What had the mayor done?

They drove on in silence. This was an attractive part of Florida, Bloom thought as he stared out the window. It wasn't purely residential, though. He recalled a newspaper article calling this area "the number-one tourist destination in the world," with 14 million visitors each year to Disney World and millions more to Cypress Gardens, the Kennedy Space Center, Sea World and other attractions. Lots of industry moving in, mostly electronics. The names of a dozen large manufacturing firms filled roadside billboards.

It was half-past two when they reached Longwood. First they drove through an area of fairly large houses on good-sized lots—*not* the low-rent district. Then the Dodge rolled into a section with smaller residences, well kept but obviously less expensive. It was there that Seigenthaler finally stopped the car.

"She's in Seven Hundred and Nineteen on the next block," he announced. "Our command post is in a truck parked next to Seven Hundred and Forty-two."

"Thanks."

For a few seconds David Bloom considered telling him who her son was and what he had done. He decided not to. Bloom didn't have to justify himself to some FBI operative whose own bosses wouldn't tell him the whole truth. Maybe they were right. Or perhaps the army had persuaded them not to.

Bloom got out of the car and walked slowly down the street. It was hot and humid. Each small residence had its own little plot of grass in front, a neatly tended minilawn with an occasional grapefruit tree or cactus. A recently washed green Datsun gleamed in the sun in front of the house numbered 719.

Bloom went over in his mind again what he would say.

Then he strode to the front door and rang the bell.

Her hair seemed grayer than the photo had suggested.

Her glance looked calm but questioning.

Up this close, her physical strength was much more evident. The short-sleeved sun dress she wore showed her muscular build clearly. There was something almost masculine about this woman.

"Mrs. Letherby?"

"Yes."

Her accent was southern, but there was still a hint of Germany beneath it.

"My name is Evans, ma'am. Captain Eli Evans. I'm with the army. May I come in, please?"

"What is it, Captain?"

"Something kind of personal. I'd rather discuss it inside."

The house was very neat—and clean. In fact, an odor of pine soap floated through the hall. The furniture didn't seem quite right for Florida temperatures and living. Most pieces ran to the overstuffed, and Bloom guessed she might have brought them from earlier homes in army posts in colder climates. There were several framed prints of large flowers on the walls. A long shelf in the living room was crowded with those vulgar European figurines in porcelain—cherubs, peasant girls, puppy dogs, shepherds, and other dismal favorites of the lower middle class. Bloom pretended not to notice them as he settled down in a brocaded armchair.

"What is it, Captain?"

"I'd better show you my credentials, ma'am. That's regulations, you know."

He gave her the fake identity card.

Something flickered in her eyes. It was more than surprise. It was fear.

"Criminal Investigation Division? I don't understand," she announced.

"I'll do my best to explain. This is kind of complicated," he told her. "It involves money."

"What money?"

"Could I trouble you for a glass of cold water, ma'am?" he fenced. He had to set the stage for the trap carefully. He had to time it perfectly.

She nodded, went to the kitchen, and returned with a pink tumbler filled with water and two ice cubes. He sipped from it and sighed.

"Thank you, ma'am. Mighty warm out there. Now the money I was talking about . . . it's insurance money."

Her eyes narrowed in uncertainty.

"What insurance money?"

He sipped more water before he answered.

"Did you receive a check for thirty thousand dollars from your son's GI policy . . . let's see . . . sixteen months ago?"

"Yes. Four months after he died."

"And you deposited it?"

"Of course. What's the problem?" she asked impatiently.

"*That's* the problem. The army has received information which strongly suggests that you may have to return that money."

She blinked several times, puzzled.

"Why?" she asked.

Bloom drank from the ugly tumbler again.

"Because it appears that your son is alive," he said.

For a second her mask cracked wide open. Something flashed out. It wasn't the astonishment of a parent who has been totally surprised. It wasn't the anger of a mother who has been hurt. It was stunned panic.

The mask closed. The real feelings vanished inside it, fleeing like thieves in the night.

"That's impossible," she said. "My boy is dead."

Bloom shook his head.

"We have evidence that he's alive, Mrs. Letherby. He has been positively identified by two armored car guards in Ohio as one of the men who stole three hundred and forty thousand dollars in Cleveland five months ago. That's a very serious crime, ma'am."

"It can't be my son. There must be a mistake," she insisted.

"No mistake. They're offering a reward of twenty-five thousand dollars for his arrest."

He could see that she was disturbed. Now he had to keep the pressure on, build it higher and higher.

"Who is?" she challenged.

"The armored car company. I hate to tell you, ma'am, but the FBI is hunting for your son right now."

"Even if he was alive, he'd never do such a thing. Never!"

"There are wanted posters going out tomorrow," Bloom said in his grimmest tone. "They'll be in every post office by next week."

"This is insane. Why can't you leave the dead alone? Have you no respect for the twenty years of good service he gave the army? Why don't you let him rest in honorable sleep at Arlington with the other fine soldiers?"

"I don't think he's there."

"You must be crazy. Of course he's there. Why do you blacken a loyal soldier's name?"

She was fighting back well. It was time to escalate the confrontation.

"There are others who don't believe that he's there," Bloom announced. "Several of those people are in the Newark, New Jersey, police."

Another flash of fear. Just a glimmer, but it was promising.

"My son sleeps with the heroes in Arlington, Virginia," she answered defiantly. "Why should I care about some fools in . . . in New Jersey?"

Bloom noticed her hesitation.

New Jersey? The phone booth she had called was there.

More pressure.

The kind she would like least.

"The Newark police have a warrant out for him on a charge of rape, Mrs. Letherby."

She looked completely incredulous.

"*Rape?* My Ernie?"

Bloom nodded solemnly.

"A fifteen-year-old black girl."

Her lower lip trembled.

Then her face started to twitch.

The mask was cracking again.

Suddenly, the calm and sensible perfect neighbor was on her feet screaming. The indignant mother was gone. Someone bitter and savage had taken her place.

"A *black* girl? That's disgusting! My Ernie doesn't bother women. The thought that he'd have anything to do with some nigger whore is vile! He doesn't do those filthy things. He lives clean. I raised him right. He's a good boy."

Present tense.

Doesn't bother women. Doesn't do those things. Lives clean.

Present tense.

She *knew* that he was alive.

Then she realized her slip.

"I mean he *was*. You've confused me with these awful stories," she explained. "No, my only child is just a memory—like his father. I'm all alone."

She paused, sighed, and sat down again.

She was back in control.

She wasn't going to admit anything, but Bloom didn't mind. He hadn't expected her to. He had come with two objectives. The first was to find out whether she knew. He had the answer to that. The second was to scare her so she would make some key mistake that could lead them to her cunning son.

Perhaps she needed another shock . . . another threat.

"Captain, it must be that there's someone who looks like my poor dead son who did these bad things," she reasoned. "He was such a warm and decent person. It has to be a case of mistaken identity."

"Or amnesia, ma'am. I've thought of that. Suppose that his memory was injured by some physical trauma, and he wandered off—suddenly with a different personality. He wouldn't be entirely responsible for what he did. The army would take that into account."

She wasn't that good at hiding her contempt. She wasn't about to be fooled into betraying Otto's Boy. This clumsy CID officer couldn't trick *her*.

"No, my boy is sleeping at Arlington," she said sadly.

"We'll know for sure next week," Bloom announced as he rose. "I hope you're right, Mrs. Letherby. If you're not, it won't be only Ernie who's in trouble. The government will want every cent of that insurance money back—probably with interest."

"I don't care about money anymore, not since I'm all alone," she said piously.

"I'm afraid the army does. There could even be a criminal fraud prosecution, ma'am."

"I've done nothing!"

Bloom nodded benignly.

"Then you've got nothing to worry about," he assured her as he started for the door.

"Captain Evans?"

"Yes, ma'am."

Would she take the bait?

"Captain, what did you mean about *next week?*" she asked very casually.

Bloom shrugged.

"There's a general who's really steamed up on this case," he told her. "Says the only way we can be fair to your son's memory is to exhume the remains and check the dental work. They're going to do that on Monday."

"Is it really necessary?" she appealed.

"Think of it this way: It'll put all our minds at ease, and it could prove your boy didn't do any of these crimes."

She had to make an instant decision. If she resisted, these fools might be more suspicious—perhaps even of her. If she didn't try to discourage or stop them, who could predict what they might find?

Or were they just testing her?

Maybe it was a trap. This Evans could be a Jew. They hid under all kinds of names.

"We'll let you know what we find," Bloom promised. "And if you want to call me, I'll give you the number."

He picked up the pad beside the phone, found his pen, and wrote down the number of his direct line at the office.

"Two-one-two? That's the area code for New York City, isn't it?" she asked.

"Financial capital of the country. That's why we handle money investigations out of there. Talk to you soon," Bloom said and walked out into the afternoon sun. Federal videotape cameras followed him step by step, and two still photographers focused on his face.

Click . . . click . . . click . . . click . . . click.

Standard FBI procedure.

Inside the house Bloom had just left, the subject of this sophisticated surveillance was staring at the phone number he had given her.

She didn't trust that Captain Evans.

There was something troubling about the New York telephone number.

Could they suspect that Otto's Boy was up there?

Did the army really believe that he had done these nauseating things that Evans had mentioned—or was it the gas?

Suddenly she thought about the emergency number, the one that she had memorized and never written anywhere. It was to be used only in a critical situation. She had never called it in all these months. Even on his birthday she had phoned him at the public booth as they had prearranged.

231

Should she warn him that they were looking for him?

Should he know about the posters and the plan to dig up the coffin in Arlington?

Or were those stories all lies? She couldn't make a mistake. She mustn't put *kleine Ernst* in danger. He had been such an obedient child, never complained about the strappings she had had to give him. He had understood that she did it for his own good.

No, she wasn't going to call him now. She had to think about this for a while—very carefully. She felt so tense, so taut with the responsibility. It wasn't easy living alone among so many enemies. It was probably unpleasant for Ernst too, she thought, but he was a soldier. He was strong like his father. He was definitely Otto's Boy.

CHAPTER 33

HIGH TECH.

The large truck that the FBI was using for its command post was crammed with surveillance and communications machines. The outside of the van carried the names of a fictitious moving company. The interior was filled with video monitors, tape recorders, listening gear and two radio transmitters. There was hardly room for the shirt-sleeved agents manning the equipment.

"Hear it all?" Bloom asked.

Seigenthaler nodded.

"What do you think?"

"I'll let you know in a couple of days," the FBI executive replied. "By the way, was all that true? Did he do those things?"

"Much worse. He's a mass murderer. He's a monster."

Seigenthaler shook his head.

"Could one of your people give me a ride back to the airport?"

"Sure."

As Bloom entered the terminal forty minutes later, he wondered what Anna Letherby would do. *When* was almost as important as *what* now. There was very little time: twenty-nine or thirty hours. If she did nothing until after that, he had lost.

Bloom booked a seat on a flight leaving for Newark in thirty-five minutes, saw the phone booths and hurried through the busy terminal to call his office.

"Gabe, it's me. What have you got?"

"Bad news and bad news. You really did it this time."

"Nobody's perfect."

"Lieutenant, you've got about forty-seven reporters annoyed about that *Post* exclusive and the Chief of Detectives is sore as hell. He has the idea you did this thing for personal publicity."

"He's about fifty percent right."

"Be a good thing if you phoned him to explain the other fifty percent. He's shooting fire out of both barrels. If you don't want your ass pounded into kindling, you'd better talk to him right away. And that's not all."

"I'm listening."

"The PC's personal hatchet man, Carty, was on the horn twice. The Commissioner thinks your statement was *inappropriate* and *irresponsible*. He also said *immature*. Carty asked me if you'd been drinking or acting strange. Speaking of that, the lady psychiatrist called. She sounded very tense."

"Tense?"

"More like scared. Lieutenant, I'm a little scared myself. You see, I've figured out what the hell you're up to. I think she has too."

Bloom had expected that she might, but he had seen no alternative.

"What about the mayor?" he asked.

"He's gonna pay. Used the code phrase at an eleven-thirty conference. They're collecting the diamonds now. When will you be back?"

"I'll see you at seven-thirty."

As the jet started its descent at Newark, Otto's Boy was re-reading the FINAL edition of the *Post* some thirty miles away.

He had been angry when he had first seen the article. His throat had knotted with rage at the vicious insults. Sitting in the bus on the way home, he had nearly lost control when he saw those vile words:

A man of no principles?

A cage in a zoo?

A sick animal?

But he understood what Bloom was attempting to do to him. The Jew was trying to outsmart him. It was all a question of control. Bloom wanted to trick him into losing his control. Whoever lost control would lose this war.

Control—that was it.

Bloom wanted to control him. *They* controlled the media and the banks, the schools and the politicians. They were dirty manipulators, always scheming and conspiring for power. They were rich and sly. They were all liars. They had made up lies about the SS and the so-called massacre at Malmedy. They had fabricated disgusting falsehoods about his father. Now they were spreading poison about him.

But he was too clever for them.

He had made a perfect plan. They couldn't stop it. Nobody could. It provided for every contingency. He had moved the two big cylinders into place weeks ago. It had been easy. He had said that they were oxyacetylene tanks for welding, and the dumb watchman at the loading platform had believed him. No one had asked any questions as he rolled the dolly down the corridors. He had worked there for over a year and had a pass. None of them wondered what an electrician was doing with such a tank. Nobody cared.

Tomorrow night would be his greatest triumph.

Two hundred fifty-two? That was *nothing*.

He would teach Bloom who was in control. He would show them all.

Now he was absolutely calm. Seated in his kitchen, he went over his checklist again. He had been to the post office, paid his bills, and taken care of his other duties. He looked at the open suitcase. In the morning he would put in his toilet articles and carry it out to the rented car. The tank was full. He had checked the tires and the spare.

He had the airline ticket. He wasn't going to fly from a local airport. Even though the police didn't know who he was, it would be safer to drive up to Boston to board the overseas flight there. It really hadn't been that difficult to get the false passport in the name of Kenneth Sears, whom he had known in the army. Sears, an orphan, had died three years ago. Ernst Henke had secured a copy of his birth certificate by mail and used it to get the passport.

He would disappear. He would leave nothing but corpses and fear—no clue they could use to trace him.

Mama would join him in a few weeks. They would be together at last. He had been waiting so long for that. No one would ever separate them again. Together they would honor the memory of the great SS hero whom the Americans had murdered. They would build a monument at his grave—a great one of marble and steel. It would last ten thousand years.

Otto's Boy went from room to room wiping every doorknob clean of fingerprints. The clothes that he wasn't taking would be destroyed later. Nothing must remain for the police. He certainly wasn't going to leave the other three cylinders. He had already buried them in the woods twenty miles from here. If he needed them again, he would return.

Not for at least a year.

That was in the plan too.

He stripped to his shorts for the exercises. He might not have the opportunity to work out during the next few days, and he had to keep fit. Mama might have more for him to do. It would be different now. She wouldn't have to take the strap to him anymore. He understood that she had done it for his own good because she loved him. He had learned her lessons. Now he would do everything right. He would be the perfect son she deserved.

When the exercises were done, he went into the bathroom

for the enema. Mama had never explained why it had to be ice cold, but he knew that she was right. The freezing cold water hurt. It always did. At first he used to scream at the impact, but he had learned to stand it. The son of an SS hero had to bear pain bravely.

Even after all these years, the shock made him gasp.

His body twitched and shook, but then he was in control again. The hurting was necessary. Mama had explained that part. Suddenly he remembered how it had been when she first taught him about the enemas, how she had smiled and held his hand.

After his body had emptied out the water and wastes, he took a shower. As he towelled himself dry, he thought about how happy Mama would be to hear that it was almost done. He hadn't spoken to her in so many months. He had been lonely for such a long time. *They* had done this thing to him. Even those thousands of bodies tomorrow night couldn't make up for that.

He would be going in to work in the morning in the car.

He would call her just before he left.

CHAPTER 34

THE ANTITERRORIST UNIT'S OFFICE seemed oddly quiet.

There were four detectives in the outer room, but none of them were on the telephone.

"The calling's over," Gabriel Velez said. "We finished with the last of the shrinks. Perfect score. Zero for three thousand one hundred and ninety-four."

"Come on inside," Bloom said, and Velez and Gillespie followed him into the private office.

"The Chief of Detectives phoned again, in case you're interested," Velez reported. "He expects you in his office at nine tomorrow morning."

"I'll be there. Anything else?" Bloom asked as he took out a cigar.

Velez held up two fingers.

"A deuce. You got a pair from Washington. Just after I spoke to you, word came in on those prints we lifted off the bugs Tony found. The FBI says they have no matching ones in their computer."

"It's a lie," Bloom judged and lit the corona. "I don't like being lied to, even by the federal government. They're covering up for the army. We'll get to that later."

"Here's one for the sooner file," Gillespie said and handed him a folder. "It's the stuff the BKA dug up on Letherby's parents. You might find his father kind of interesting."

Bloom sat down behind the desk, flipped open the folder, and began to read. After about a minute he stopped.

"That's it," he announced.

Gillespie nodded in agreement.

"That's what I've been looking for—*why*. It didn't make sense until now. It still doesn't make a lot of sense, you know," Bloom said.

"Makes sense to me," Velez declared. "His father was a fucking Nazi war criminal. Those SS guys were loonies."

Bloom puffed on the Don Diego. "Thousands of them had sons who didn't grow up to be mass murderers," he said. "Probably lots of their kids are pretty ordinary citizens in Germany today."

"Which side are you on anyway?" Velez challenged. "Are you into that saint number again?"

"Please, don't play amateur psychiatrist. I've got a professional I can talk to."

"You'd better," Velez responded. "She called again an hour ago."

David Bloom pointed toward the door. The others left as he picked up the phone.

"I'm sorry that I couldn't get back to you sooner," he apologized, "but I've been out of town."

"I saw the statement you gave to the *Post*. You shouldn't have done that," she said.

"It seemed like a good idea . . . well, a *fair* idea. Actually, it was the only one I had," he told her.

"It could be a dangerous idea. I suppose you knew that before you did it."

"Look, I wasn't trying to be a martyr, damn it. I thought

that I had to draw the O. B. leader out into the open before he collected the ransom. I was wrong."

"Thank God for that," she said. "I was shocked when I saw the paper. And if it makes you feel important, I was frightened."

"I'm sorry. That wasn't the idea."

"You said that you'd be careful," she accused, "and I believed you. I didn't come all the way from Galway to get involved with a policeman, certainly not a suicidal policeman."

"I've got to stop these murderers."

"No, the New York City Police Department, an organization of thousands of people, has to. You don't have to do it all yourself. That's just . . . well . . . immature."

"A senior official of the department called me that today," Bloom told her.

"But it didn't change you, did it?" she demanded.

"I didn't do this out of ego. If I was smarter, I'd have come up with a better idea."

"And now I suppose you need my help?" she asked.

"Very much. I . . . we . . . can't let these terrorists get away."

"I hope they go to the Antarctic . . . to the moon," she answered bitterly.

Bloom sighed.

"You're the expert," he said quietly. "I think that they'll kill again. What do you think?"

She didn't answer immediately.

"They might," she finally replied. "The pathology is there, and having those terrible weapons must excite them. And the leader could still come after you. That kind of psychotic is very good at holding grudges. I'll be honest with you. You won't be safe until he's dead."

"Can I come up to talk to you now, Maeve?"

Hearing him say her name made something ripple within her. It was preposterous to think that this man she hardly knew could affect her so, but it had just happened. She liked it too.

"Come ahead . . . David."

They spoke for more than two hours. She brought out cold

chicken and a bottle of Sancerre, and they talked about paranoia and the terrorist mind for quite a while. She mentioned many groups that used violence for political purposes, including the Irish Republican Army.

"They're one of our lesser problems," Bloom said as she poured the coffee. "This is where they buy arms, not where they fight."

"Let's get back to O. B.," she suggested. "They could go underground for a while after they collect this ransom. Or they might leave this part of the country. They could even go abroad."

"We might put extra men at the airports and railroad stations to watch for them," Bloom said. "We've got pictures of one of them."

Then he told her about the theft of the gas, Ernest Letherby, and his parents.

"This is fascinating," the psychiatrist said. "You think that his mother knows he's a mass killer and doesn't mind?"

Bloom nodded.

"What does that say about *her* mental health?" he asked. He sipped the coffee and then smiled. It was excellent.

"Now about tomorrow night—that could be crucial," he warned.

"What do you mean?"

"O. B. is supposed to pick up the ransom after nine o'clock, and I'd like you with me from seven on," Bloom said.

"What could I do?"

"Give your best professional judgment on the spot as to what they might do."

"It'll be an informed guess at best," she reminded him.

"I'll settle for that."

Then they stood up and kissed. At the door before he left, they embraced and kissed again, gently but stirringly. In the descending elevator Bloom closed his eyes and thought about Maeve Cathleen O'Donnell and her mass of reddish hair. He wondered when he would see it tumble free—a chestnut mane.

He hoped that it would be soon.

CHAPTER 35

OTTO'S BOY looked around the house that he would never see again. Yes, everything had been done. The charges were set and the clothes and furniture soaked in kerosene. He could leave this place with full confidence that he had done his job well.

Now it was time to call Mama.

He had never spoken to her on this telephone. He felt almost naughty as he dialed her number. She should still be home. She didn't depart for work before eight. He grinned as he heard the ringing of her phone. Mama would be so surprised, so happy.

"Yes?"

"It's me, Mama. I'm almost finished. Tonight's the big event," he said proudly.

"You shouldn't have called."

"I wanted you to know. We can meet in three weeks at the cemetery, Mama. We can tell Papa that his honor has been restored."

"Ernst, they were here yesterday. An Army captain came.

242

He said the police were looking for you for robbing an armored car—in Ohio, I think—and for something filthy in Newark."

"That's stupid."

"They're going to dig up that coffin in Arlington," she warned in an urgent breathy tone. "They suspect that you're still alive."

They were up to something.

They could be watching Mama now or tapping her phone.

"Good-bye, Mama," he said quickly and put down the telephone.

The sun was pouring in through a kitchen window. It was a fine spring morning and a special one. He wouldn't depart through the front door as he usually did. He didn't use the back door either. He opened a rear window, put the suitcase out onto the ground, and wriggled out after it. Then he closed the window and applied four squirts of Magic Glue so it would soon be impossible to slide open.

Then he saw his face and head reflected in a pane of glass. His hair wasn't neat at all. He paused to comb it carefully before he got into the car and started his last journey to the city he loathed.

A thousand miles to the south, Seigenthaler repeated the last four digits of a phone number.

"Right: eight-one-five-nine. It's your deal now," he told Collery.

Three minutes later, a special operator at the telephone company headquarters in northern New Jersey provided the address: 114 Oak Lane, Montville.

"We've got him!" Collery exulted.

Leonard Fredericks hesitated for a few seconds. The Bureau had found Letherby. It was entitled to the "bust"—but there was a policy problem. The Director had said in a memo three months ago that every effort should be made to maintain good relations with local police. There would be no harm in bringing Bloom along. He had no jurisdiction in New Jersey anyway. The FBI could still make the arrest.

Some fifty minutes later, six cars pulled to a halt on Oak

Lane in Montville, New Jersey. Five were filled with federal agents. One car blocked each end of the street. The passengers poured out and took positions behind their vehicles. Within moments, half a dozen submachine guns and rifles equipped with armor-piercing ammunition were pointed at 114 Oak Lane. More heavily armed agents rushed from the other cars, taking up positions all around the small house.

"Lot of fire power," Gillespie observed professionally.

"Let's go," Bloom said.

They got out of his car and walked to join Fredericks.

"Congratulations," Bloom said. "Is he in there?"

"We'll find out," the FBI executive replied. He reached for the radiophone in his sedan and gave the number Seigenthaler had supplied to the mobile operator. After twenty-six rings he hung up.

"If he's inside, he's not answering. Maybe he went to New York," he said.

"Shall we search the house?" Collery asked eagerly.

Fredericks nodded.

"Be careful," Bloom advised. "He's tricky."

Collery glanced at him coolly. It was pretentious for some local cop to tell federal agents how to do things.

"You take the front door with Archer and Keveson," Fredericks ordered. "McIvor, Eliason, and Porter can go in through the back. Check your watch. One minute."

The federal agents approached the house. At precisely 8:42 A.M. James Collery tested the front door and Martin McIvor tried the back one. They were locked. Collery turned and looked at his supervisor for instructions, gesturing with the butt of his machine gun toward the door.

Fredericks nodded permission, and Collery broke the wooden panel above the doorknob. Then he reached in, twisted the handle, and pushed against the door.

It stuck for a few moments.

He pushed harder. It moved.

Then Collery was dead.

So were the two agents beside him.

The house at 114 Oak Lane exploded with a tremendous roar. The boobytraps attached to the rear door went off a split second later, killing one of the FBI men there and hurling the other two a dozen yards.

The fire came next—a terrible yellow ball. Then another and another as the kerosene-soaked furniture and clothes ignited. Now the whole house was ablaze, flames spouting from every room. Then there was another explosion, throwing chunks of burning debris in a wide arc.

Men were shouting. Neighbors were screaming. Several courageous FBI agents rushed forward to their fallen comrades, risking the chance of another blast in desperate efforts to move the bodies away from the ruined house. It wasn't a residence anymore. It was a pyre.

"Jesus H. Christ!" Velez gasped.

Gillespie started to speak—but couldn't.

"We found the right house," Bloom said slowly.

The ambulances and fire engines arrived ten minutes later. Five minutes after that, Bloom and his men were on the way back to the city. Their only lead had gone up in smoke. Now there was almost no chance that they would find him before the deadline. Letherby and the O. B. gang would collect the money and escape, fleeing from the region.

They might go anywhere.

And they might kill again before they left.

CHAPTER 36

THE CHIEF OF DETECTIVES was very angry.

When Bloom explained why he was late for the nine o'clock meeting, the Chief understood, but he was still furious. An official reprimand for the "idiotic" *Post* interview would be placed in Bloom's file. There'd be a departmental hearing on further discipline next week.

"How many of the FBI did you say got wasted?" he asked in a gentler voice.

"Four—and another one's critical."

"Christ. Okay, get out of here."

Bloom returned to his office to wait. He tried to focus on other problems coming in: the rumors of another series of attacks by the Puerto Rican FALN organization; the report that a suspected member of the Armenian Secret Army had been seen near the Turkish consulate; the complaint from the Police Department's finance section that his budget was late.

It didn't work.

All he could think about was the terrorists out there with more nerve gas, and probably not very far away.

And those dead FBI men strewn like puppets around the burning house.

He would never forget that sight.

At six o'clock he called her, and they met for dinner in Chinatown half an hour later. They entered Fredericks' office at eight. The task force members and the three army officers eyed her with undisguised curiosity. Bloom introduced her, explained who she was and looked at his watch. Then they all waited for the phone to ring.

It was another telephone that rang at nine o'clock.

O. B. was right on schedule again.

"This is Mayor Warner."

"We've already planted two cylinders. They'll go off at ten if we don't stop them. If you try to grab any of us, thousands will die."

"I understand."

"Here are your orders: Give the package to a policewoman. She's to stand on the southwest corner of Broadway and Fortieth Street at nine-thirty. No jacket. No gun. No walkie-talkie. We've got people watching. If you try to flood the area with cops, O. B. will know it."

Then the mayor heard the soulless hum of the dial tone.

Vincent Grady called for a policewoman and then relayed the terrorist's message to the Joint Task Force. It was for information only. There was to be no attempt to catch the O. B. group tonight.

There was very little conversation in Fredericks' office after that. Everyone was grim-faced and uneasy, and nobody knew what to say. So they sat or paced, sipping cups of cold water or smoking or trying not to grind their teeth.

Policewoman Geraldine Bonomi arrived at the corner at 9:25, looked around, and waited. She began to perspire, and not because it was a warm night. She walked up and down. One passerby came toward her, thinking that she might be a streetwalker available for some quick anonymous sex. Then he recognized her uniform and hurried away.

At 9:32 a taxi pulled up beside the policewoman.

"You got the mayor's package?" the driver asked in a heavy Canarsie accent.

She looked at him carefully, trying to memorize the face. She gave him the package. As the taxi sped away, she studied the license plate. She recited it three times. Well, at least they hadn't killed her. She felt the sweat dripping as she walked to the unmarked police car parked on the next block.

The taxi went down to 35th Street, then west to Ninth Avenue. The driver stopped and spoke to the man waiting there.

"Here it is, Jack. Now where's that other twenty bucks?"

Otto's Boy took the package and reached inside his jacket. "Thanks," he said.

Then he took out the snub-nosed Beretta .32 and shot the driver between the eyes.

Perfect. It had gone exactly as he had planned, Otto's Boy thought triumphantly. He would be out of this mongrel city within the hour, leaving behind a mound of corpses America would never forget.

His car was parked on 31st Street. He walked down Ninth Avenue quickly, trying to ignore the panhandlers, radio players, winos and everyone else. He didn't like this street. Ninth Avenue—even at night—was simply unsanitary.

They approached him from both sides. There were four of them—dark-skinned and in their late teens or early twenties.

"Whatcha got there, baby?" one asked in a nastily cheery voice.

Otto's Boy looked up—surprised. He had no time to waste on this human garbage. Then he got another surprise. One of the hoodlums behind him rammed an icepick into his back. As he gasped in pain, the mugger plunged the long thin blade in twice more.

Otto's Boy fell to the sidewalk. Shuddering under the awful pain, he heard them laughing as they picked up *his* package. They had no right to it. Peering up through agonized eyes, he tried to make out who they were. Were they light-skinned blacks, Latins, or some other dark-complected group? He couldn't tell. The pain was too sharp.

Help me, Mama.

Then he found new strength. With the holes in his back burning white-hot, he managed to reach the Beretta. He was panting as he tried to take aim. For a few seconds everything was a blur. He could still hear the vermin laughing. He pointed his gun a foot below the sound and fired twice.

Somebody screamed. One of the shadowy figures reeled and collapsed. The others turned toward Otto's Boy, but he knew what to do. He fired two more shots at the blurs. They grabbed the package and ran. He heard their footsteps receding somewhere out into the night.

Otto's Boy tried to struggle to his feet. He couldn't, and the burning was worse. He made another attempt, rolling on the filthy sidewalk. He could smell the dog urine and clots of sickeningly sweet chewing gum only inches from his nose. He had to get up. He couldn't die here. He had one more thing to do.

I'm sorry, Mama.

He wouldn't meet her at Papa's grave. He wouldn't deliver the diamonds for the great marble-and-steel monument. He wouldn't be reunited with her—ever.

But there was one thing he could do. He would die with honor, like a soldier of the Führer's First SS Panzer Regiment.

And he'd take thousands of his enemies with him—19,501.

He struggled to his knees. Finally, with an awful effort, he stood up and leaned against a storefront. After a minute he started to walk very slowly down Ninth Avenue.

At 9:38, David Bloom was called to the telephone. The cab driver who had picked up the ransom had been found dead—shot in the head. And there had been another shooting not far away. A cruising radio car had spotted three young men, one lugging a large bundle, another barely supporting their companion, who had a bullet hole in his back.

When the police examined the bundle, they had found a huge amount of cash.

"In one-hundred-dollar bills, and there were two sacks of diamonds," Terence Carty reported. "The PC thought that you ought to know. The radio boys followed a trail of blood three blocks up Ninth; found another stiff with a slug in his spine. They figure these punks tried to heist somebody who was carrying a gun. He may have been hurt too. One of the guys was carrying an icepick still wet with blood."

"That blood could be Letherby's," Bloom said.

"We're checking local hospitals now," Grady's personal assistant reported. "If we come up with anything more, we'll call the task force right away."

Bloom told the others what Carty had said.

"He's lost the ransom and he's been hurt, probably badly," Bloom thought aloud. "Where will he go? What will he do?"

"Maybe it's some other member of the O. B. gang?" Colonel Mills suggested. "We can't be sure it's Letherby."

Bloom turned to Maeve O'Donnell.

"What about the cylinders?" he asked.

"It doesn't matter which member of the group was hurt," she replied. "One of their small close unit was injured, maybe even mortally, and they've been cheated out of the fortune they worked so hard for. They'll want vengeance."

"You really believe they'll set off the gas?" Fredericks asked.

"It's possible—maybe likely."

"And we have no idea where it is," Mills said.

The psychiatrist shook her head.

"We have a chance to think it out. Long shot—but possible," she told them.

"He said thousands," Fredericks reminded them.

"That's the cue. Think big," she urged. "They'd want to end

their war on New York—the biggest city in the country—with something enormous."

"Radio City Music Hall!" Fredericks suggested. "Seats over five thousand."

They all looked at the psychiatrist. "Maybe," she said. "What do you think, David?"

Suddenly, starkly, Bloom saw the problem. Black to move and mate in two. O. B. had already moved once, and Bloom knew it. He had set the timers for 10:00. And the Music Hall wasn't big enough for this end game.

"It's got to be bigger," he said.

"What's bigger?" the psychiatrist asked.

"Madison Square Garden," Bloom said. "More than that, the Knicks and Lakers are playing there tonight for the NBA championship. It'll be a sellout."

"The Garden holds more than nineteen thousand for basketball," Gillespie said. "I heard it on a quiz show last week."

"Suppose it *is* the Music Hall?" the FBI supervisor broke in.

"You take your people up there. We'll cover the Garden. Let's roll." Bloom said and started for the door.

Colonel Mills insisted on going with Bloom, the doctor and two detectives. As the sedan raced north from 26 Federal Plaza, Bloom realized that someone at the FBI office had been in touch with Grady. Radio car after radio car was being ordered to the Garden.

Streetlights and intersections flashed past. The cylinders could go off right now, Bloom thought. Move two and mate. But O. B. played with steely precision: he had said 10:00. Where were they? Where could they and their nerve gas win the whole fucking game? Sweep all nineteen thousand pieces into the box?

It came to him as the sedan plunged through the 14th Street intersection.

"The cylinders," he said. "He's planted them in the air-conditioning ducts."

"But what if we can't find them in time," the colonel asked. "Wouldn't it be wise to clear out the arena?"

"In the middle of the deciding game?" Velez responded. "You'd have to set the building on fire to get those crazy fans out of there. Just the *possibility* of gas—and that's what it is—won't do it."

There were sixteen radio cars parked in a jagged arc when they reached the Garden.

"What the hell is it, Lieutenant?" one policeman blurted.

"Bright blue cylinders. Metal—maybe big ones. They're full of nerve gas."

The policeman stared in shock.

"Blue cylinders and this man," Bloom continued, showing one of the pictures of Letherby. "Keep it. Here are some more. Spread them around. I want half of you guys to go through the crowd and the corridors, and the rest come with me. This man's already killed five Feds today. He's probably armed, and he may have a wound. Icepick. Watch your step."

"That's for sure."

They stormed into the building. Security guards stepped aside as they saw dozens of uniformed police charging through the door. They sprinted up the ramps, breathing hard as they rushed to find one man among more than nineteen thousand people. Suddenly they were looking down at the game below.

"Dee-fense! Dee-fense!" thousands of excited Knick fans were screaming. Men and women were on their feet, gesturing and bellowing frantically. It was an astonishing sight—bankers, judges, professors, rock stars, novelists, business men, TV executives, models, waiters, clothing manufacturers all yelling madly: "Dee-fense! Dee-fense!"

The Knicks led 88 to 84, and the Lakers had the ball. The sound level was shattering as they came charging down the court, and the emotional pitch was even higher. Velez had been right. Nothing anyone could say or do would clear these fanatics out in time. It would probably take at least twenty minutes to empty this packed arena. They didn't have twenty minutes.

Half the police fanned out through the crowd, searching for a face that was even close to the one in the pictures. Bloom led the other half to a security post manned by a guard with a walkie-talkie.

"Where's your security chief?" Bloom demanded.

"What's the problem?"

"I want to talk to him in fifteen seconds, or you're under arrest for obstructing an officer."

"You're crazy," the guard replied indignantly. But he pressed two buttons and gave Bloom the radio.

"This is Lieutenant Bloom, NYPD. This is an emergency. Lives are at stake. Where's your air-conditioning center?"

"The main machinery's next door in the office building. Same setup serves us and that one. The cool air feeds over by underground pipes."

"The basement?" Bloom demanded.

"There are pipes and booster pumps there. What the hell's going on? I see cops all over the place."

"Nerve gas. It may be here. Can you clear the arena?"

"*Now?*"

"Try," Bloom urged and sprinted for the ramp down. The others followed, with Colonel Mills and Maeve O'Donnell bringing up the rear.

Down . . . down . . . down.

It was 9:57—three minutes to checkmate.

Steps and more steps.

An intersection where four passages met.

Which way?

The answer was on the cement floor: drops of blood.

"This way," Bloom called out and drew his gun. He was running as hard and as fast as he could. More blood . . . bigger drops. He was hurt badly all right.

The door was marked AIR CONDITIONING—NO ADMITTANCE. Bloom tried the handle. The door opened. He swung it in and stepped aside quickly.

9:58.

The hum of the compressors was a low, steady sound. This was a large room. The main air-conditioning facility in the next building was many times bigger, but this chamber was more than thirty feet long and nearly as wide. It was full of machinery. The wounded terrorist might be behind any one of them, gun in hand.

There were rules as to what to do in this situation. There were standard police procedures—tested and sensible. But there was no time to be sensible now.

Bloom crouched low and dashed into the room, racing for the protection of a nearby machine.

"I know you're in here," he called out loudly.

Silence.

"You can't get away," he said. "We've got every exit covered, and we're evacuating the building at this moment."

Silence.

Bloom braced himself and ran for the next compressor.

A bullet hit it within an inch of his head.

"Come out, Letherby. It's over."

"Don't call me by that name. . . . I'm Otto's Boy," a weak but bitter voice replied.

"Otto's Boy? O. B.?"

Coughing and a muffled moan.

"That's me—O. B. . . . O. B. the avenger. I fooled you all, didn't I?"

There was blood at Bloom's feet.

A rivulet leaking from a ruined body behind the next pump five yards away.

9:59.

Just sixty seconds and only one thing to do.

Bloom had to stop him and the gas now.

The detective charged forward. For a split second he saw the whole nightmare framed like a still life: There was an ashen Ernest Letherby, slumped against the wall, barely able to stand. There was a crimson pool at his feet and two blue cylinders in an open wall duct.

Otto's Boy peered at his enemy through half-clouded eyes. It was hard to make out the detective for sure.

It hurts so, Mama. My whole back is burning, and inside the pain is terrible.

Where are you, Mama?

I'll take him with me, Mama.

The murderer raised his automatic and fired. The bullet struck David Bloom in the chest just a moment before Bloom's slug tore out the killer's throat. Thirty seconds from death, Otto's Boy turned and fired a final bullet into one of the lethal cylinders.

Bloom spun under the impact of the maniac's slug. He reeled back. He had to reach the timer. Even if the murderer's bullet had pierced the cylinder, Bloom had to stop that clock.

In twenty seconds the gas would flow and nineteen thousand people would start to die.

Bloom took one step forward.

Then the nerve gas got to him, and he fell.

He heard her cry out his name.

A moment after that, everything went black.

CHAPTER 37

FOUR DAYS later. A large building on Fifth Avenue at 100th Street. Room 522.

The door opened, and two officers in the uniform of the U. S. Army entered. One was Colonel Stanley Mills; the other was General James Raleigh Younts.

"How're they treatin' you?" Younts asked.

"The coffee here is lousy," the man in the bed replied.

"He's okay, Stanley," the general assured. "He always bitches about coffee. Well, I guess you owe Stanley one—right? Saved your life, didn't he?"

Bloom nodded.

"You always carry atropine kits, Colonel?" he questioned.

"Only when I'm on a mission involving nerve gas," the Chemical Corps officer answered. "It was a damn near thing. Another forty or fifty seconds, and you'd have bought it."

"Thank you, Colonel."

"You can thank your two friends too," Mills suggested. "If

Gillespie and Velez hadn't risked their necks to drag you out of there, you'd be in an urn right now."

"And if the Garden engineers hadn't knocked off that air-conditioning circuit, so would a lot of other people," Bloom said.

"Still worrying about other people?"

Bloom turned his head and saw Maeve O'Donnell in the doorway.

"Come in and join the army," David Bloom invited. "I don't think that you've met General Younts."

"I saw him on the news yesterday. He was testifying about the need to start making some new nerve gas."

"Still pushing for the binary?" Bloom asked.

Younts nodded.

"I'm not going to wish you good luck on that," Bloom said.

"That's okay. You do the detecting, and I'll handle the protecting. That's the army's job, son. I'm grateful for what you've done already. We're looking around for some kind of medal for you. So's the President."

"He called yesterday," she announced.

"The President phoned?" Younts asked.

Bloom nodded.

"You're gonna be a hero," Younts predicted.

"He *is* a hero—almost a dead one," she said.

The general hesitated and remembered.

"Brought you some flowers," he announced. "Pretty little Chinese nurse is putting them in a vase now. Hell, I see you've already got a load."

"Those are from the mayor," she told him.

"That's just fine. By the way, the FBI has arrested Letherby's mother. They tell me she's good for ten years. I've got to go now. Giving a speech to the newspaper editors' convention in half an hour."

"About the binary?" Bloom asked.

"Among other things. Mostly the Soviet chemical weapons buildup. I'll see you, Lieutenant."

He started for the door, stopped, and walked back to the bed. After a moment he held out his hand, and Bloom shook it. Then the army officers left.

Barely a minute passed before the nurse arrived with the flowers. Velez and Gillespie walked in right behind her.

"How're you feeling?" Gillespie asked.

"Grateful . . . to both of you. I've heard what you did."

"Good lieutenants are hard to come by," Velez said. "We've just got you broken in right. You can thank the Chief of Detectives too. If he hadn't made you wear that bulletproof vest, you'd be in a box."

"General Younts said an *urn*."

"Chief's coming up to give you a heavy medal tomorrow," Velez reported. "With Grady."

"And some TV cameras?" Bloom asked.

"Of course. There could be something else. I heard they're talking about making you a captain when you get out of here. When are you coming back?"

She answered for him:

"Not for at least three weeks."

"Three weeks?" Bloom asked.

"That's right."

"Good. My parents should be back from visiting my sister in Brazil by then. She's in the Peace Corps," Bloom said. "They're very nice people."

"I'm sure they are," she agreed.

Bloom smiled.

"You're going to like meeting them," he predicted.

"Don't rush me," she said.

"You hear how the game came out?" Velez broke in briskly.

Bloom recognized the effort to avert a dispute. Only his eyes showed his amusement.

"Tell me about it, Gabe," he invited.

"The Knicks played *terrific* ball. It went to double overtime."

"Did they win?"

"Final score was one hundred and twenty-two to one hundred

and twenty. One of the best playoff games in league history!"

"Did they win?" Bloom repeated.

"Tell him," Gillespie blurted impatiently.

Gabriel Velez hesitated before he shook his head.

"They gave it a great shot, though," he said. "Double over-time!"

Bloom nodded in silent disappointment.

"Is winning that important, David?" Maeve O'Donnell asked.

"Yes."

"We'll get 'em next year," Velez predicted enthusiastically.

"Sure," Bloom agreed. "I'm feeling tired. I think I'll take a nap."

After they had left he closed his eyes. For a few moments he reconsidered her curious question about winning. Then the fatigue began to blur his thinking. When the nurse arrived with Younts' flowers, he was deep in sleep.

CHAPTER 38

IT WAS five o'clock on a humid Friday afternoon when Bloom returned to his apartment. She was with him. They entered the eighteen-storey, red brick building on West 79th Street, and he went to check his mail.

"I have it in my office," the mustachioed superintendent told him. "You got all kinds of stuff in three weeks, so Max asked me to keep it for you. Your mailbox couldn't handle the load."

Letters, magazines, bills, circulars from department stores, solicitations from the Columbia College Fund, two packages, assorted brochures, postcards from friends, and a lot of junk mail.

"I've put it in a couple of shopping bags," the superintendent said.

"Thanks, Joe."

"You're thanking me? My brother was at that game."

When they entered the apartment, Bloom put the two bags of mail on the light elm dining table. Then he hung up his jacket and looked around. Neighbors had come in to water the plants. Everything seemed fine.

"Would you like a drink?" he asked.

"Haig Pinch and water," she replied. "Where's the loo?"

He chuckled.

"That word has two meanings. Some cops use it as short for lieutenant," he explained, "but you mean bathroom. It's back there."

When she left the room, he mixed her drink. Then he couldn't resist examining the mail. He had never been able to do that. After scanning two letters and a postcard, he threw away brochures from vitamin companies, clothing stores, discount record firms and a travel agency.

Then he paused to make himself a very dry martini. He sipped, appreciated his skill and picked up one of the packages.

"That can wait," she said as she returned to the dining-living room. "Say, you've got a very good view here."

He gave her the Scotch and water.

Then he noticed that the package had come from the Marshall Chess Club. It seemed heavy. A gift? The trophy from that last tournament?

"It's a nice apartment," she said, "and the drink's good too. Who decorated it?"

"I did. I wonder what this is," he thought as he started to untie the string.

"David, would you forget the mail for now?" she appealed.

"Sure," he replied and went ahead unwrapping the package.

"There's something that I have to talk to you about, David. It's not a criticism."

"I can take criticism."

"I'm telling you this because I like you a lot. I wouldn't be here if I didn't. David, you're a wonderful person, but you can be a bit obsessive."

He thought, frowned, and stopped. He went to a drawer and took out a Swiss Army knife.

"You've set yourself very high standards," she continued.

He pried open a blade and began sawing a slit in the side of the package as she paused to sip her Scotch.

"David, let me put it this way. You're an outstanding person, but you don't have to be the best at everything. Are you listening to me?"

"Of course."

He cut a slash three inches wide, then turned the blade up to open a hole.

"What in the world are you doing?"

"Almost finished. Go ahead," he urged.

"What I'm saying is you don't have to be perfect. I like you just the way you are. Don't be an overachiever. That maniac is dead. You're safe—and a hero. And I'm falling in love with you. Isn't that enough?"

He sawed away until the opening was three inches square.

"You don't have to be perfect for me, David. It's a strain. It's bad for your mental health."

He pointed at the package.

"Oh my God!" she cried out.

Through the opening he had cut she could see it clearly:

Blue and metallic.

She stood there—stunned.

"It's okay," Bloom said calmly. He carried the package into the kitchen, opened the nearly empty refrigerator, and put the nerve gas bomb inside. Then he closed the door and rejoined her in the next room. Her glass was empty.

"Guess he sent that as a going-away present," Bloom said. "Mean little shit."

She was rigid with fear.

"He rigged it to go if I opened it normally," the detective reported.

"That thing could have killed us, David."

Bloom nodded and savored his martini.

Several seconds passed before she could find the right words.

"David," she said earnestly, "I've changed my mind. Stay just the way you are. If you want to be perfect, *be* perfect."

And he was.

An hour later she was lying in his arms in the big bed. Her silky hair was spread across his shoulder and over her upper arms. She felt warm, complete, luxurious. Then she sensed the tension returning to his body.

"Is something bothering you, David?"

"Not really," he replied and gently stroked the long red-brown tresses.

"Please—what is it?"

"Loose end. I hate loose ends. Can't help it," he said.

She turned and looked up into his eyes.

"What the hell is it?"

So she had a temper.

"I was just wondering," Bloom explained. "Wondering where he hid the other three cylinders."